DEATH OF A NEWSPA-
PERMAN

The editor has no clothes

chronicling the lonesome...

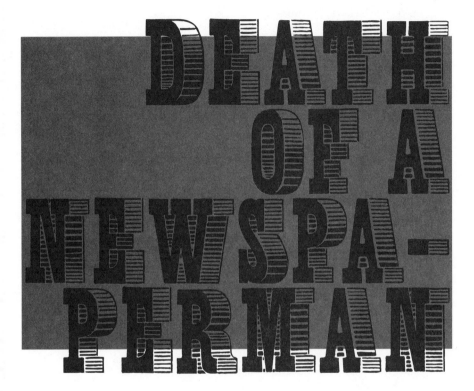

DEATH OF A NEWSPA- PERMAN

a novel by *Delfin Vigil*

Illustrations by *Scott Bradley*

• *A Vireo Book / Rare Bird Books* •

This is a Genuine Vireo Book

A Vireo Book | Rare Bird Books
453 South Spring Street, Suite 302
Los Angeles, CA 90013
rarebirdbooks.com

Copyright © 2015 by Delfin Vigil

FIRST TRADE PAPERBACK ORIGINAL EDITION

All rights reserved, including the right to reproduce this book or portions thereof
in any form whatsoever, including but not limited to print, audio, and electronic.
For more information, address: A Vireo Book | Rare Bird Books Subsidiary Rights
Department, 453 South Spring Street, Suite 302, Los Angeles, CA 90013.

Set in Minion
Printed in the United States

deathofanewspaperman.com

A passage from Herb Caen's *One Man's San Francisco*, (Doubleday, 1976) is
included on page 222.

10 9 8 7 6 5 4 3 2 1

Publisher's Cataloging-in-Publication data

Vigial, Delfin.
    Death of a Newspaperman / by Delfin Vigial ; illustrations by Scott Bradley.
    pages cm
    ISBN 9781942600077

1. Journalism—Fiction. 2. Newspapers—Fiction. 3. San Francisco (Calif.)—
History—Fiction. 4. Barbary Coast—Fiction. 5. Reincarnation—Fiction. 6.
Caen, Herb, 1916-1997—Fiction. 7. De Young, Charles—Fiction. 8. Hearst,
William Randolph, 1863-1951—Fiction. I. Bradley, Scott M. II. Title.

PS3622 .I459 D43 2015
813.6—dc23

For Tiffany, Monty, and Paloma

"If the world is cold, make it your business to build fires."

—Horace Traubel

Prologue ▶

R ichard Leech was not a bad editor. He was a bad person.
Far be it from me to sum up the quality of a man's character
with the whim of so few words. But I'm a newspaper reporter, and
that's my job—to separate the right from the wrong, the winner
from the loser, the victim from the suspect.

And the good guys from the bad.

As a newspaper reporter, my assignments involve targeting
people of interest. I interview them. Take notes about what they
wear, how they talk, and the way they walk. I speak to their friends.
I question their enemies. And in the end, they are either validated
or, otherwise, nullified with some kind of black-and-white
conclusion, usually in about two thousand words or less. But in
the case of Richard Leech, his story can be told in just four words:

Good editor. Bad person.

This is not just according to me. It's a determination that can be attributed to several reliable sources who have all worked with, for, under, or against Richard Leech during his more than twenty-five years as editor of *The San Francisco Call*'s daily features pages. Each morning, Richard Leech navigated the cubicle maze at his end of the newsroom like one of those ghosts in Pac-Man. There, he would corner and smother anyone carrying an aura of insecurity. Or he would visibly change color and run for temporary cover when anyone confronted him with a sudden power pellet of confidence and contempt.

It's like Happy Hamilton used to say, "Richard is just a cardinal in the Vatican checking to see what color the smoke is. And he's always going to be one hundred percent behind you—either kissing your ass or stabbing you in the back."

Happy Hamilton not only had the coolest byline at the paper, but he had also been with *The San Francisco Call* long enough to criticize Richard Leech aloud in the hallway. Richard Leech was known to prey upon more insecure careers. And Happy knew his storied career could never be considered endangered. So, the scarf-and-beret-wearing jazz writer who snapped while he walked always laughed Leech off whenever the editor tried to take him to task on anything. Happy enjoyed snapping the upper hand fingers of this relationship for what felt like forever.

However, reports that Richard Leech was unqualified, incompetent, or the altogether wrong person for the position of top features editor have always proven to be false. Aside from the trail of a half-dozen deputy editors exiled to smaller markets in the Midwest for failed coup d'états against him, Richard Leech had, since the mid-eighties, supervised some of the more compelling and most popular pages of *The San Francisco Call*. In comparison with the news, business, and sports sections, and as the prominently displayed editorial trophies and plaques on his office wall attested to, the features pages consistently won more awards, made fewer errors, and told better stories.

Perhaps what most set him apart from other masthead editors could be attributed to what Richard Leech did not have and did not do. Richard Leech had no mortgage. No marriage. No children. No car. He hated golf. He rarely drank. He spent vacation days in his apartment (a fifteen-minute subway ride from the newsroom), choosing which stories to submit for journalism awards. Richard Leech loved his work as much as some hated working for him. There was no more important commitment in Richard Leech's life than making a copy editor cry for misspelling a name in a photo caption.

The man had found his dharma in spite of his karma.

If the secret to his longevity could be narrowed down to something singular, it was that Richard Leech always did what other top editors apparently didn't.

He actually read the newspaper.

I took note of this on the day I met Richard Leech. It was an encounter that I am certain he would never remember. ◻

PART I
Be True to Your School

Chapter 1

I started working for The Call when I was twelve years old. That's when, each weekday morning, I would break into the city's newspaper racks and steal copies of *The Call* before making my way to Westgate Middle School. Because I was usually either late for class or missing my homework, each section of the newspaper often came in handy as a sort of peace offering.

Mr. Corbett, our real swell guy of a principal, always enjoyed the comics, as the outdated lives of the *Peanuts* gang represented the fifties world he could only wish to see in our dilapidated neighborhood on the southern outskirts of San Francisco.

Mr. Bosworth, the physical education instructor, got the sports section and pretended he liked to read. Science and math teachers would get the business sections, presuming they were the only ones who opened them anyway. Mr. Girard, both my history and drama teacher, always appreciated the arts and features pages. And, no, not just because he was gay, but because he hoped (sadly, in vain) to find a review or calendar listing of his local theater group. And Miss Gambier would never mark me absent in home economics class on Wednesdays so long as I left her copies of the home and garden sections atop my otherwise empty seat.

By no means did these special deliveries entitle me to fixed report cards. They all still failed me on exams that I'd invariably complete with smart-ass answers. But unlike the whereabouts of Alistair Martinez, our valedictorian who was secretly selling sheets of LSD in-between classes, my teachers knew exactly where I was and what I was doing. I could always be found coming in or out of the portable newsroom/classroom of *The Tiger Paw Press*. There is where, every morning, I would tape up the front page of *The Call* as inspiration for the rest of the usually indifferent and unimpressed Westgate Middle School journalism students. And there is where I first declared that I, Desmond de Leon, would someday become a reporter for *The San Francisco Call*.

My allegiance to *The Call* was pledged upon me circa 1978 by my Uncle Lalo, who for many years operated a newspaper stand at the Twenty-Fourth and Mission Street BART station.

Excuse me.

"*Newsstand*," as Lalo often corrected people in his unapologetic way.

In addition to the complete morning, afternoon, and evening editions of all the Bay Area and San Francisco city newspapers, Lalo's newsstand included international publications like *Le Monde* and *El País*, national news magazines like *Time*, *Newsweek*, *U.S. News* and *World Report*, "*basura*" like *Rolling Stone* and *Playboy* and even the latest copies of *The Watchtower* and *Awake!* which Uncle Lalo allowed the elderly Jehovah's Witness ladies to leave once a week.

An immigrant from Chile, Uncle Lalo read them all, teaching himself basic and unbroken who-what-where-when-why English along the way. He was particularly proud to make a living as part of what he saw as an intellectual labor force that sold the truth at a price everyone could afford. According to Uncle Lalo, *The San Francisco Call* was the city's newspaper of record and therefore the only logo he would agree to endorse on his change-dispensing apron. *The Call*, Uncle Lalo noted, also ran the fewest corrections. And so, during the late seventies, when I was about four years old, climbing up and down bundles of periodicals, Uncle Lalo would only shoot me that sharp blue-eyed glare from beneath his herringbone tweed cap whenever I stepped near a morning *Call*.

"Oye! Desi! Go play on top of *El National Enquirer!*" he would shout, shooing me away to look for the only publication he refused to sell.

My uncle had left Santiago de Chile to live with us in San Francisco around the time President Salvador Allende was assassinated and General Pinochet's regime was rounding up pesky university-type intellectuals like Lalo and making them disappear. The funny thing is that Uncle Lalo was never enrolled as a student. My father's side of the family in Chile couldn't possibly afford to send Uncle Lalo to a university. But on his days off from dishwashing at the downtown Santiago hotels, Uncle Lalo could be found over at the campus cafés. It was, he explained, the only place where one could engage in conversations that weren't about "men playing with their balls." Uncle Lalo may not have been a student, but he was astute enough to skip town for his brother's house in California the day after two of his best friends were thrown into the backseat of a shiny black Ford Falcon and never seen or heard from again.

Uncle Lalo died an unglamorous death of lung cancer in 1988. It was not unexpected considering that he began smoking at the age

of ten and didn't stop with the diagnosis in 1986. But the biggest tragedy was that Uncle Lalo outlived his newsstand by about five years. Those were by far the most miserable days of his life—even more so than his impoverished childhood in Santiago, when he and my father were forced to drop out of school to work on fishing boats and cargo ships in nearby Valparaiso. The newsstand was his entire livelihood, and when it was taken away because of sporadically enforced city permit laws, Uncle Lalo's whole sense of purpose went with it. It mattered little to my uncle that he would make much more money working alongside my father, a longshoreman, who got him a job unloading container ships at the Embarcadero. Uncle Lalo hated the mindless monotony of not learning anything new at the end of each day. He had grown to detest container ships and sailboats, as they reminded Uncle Lalo of choices being made for him. San Francisco's smell and taste of the Pacific was far too similar to that of *Sudamérica*'s. And it all made Uncle Lalo feel like just another drop in the ocean.

I was thirteen, with one year of experience working on *The Tiger Paw Press*, when Uncle Lalo finally succumbed to cancer. Although he insisted otherwise, my news briefs about delayed construction on the school gym and previews of Mr. Girard–directed school plays did little to cheer him up. Even though Uncle Lalo bought me this tape recorder to encourage me to conduct better interviews, he worried that I, too, would someday be destined to deliver other people's dreams from a cargo ship or diesel truck. Of course, that didn't stop him from pointing out all of my typos and buried ledes. The one story I wrote that I knew he would have loved was his obituary.

My junior high journalism teacher, Mr. Gibb, tried to get *The Call* to write a news obituary on my uncle. It wasn't that an editor passed on the story: aloof newsroom assistants kept putting us on hold before we could ask to leave a message. We settled for a paid obituary, which I wrote and Mr. Gibb edited. My widowed father, a private, unsentimental, and very untrusting man, reluctantly paid for it. Technically, that was the first story I ever wrote for *The San Francisco Call*. I kept my byline out of it, though it certainly included some of my most thorough and thoughtful reporting.

Chapter 2

Imet Richard Leech the same year that Uncle Lalo died. It was
1988, and the first week of eighth grade. Mr. Gibb booked a field
trip tour of the *San Francisco Call* newsroom for the new *Tiger Paw
Press* staff, of which I was the only returning member. Although
Mr. Gibb had no problem playing up the educational value of the
trip with Principal Corbett, I knew part of his plan was to help
keep Uncle Lalo's death off my mind.

We took the trip across town in a school bus. This was a
pleasant surprise. Most of us had never been in a school bus, since
the majority of Westgate students lived within walking distance or
near a city bus line. The dozen of us attending the field trip spread
out, staking claim to entire sections of the oversized banana boat,
which had a capacity for twice as many suburban kids.

At first, we enjoyed the unfamiliar feeling of not stepping on
top of one another, as was more customary to us on smelly city

busses. But something just didn't seem right. Within minutes we were all huddled toward the back, our limbs tangled, daring each other to throw things out the windows at passing pedestrians and nervous drivers. Riding inside that yellow submarine thing was by far the most exciting part of the trip for most of the students. Phony warnings from Mr. Gibb and the cranky bus driver that they would cancel the newspaper tour were hardly threatening, if even heard at all. The amusement ride ended outside *The Call*'s main entrance near the corner of Third and Market Streets, where we reluctantly disembarked, leaving gum on the bottoms of seats and pen-marked initials at the tops.

The Call's façade felt equal parts familiar and unwelcoming.

"Damn. Kinda looks like San Quentin," said Marcos Aguilar, one of our four new sports editors. Marcos would know, since he often spent Sundays visiting his older brother, Tony, at the state prison across the Bay.

A tubby, balding, and noticeably sunburned man in wrinkled slacks yet a perfectly pressed dress shirt approached.

"Well now, you may be onto something there, young man."

He held open *The Call*'s glass front door, gesturing for us to enter.

"And you might be interested to know that all of these windows are, in fact, bulletproof. They were installed after Miss Cynthia Apperson was kidnapped many years ago. Any of you know that name?"

As with most people's first impression of a newsroom assistant, Marcos and the rest of us weren't sure what to make of Lester Braun's sense of humor. Was he being sarcastic? Condescending? And why was he staring so intently into Jason Chan's eyes? No, none of us knew who Cynthia Apperson was. But we did know a thing or two about windows that weren't bulletproof. We lived in the Ingleside and Excelsior Districts, where gunfire was common. There was a fatal student shooting a few years back in the Westgate cafeteria, but that was when we were all in elementary school. Still, we'd heard all about it from our older brothers and sisters, who in some cases (like with Marcos) were accused of pulling a few of those drive-by triggers.

Although I didn't immediately let on, I was very interested in the bulletproof window story. But I was equally intrigued with Lester Braun. Since I had already declared, albeit a bit presumptuously, that I would someday be a reporter with *The San Francisco Call*, I wanted to know what I was getting myself into and what kind of people I would be working with. With all due respect to Mr. Gibb's stint as publisher of an underground political fanzine in the forests of Vermont during the late sixties, I had never met a professional journalist. I pictured the typical reporter as looking like they did in Uncle Lalo's favorite old movies—guys in sharp suits and fedoras, with pencils tucked atop their ears, uttering things like, "Say, Mac, whatta ya know?" The sight of Lester Braun's underarm sweat rings at ten o'clock in the morning was a disappointing first impression. But truth be told, he was an excellent guide.

Still staring at Jason Chan much of the time, Lester Braun gave a thorough tour of the Call Building, beginning with a crash course in San Francisco's colorful newspaper history.

"Our story begins January sixteenth, eighteen sixty-five," said Lester, raising his voice to that of an uninhibited tour guide and pointing to a dusty bronze plaque partially obstructed by an unwatered plant at the corner of *The Call*'s main lobby. Our class, still blocking the front entrance, gathered around the plaque, while annoyed *Call* employees made their way through the lobby to the nearby elevators. Lester placed his finger on the etched nose of a thickly mustachioed nineteenth-century man.

"Meet Mr. Charles Sansome." Lester then placed his finger on the more clean-shaven face of a second man. "And his brother, Michael Sansome. These two gentlemen were, in fact, not much older than all of you when, on January sixteenth, eighteen sixty-five, they published the first edition of *The San Francisco Call.*"

It began as a one-page newssheet that the two brothers put together with a ragtag team of writers paid mostly in whiskey, and then distributed in saloons and such around town, Lester told us. *The Call* became the best-known paper in California overnight when it delivered the West Coast scoop on the assassination of President Lincoln. This was thanks to Charles, who, during a routine visit to the Western Union office, happened to arrive at the very moment the clerk received the news of the president's murder. While the clerk went into panicked hysteria, the quick-thinking teenaged copublisher memorized the information and ran back to the *Call* newsroom. On his way out the door, he hung a handwritten sign in the window that read:

Closed due to measles outbreak.

•••

SAN FRANCISCO'S NEWSPAPER COMPETITION remained stiff throughout the late eighteen hundreds. The city had nearly a dozen respectable morning, afternoon, and evening papers, making it as big a newspaper town as London or New York City—and even bigger when counting the non-respectable ones.

"What would you do if someone called your mother *a whore?*" Lester asked us, pausing to take pleasure in Mr. Gibb's tense expression.

"Well, when someone started speaking unkindly of the Sansome boys' mother, Charles here did what any respectable San Francisco gentleman of the era would do and went for his gun."

When one of his former reporters betrayed him by writing stories in a rival paper suggesting that the elderly Sansome matriarch was once the "prettiest of prostitutes in Paris," Charles stalked the traitor through the streets of San Francisco, unloading countless bullets from his pistol's chamber, yet missing his target every time. It was one of nearly a dozen gunfights the Sansome brothers engaged in during an era when San Francisco newspaper publishers were expected to handle editorial differences within twenty paces. Several of these "newspaperman negotiations" were even settled in the newsroom near where we stood, including the most tragic, which ended with a fatal bullet landing in Charles' bushy moustache. The guilty shooter, Abraham Judah, was a sex-scandalized preacher running for mayor of San Francisco. He took revenge on Charles Sansome for *The Call*'s unflattering political editorials that denounced his campaign.

It was one of many pen-turned-pistol duels between the two. The final confrontation ended with Abraham cold-bloodedly killing Charles inside *The Call* newsroom. Abraham Judah went on to be elected as mayor of San Francisco by a suspiciously narrow margin, while Charles Sansome's newspaperman legacy would forever hover in obscurity, preserved by only the geekiest of San Francisco history buffs and a handful of junior high school students who actually paid attention during Lester Braun's tours.

"Are there any questions?" asked Lester, while we looked for evidence of blood and bullet holes.

"Yes," I said, just as everyone was set to scuffle along. "Did you notice that journalism is spelled wrong?"

"Excuse me?"

Lester did not like being cut off of his own caffeinated rhythm.

"Right there. On the plaque. It says the 'The Sansome brothers practiced a bold and brave brand of *jounalism*.'" I pronounced the misspelled word as join-a-lism, the way Bugs Bunny might have done. I wasn't trying to be funny. That's just how I read it.

Lester Braun was not amused. Taking his hand off of Jason Chan's shoulder, he walked back toward the unpolished bronze plaque at the corner of the front entrance, where I was still standing. He glared at me. Putting on the reading glasses hanging from his shoulders, Lester looked closely at the typo, and then again at me as if to make sure I didn't somehow steal the missing letter. Saying nothing, but breathing noticeably heavier with concentration, Lester pulled a black marker out from his pocket. On the misspelled plaque he carefully wrote:

r

JOUNALISM

^

"Now then!" he pronounced, back in his tour guide tone and controlled breathing. "Follow me. Single file. Up the stairs. Please. Now."

The rest of the newspaper tour was uneventful for most of the class. But I was still intrigued. Our first stop was the 10:30 a.m. news meeting in *The Call*'s not-so-bustling main newsroom on the top floor. We entered the bland conference room where all of the top editors decided "what went well with today's paper and what to do better with tomorrow's," Lester said. Outside of the classroom element, our preteen entourage behaved uncharacteristically well as we huddled toward the back and quietly waited for the room to fill with about fifteen men and six women. We watched in awe as several in the group of grown-up professionals seemed to go out of their way to act unprofessional and juvenile.

As the most well-dressed man in the room led the meeting from the head of the conference table, each editor waited his or her turn to read aloud two-to-three sentence synopses of main stories planned for the next morning. One woman yawned at least fourteen times. A balding, middle-aged man repeatedly fondled his thick, early eighties, already-by-then-out-of-style moustache. Some clinked pens on coffee cups, while others whispered jokes to one another with their mouths full of bran muffin bites.

And then there were the wisecracks.

LOCAL NEWS EDITOR: "The mayor is still campaigning to revive Prop ninenty-seven…Too bad he couldn't revive the homeless guys who passed out in his parking spot at City Hall yesterday."

MUSIC EDITOR: "Sting is canceling Friday's Amnesty International concert at the Oakland Coliseum due to personal conflicts…"

UNIDENTIFIED EDITOR IN THE FAR CORNER OF THE ROOM: "So that explains why that guy wearing earphones next to me on BART this morning kept saying 'Fuck the Police!'"

SPORTS EDITOR: "Looks like there's a group of investors serious about buying the Giants and keeping them in the city…shit. I'm surprised it's not the Dodgers, since they practically own the Giants right now."

It was like some kind of sarcasmathon.

You could cut the negative energy with a knife and serve it with an extra slice of cynicism. No one actually laughed or responded to any of the journalist jokes. None of the swearing or detached attention spans seemed to bother the editor apparently in charge, who appeared just as eager as everyone else to get the meeting over with. But before ending it, he turned the focus to that day's *Call*. Along with the change in topic went the tone. Suddenly on guard, everyone sat upright.

"I really enjoyed W. C. O'Farrell's column about his cat's fascination with argyle socks," said the yawning lady, now quick and alert.

They all laughed in nervous agreement.

The top editor appeared to be waiting for one more piece of feedback from that day's paper before getting ready to let everyone go.

Several awkward seconds of silence passed before the only person sitting directly next to him spoke up. He was the quietest and most attentive editor in the room, taking notes the entire time and periodically referencing a short stack of newspapers that he kept at his side.

"I thought the most interesting story was the one about Dave Dravecky having cancer in his throwing arm."

"Yeah, that's an incredible story," said the man with the *Magnum, P.I.* moustache. He, along with those who remembered to bring copies of that day's *Call*, furiously flipped through them to find the Dravecky story. The pissed-off sports editor did the same.

"It wasn't in our paper. I read about it in *The Merc.*"

The attentive editor held up a sports section from the rival San Jose newspaper. All eyes became fixed on *The Call* sports editor.

"*That* was an embargoed story. The Giants asked us to hold it until Saturday and we agreed out of respect to Dravecky's family."

The sports editor attempted to make contentious eye contact in the direction of the quiet editor, who from that point onward dedicated his entire awareness to cleaning a pair of gold circle-rimmed glasses with his blue Cal-Berkeley-insignia necktie.

"Well, looks like *The Merc* got to the family first," said the top editor, standing up and finally giving the class-dismissed signal. "Guess it's time to un-embargo it. Thanks for pointing that out, Richard."

"I'm on it," said the sports editor, abandoning the attempted eye contact with Richard, the attentive editor. "Yeah. Thanks, Leech."

As we walked single file out of the conference room to take on the remainder of the tour, I couldn't help but wonder how the Sansome brothers would've handled the meeting. Whom would they have shot? If it was about putting the interest of the paper first, I'm guessing they would have aimed at the sports editor. One thing was for certain: if the sports editor went to Westgate Middle School, nobody in our neighborhood would have blamed him for taking some kind of shot at Richard Leech after class. But this was clearly a different part of town and certainly a different kind of school. I watched as the two men avoided one another, walking down the hall in opposite directions toward their respective desks.

The rest of the newsroom tour included stops in various editorial departments that looked very much the same, and still nothing like Uncle Lalo's favorite movies. There were no fancy fedora-wearing fellas. No cigar smokers. No gruff guys snapping their suspenders. The phones weren't ringing off the hook, and I don't think I saw a single typewriter. The newsroom seemed to be divided in a sixty-forty ratio of men to women, all of whom appeared to shop at either JC Penney's or Mervyn's. For the most part, they looked happy, confident, and comfortable. One guy had his feet propped up on a desk as he laughed into a phone tucked between his head and sport-jacketed shoulder. There was no supervisor telling him to sit up straight or keep his voice down. Two ladies in pantsuits stood in the hallway arguing about something that had to do with the Oakland school district. They dropped a couple of F-bombs along the way, and no one even flinched.

This really cheered me up.

I had the sudden sensation that these could be my people. That someday I could fit in with them.

The tour ended in a spacious lobby near the main exit where Lester Braun brought us to a table buffeted with sandwiches and soda. This was the real highlight for our group, and was greeted with an uninhibited roar from the students and Mr. Gibb. Free to be back to our fully restless, prepubescent selves, conversations about who cut in line and questions about why Lester Braun gave only Jason Chan a candy bar continued through lunch. In the midst of all the middle school murmuring, a familiar baritone voice called out my name from across the room.

"Desi D! Is that you, little man?"

It was my older brother's best friend from high school, Cyrus Sherman. Big Cy, as everyone called him, used to come around our house after football practice and have dinner. If it got too late, sometimes he'd even spend the night, since he lived way across town in the Western Addition projects. This was unusual because my father did not exactly trust anyone to stay at our house, particularly not "*los negros*." But there was something irresistibly upbeat and optimistic about Cy that even my politically incorrect father appreciated. Cy was like a chiseled, six-foot-five, 200-pound Eddie Haskell from the hood. Only he actually meant all of the nice things that he said. I hadn't seen him since the night my brother got arrested for getting into a drunken brawl in the parking lot of a Daly City bowling alley a few years before. My brother was supposed to be with Cyrus that night. But Big Cy didn't like to drink, so he left and went to the movies by himself. My brother blamed Cy for a lot of his problems, especially after Cy got a scholarship to play linebacker at Auburn University.

"Hey. It is you," said Cy. He set down the two big boxes of mail that he was carrying on his shoulders and walked over to shake my hand. "How you been, Desi? How's the family? How's Hector?"

"He's cool," I lied. I didn't feel like talking about my brother in front of my friends. Cy grabbed a sandwich before I could.

"Hey, I heard about Uncle Lalo in the paper. Hey, was that you? Did you write that?"

I blushed.

"Look at you! How about that! You gonna be a big-time reporter someday? Hey, that's great! Good for you!"

The man with the Tom Selleck moustache and one of the sailor-mouthed ladies in a pantsuit walked toward us, not to say hello, but to reach in and grab sandwiches.

"So, Cy. You work for *The Call* or something?"

I went to grab the last sandwich, but the best-dressed top editor from the meeting walked by and beat me to it.

"Yeah! I'm an editorial assistant. Just started this summer after I got back from Auburn. It's a great gig. Answer phone calls from all kinds of crazy people. Organize press release materials. Lotta fun. Lotta action. You know. It's a different story every day. Ha! Literally. And it's a union job. Now I know your pop would appreciate *that*," he said, pointing at me with his sandwich hand.

Cy reached for the last Coke just before I thought of doing the same.

"Hey, I gotta get back to work. Now you make sure you send my regards to Hector and your pop." Cy picked up his boxes of mail and continued the conversation as he headed out the lobby, shouting even louder along the way.

"And hey, Desi! When you got that reporter résumé ready, you come bring it to me, you hear? I'll make sure it gets delivered to the right people! You take care now!"

As Big Cy's voice trailed off into the main newsroom it occurred to me that I was hungry. But more importantly, I was happy.

These really were my people.

Chapter 3

We're loyal all and ever true,
a pledge of faith we give to you,
We follow where our colors lead
our Orange and our Blue!

—*"Oh, Hail Vasco"*

When construction of Vasco High School was completed in 1931, it was hailed as the jewel of a neighborhood that even back then didn't have much of a crown. Far from the familiar San Francisco city icons, the school was built way out on the outskirts of town on a street that some maps might place in the Excelsior, others in Mission Terrace, and still others in neighborhoods or districts with names that even many San Franciscans have never heard of.

The brightly painted Spanish Colonial structure was a warm welcome to one of the coldest, drabbest, and foggiest corners of the city and county of San Francisco. No, not the romantic kind that chilled Tony Bennett's morning air. And no, not the fog that might have rolled into Otis Redding's wasted day on the dock of the Bay. This fog is dense, depressing, a sun-will-probably-not-come-out-tomorrow-or-the-day-after-that-as-it-drenches-and-drains-your-spirit-even-in-the-summer kind of fog.

There was nothing golden or gated that a thick and cozy kind of fog could wrap around on Cayuga Avenue, where Vasco High was centralized. There weren't any skyscraper tops that could be mystically made out of the low misty clouds covering nearby Alemany Boring-Levard's gas stations and chain grocery stores. It was just row after row of ordinary two- and sometimes three-story houses that literally blended together. Some were built so close that only a little stucco and dampened wood frames divided neighboring family living rooms. People often tried to brighten up the streets by painting their single-family homes with mint green or hot pink paint in hopes of making them stand out. But through the years they all somehow still felt gray as the grayest day. Vasco High immediately brightened up the neighborhood when the first classes took session in 1928.

"*Vasco Núñez de Balboa, the mighty conquistador himself, would most certainly raise his sword with pride at the sight of this glorious educational institution that is…'the First on the Pacific,*'" wrote then-senior Kenneth Basper in his 1931 departing editorial for the school's newspaper, *The Galleon*. I had found the article stuck to the bottom drawer of a desk that was still being used when I was a freshman in 1990. Mr. Basper's positive outlook, I'm guessing, might have had something to do with the fact that he was among the school's inaugural graduating class and therefore one of the first to get the hell out of "Vas" and head for the sunnier suburbs, as those of his generation were known to do.

You can't really see the Pacific Ocean from Vasco High School.

Not even on the clearest day while on top of the roof with a set of binoculars stolen from the science department. I know because I've tried. I've also tried to understand the meaning of the school's motto, "First on the Pacific," when in fact there is another San Francisco high school that is closer to the ocean, has a much clearer view of the sea, and was founded long before Vasco High.

Having a Buccaneer as our school mascot—well now, that made sense. When I arrived as a freshman at Vasco High in 1990, the campus looked as if pirates had indeed pillaged through the school over the summer, leaving their marks with spray paint, broken windows, and clogged plumbing. They took treasures in the form of stolen sports equipment, computer parts, fire extinguishers, and anything else of random or ridiculous value. My older brother, Hector, attended Vasco a few years before me, just as the school began sinking into its degenerated state. Although Hector technically never graduated, he left with some good memories, including the school's last city football championship trophy as well as a couple of fire extinguishers that I now understood how they ended up in our basement. From the perspective of a student reporter for *The Galleon*, there were plenty of campus stories to keep busy.

• • •

COME... GET YOUR CONDOMS

ON MY FIRST DAY as a freshman at Vasco High, students arriving from varying levels of sexual awareness lined up around all corners of the cafeteria to collect handfuls of fluorescent-packaged "*Hecho en Mexico*" condoms. These glow-in-the-dark prophylactics were distributed by (sadly, out-of-uniform) school nurses. This was no senior prank. Teen pregnancies and syphilis were big problems at Vasco. The faculty and staff were proud to announce a new sex education program in 1990 that made Vasco High the first public school in California to make condoms available to students, via the new Teen Health Center on campus. To the staff and city politicians who diligently campaigned to make it happen, this was serious stuff. To us students, it was...

"*Hella* funny."

That's the most common quote I collected while reporting on the story for *The Galleon* during lunch hour.

"Yo, Desi. Check it out," said Anthony Mendoza, a fellow freshman. He covered his mouth in anticipation of letting out a loud and potentially fruit-juice-spitted laugh. "You should write about Jamal—I mean...*Captain Condom!*"

Anthony caught the Capri Sun spit with his bottom lip just in time, while a Filipino contingency in the crowd cracked up and pointed in the immediate direction of Jamal, a black sophomore. Jamal was wearing a blindingly bright yellow pair of overalls complete with matching yellow basketball shoes, yellowy polo shirt, and with a somehow even yellower baseball cap on his head. He looked not unlike a five-foot-five Hi-Liter marker. Nevertheless, Jamal continued to carry himself with the confidence of a Crayola Crayons CEO. This not-so-mellow-yellow outfit was obviously the pride and joy of his new back-to-school clothes collection.

Unfortunately for Jamal, his fluorescent essence also happened to be the exact color as the condoms. Not making things any easier for him was the fact that Jamal's last name was Condon.

Considering that these insults were coming from freshmen on their first day of high school, Jamal had to do something to establish his sophomore superiority. This was challenging, in part because no one had ever been intimidated by Jamal Condon since the time in elementary school when we all found out that he was deathly afraid of fruit.

That's right. Fruit.

Apricots. Apples. Oranges. Avocados too, which Jamal always insisted be categorized as a seed-bearing fruit. For Jamal, it was all one big basket of grossed-out fear. It escalated to a full-on phobia after too many students dangled tangerines and things in Jamal's face—or worse, left apple cores on his desk, causing everyone else to delight at his shrieks. Even Jamal's little sister could control her big brother just by chasing him around the school playground shouting words like "Papaya!" and "Pineapple!"

But this was Vasco High School, where, on the fruity level, Jamal was safe. Anyone caught running around campus with fruit in hand would just as likely be ridiculed, or possibly pummeled. In order to get his year started off the right way, Jamal immediately took things to another level.

"Shut the hell up, Mendoza. You're just jealous 'cause my clothes cost more than your mail-order mom."

With that, Mendoza and Jamal were officially fronting. Shoulder to shoulder, nose to nose, a familiar staring contest had begun. We all knew this was a big charade. The odds that Jamal would throw a punch were about as likely as he'd ever get to use any of those condoms he'd stuffed in the outrageous number of pockets of his yellow overalls. Not a chance. And the fact that Mendoza was still holding a Capri Sun in his hand made it easy to call his bluff as well. Both boys were simply hoping that enough people were watching the confrontation so that word would get around that they *almost* got into a fight.

"Come on now, fellas. Let's talk about the rubbers," I said, positioning my notebook in-between the both of them. Mendoza pushed me out of the way with his Capri Sun hand, leaving Mountain Cooler–colored stains on my notepad. Now it was my turn to show that I wasn't afraid to take it to another level either.

"Okay, you both know neither one of you would even be here today if *your* parents had condoms in high school, right? How's that make you feel, you know, to know that the both of you could have been prevented?"

Mendoza's half-smile triggered the same reaction from Jamal, and the flinch-off was soon over. These two had known each other since elementary school back when they began trading baseball cards, a practice that they more than likely still privately participated in, as opposed to Vasco's less petty or more public problems of drugs, guns, knives, and gangs.

"Hey, Desi," Jamal said. "Just put in the paper that I'm surprised they actually had a supply for my rather large size."

"Whatever you say, your yellowness."

When the condom news story ran the next week, Jamal's quote read somewhat differently:

"'I am particularly proud that our school is not afraid to step into the nineties. To ignore the fact that teenagers are sexually active would be a big mistake. I think Vasco is doing the right thing by promoting sex education,' said Jamal Condon, a sophomore who waited patiently in line during lunch hour to collect his supply of condoms."

There was no experienced journalism teacher at Vasco High School to tell me there was anything wrong with fabricating a quote like this. In fact, it was Miss Lars, the school's speech and debate teacher turned makeshift journalism advisor, who insisted on it. The words were hers. She wrote them during one of her editing sessions that took place after student reporters turned their stories in and left for the day. I read the faux-quote for the first time along with everyone else who picked up a copy of *The Galleon* on campus.

Furious, I stormed into *The Galleon* newsroom that morning and confronted Miss Lars about her "editing."

"Well, hello, Desmond! You're just the person I was looking for," she said, oblivious to my anger.

"Me? What did I do?"

"You…did…an absolutely stupendous job on your *four* stories in today's paper!"

She placed several red stars next to my name written at the top of a chart taped to the blackboard.

"A front-page news story on the new Teen Health Center. A wonderful little profile on Jorge, our new morning janitor. A news brief on the deadline for ordering yearbooks, and yet another about the lunch menu. No misspellings. No fragments! You're my little star reporter, aren't you?"

"But what was all that about Jamal's quote? About the condoms?"

"Well, I wasn't going to say anything, because I don't like to focus on the negative. But, yes. There is room for improvement with your quotes."

She went on about how receiving five "Lars-Stars" in the first week was an unprecedented record for her student reporters. Only three other students received any stars at all for this issue, one of which was a half-star. The red Lars-Stars represent an "A" grade. I received an extra-credit fifth (gold) star for not having any typos or misspellings. Whoever ended up with the most stars at the end of the school year would receive the special treat of having lunch with Miss Lars. It occurred to me that calling Miss Lars out on her cavalier editing would most likely make my life more complicated. And, for a moment, I considered graciously accepting the goddamn gold star. But thanks to the voices of Uncle Lalo, Mr. Gibb, and the other editorial ghosts clamoring in the collective unconsciousness of my head, I simply could not.

"Miss Lars, I know you majored in creative writing and all. But isn't it, you know, unethical to make up quotes?"

"Excuse me?"

She stopped just short of stapling through my gold star.

"Unethical? That's a very heavy word to throw around. Are you sure you're aware of its meaning?"

"Mr. Gibb over at Westgate always told me to be careful when quoting anyone because, you know, it's—it's their words, not mine. And not yours."

"Are you suggesting we mischaracterized a student's position in print?"

"We? You're the one who wrote it! There's no way Jamal would say any of that shit—I mean—stuff—about safe sex or whatever."

"First of all, watch your mouth, young man. Secondly, the way you describe 'stuff about safe sex or whatever' is precisely why you need a good editor. Your job is to report on the views and news of the campus, and, with a little guidance, that's exactly what you did."

Just then, Jamal walked in.

Wearing all orange and carrying a stack of *The Galleons*, he shouted in my direction. "Yo! Desi! Come here, man."

I froze like a bag of blueberries. Before I could think to apologize or explain, Jamal reached over in my direction, not to hit me, but to deliver a high-five.

"Man. That article you wrote on me was tight! For reals, man. You made me sound *hella* cool. I been getting all kinds of looks from girls today. I'm pretty sure one of them's going to ask *me* out to the dance. Man, Desi. You did me a solid. Where can I get more copies?"

Miss Lars, listening to every word, stepped down from her ladder to hand over a half-dozen more copies of *The Galleon*.

"Here you are, Jamal."

He thanked Miss Lars, grabbed the extra papers, and paid me another high-five while making an orange-slice move for the door. The bell for the next class rang and several students began pouring into Miss Lars' next debate class. Miss Lars turned her back to write something about the pros and cons of abortion on the blackboard.

I looked up at the Lars-Stars chart and saw that my gold star was no longer there.

Chapter 4

While Vasco's teen pregnancies and STDs ranked among the highest in the country, our 2.17 student GPA was among the lowest in the Bay Area. We had dress codes not only to prevent conflicts from kids wearing rival gang colors, but also to keep others from wearing fast food uniforms to school, since many Vasco students spent more time working night shifts flipping burgers at McDonald's or loading UPS trucks than studying on campus. With enough common sense and a relatively reasonable family upbringing, the majority of us could still stay out of serious trouble.

When it came to Vasco's real gangster thugs, I had a couple of things in my favor: many of these hoodlums were friends with my brother, and most of the others were afraid of him. These were defense mechanisms that I never needed or wanted to test. It seemed obvious to me that the way to get caught up in gang politics was to care about them. I sure didn't. But there was one problem at Vasco that neither an A-plus student nor a kid with an AK-47 could avoid: the bathroom.

There were eight sets of boys' and girls' bathrooms at Vasco High School, and each one somehow seemed nastier than the next. The toilets that didn't have clogged plumbing had doors taken off hinges, providing no privacy. Even the most obsessive-compulsive graffiti artist avoided the otherwise irresistible canvas of bathroom walls due to an inability to not drop a pen into a puddle of piss while gagging at the stench. And it wasn't one of those deals where the girls' bathroom was any less decrepit than the boys'. Those of us not lucky enough to live within walking distance of our homes often made a two-block trek to the nearby gas station, where the toilets were clean(er). Sometimes we'd go to the junior high school that was connected to Vasco by a wide alley. Eventually, the neighboring principal or gas station attendant would catch on and kick us out. The only time I remember using a Vasco High (student) bathroom was while covering a basketball game for *The Galleon* that went into overtime.

•••

I DIDN'T SEE HER at first. We were in the boys' bathroom, after all. Naturally, I was a bit flustered when her voice called out from inside one of the stalls.

"Hi. I'm writing a news story for the Union High School newspaper on the poor conditions of Vasco High's bathrooms. Do you mind if I ask you some questions for my story?"

Abiding by instinctive guy code, I continued to face the urinal wall, avoiding eye contact until fully fidgeting my zipper back into place. Gathering composure while keeping my tape recorder from falling out of my pocket and onto the cracked porcelain, I adjusted my belt back into place and turned around to face her.

"I'm sorry. What exactly are you doing here?"

"*I said*: I'm writing a story for the Union High School newspaper on the—"

"Yeah, yeah, yeah. I heard that part. But aren't you, you know… in the wrong bathroom? And the wrong school, maybe?"

"Not at all. I've been assigned to cover tonight's Vasco-Union basketball game. I had to use the bathroom—and my god! I mean. Wow! This is the real story here. These bathrooms are horrendous. How can anyone study in these kinds of conditions? I can't believe someone on the faculty hasn't called the mayor about this. Or *The Call*. I bet Don Royce over at Channel Seven will be all over this. *So?* Can I quote you or not?"

"Well, I'm covering the basketball game for our school paper, too. So you know. Might be kinda weird quoting another student reporter, don't you think? I'm Desmond, by the way."

I reached out to shake her hand before realizing it was not the most appropriate thing to do. I followed her perturbed signal out of the bathroom and into the dark evening campus.

"*You* write for *The Galleon*?"

"Yeah," I answered, surprised that she was surprised—but even more surprised that she knew the name of Vasco's school newspaper when many of our own students didn't.

"Why haven't you written about this yet? I mean, come on. This is a great story!"

"Great? Well. I never thought of it that way. Sorta sucks more than anything, you know?"

She gave my entire presence a second read.

"Wait a minute," I said, defensively. "I did write something on the bathrooms. I did a brief last month on how some students complained…and the principal promised to address the issue…

after spring break…or something like that. I dunno. Can't exactly remember the details."

My memory had faded after this "news" was heavily edited by Miss Lars. It was another early lesson that any story with teeth to it would no longer have much bite once Miss Lars put one of her gold star edits on it.

"That was you? You call that regurgitated faculty fluff a news story? Give me a break!"

It was then, under a cracked and dimly lit lamp fixture dangling outside the gymnasium, that I realized that this girl was impeccably pretty. Yet somehow I was not at all nervous around her. Not in the way a clumsy teenaged boy ought to be when standing next to a girl who lived far further down Puberty Way. She looked like one of those television news anchors that Uncle Lalo told me to never trust because, as he insisted, they lived "inauthentic lives."

But she was right. My story was fluff. And the Vasco bathroom debacle would indeed be a "great" Bay Area news story.

"Yeah, well, you know. *Editors*," I said, in my best irreverent tone. "Miss Lars, my editor, she has this thing where she grades you with these stars and—wait a minute. You read that story? You read *The Galleon*?"

"Of course. I read all the city's high school papers—public and private. Mission High, Galileo High, Sacred Heart. I mean. Come on. How else would I know what stories I might be missing? Obviously, I want to know how my work compares with other candidates for the San Francisco Newspaper Agency's City High School internship."

"The what?"

"You don't know what an internship is? Well, I guess I don't have to read *The Galleon* anymore, now do I?"

"No. I mean, I know what an internship is. But what's the thing? You know. The one you're talking about? Is that with *The Call*?"

"The San Francisco Newspaper Agency? The JOA?" she said, overtly rolling her eyes at my ignorance. "The Joint Operating Agreement? That's how *The Call* and *The Inquirer* work to share the same building and presses. So there are actually two internships, one with *The Mornin' Call* and one with *The Afternoon Inky*."

I hated the way she gave the papers nicknames, like she knew them better than I did. But clearly, she did.

"Oh. Right. That internship. I'll check it out. Thanks for the tip. Hey, shouldn't we get back to covering the game?"

"Nah. There's another four minutes left in O.T. I'm not in a rush. Union's gonna win. Coach Garcia told me he'd put Kevin Simmons in the game for the final minutes. He's just trying to give the benchwarmers some playing time to get ready for Washington next week. Once Simmons gets court time he'll take over."

Outside the gym's main entrance, we heard a collective groan come from Vasco fans as Mr. Bruno's voice on the PA shouted, "Simmons for three."

"Well, Desmond. I'm going to go take some more notes in the bathroom. You'll be covering next month's Union-Vasco game at our campus, I trust? Look for me in our newsroom after the game. I'll give you the paperwork to apply for that internship."

"Wait," I called, as her silhouette blended back into the darkened dankness. "What's your name?"

"Maryanne," she said, swooping her long, feathered red hair from one shoulder to another. "My name is Maryanne Miller."

•••

During the weeks leading up to the next Union-Vasco basketball game, I studied up on the politics and history of the San Francisco newspaper business by playing hooky at the public library. The downtown public library is not the easiest place in San Francisco for a student to cut class in. This is sadly ironic, considering that no one in the SFPD would give much of a second glance to school-aged kids hanging out around any other part of the city in the middle of the day. But at the library, it's a different story.

There are several ways for a student to be barred entry by library security guards at the entrance. Chief among them: carrying a boombox, wearing empty backpacks blatantly intended for stealing, or for just plain "actin' hella dumb." Young couples holding hands wouldn't stand a chance. Not since librarians finally caught on that the hormonal kids were using the back rooms to study biology without books. But then again, if you were too unassuming, they'd just as soon throw your preteen ass back onto the Tenderloin drug-dealing streets, too. There was, however, a simple, fail-safe solution.

"Homeschooling." The security guard immediately backed off as if he'd encountered an insect that he was unfamiliar with. With that came a free pass to spend the day watching a VHS tape of *Citizen Kane*, a film Mr. Gibb repeatedly insisted I watch.

"Ahh," said the homeless man in the adjacent viewing booth. "Greatest American film of all time."

Even his (cilantro-scented?) B.O. couldn't distract me from every mesmerizing moment of the life and times of George W. Apperson. The dramatic proclamations set against the imagery of newsreels…the chicks in fancy fur coats…the sprawling mansion… the dudes with press passes in their hats…*starting a freaking war*. I watched *Citizen Kane* twice that day and was about to make it a third when the homeless guy still sitting at my side interrupted.

"Come on kid, it ain't *that* great."

I adjusted my headphones and pretended not to hear him.

"You know that cat was born here in San Francisco, right?"

Using mostly my shoulders, I answered with an ambiguous scoff.

"Don't ignore me, man. I know what I'm talking about. I'm speaking the truth."

"Who? Orson Welles?"

"No man. I'm talking about Apperson. Citizen Fucking Apperson."

The homeless man laughed. As a nervous reaction, I laughed along with him.

"Seriously, man. Apperson was a *total* San Francisco son of a bitch. And a real bastard. He was the fucking Chief. The fucking *San Francisco Inquirer*, man? The fucking Apperson building off Market Fucking Street? I'm not making this up, man. You might as well get your non-fucking-fictional names and facts straight if you're gonna watch this movie a hundred fucking times, kid."

After dropping too many audible F-bombs, the homeless man grabbed the attention of a chafed librarian. We split into different directions to avoid security. The homeless man headed for the bathroom, and I headed for the biography section. Although he may have looked like a surfer version of Charles Manson, the man proved trustworthy. That day I checked out two books about the life of George W. Apperson and another on the history of American journalism.

In real life, George W. Apperson was indeed a San Francisco son of a bitch. Born in 1863, the son of Southern-born silver magnate and US Senator George Apperson, Charles picked up his love of newspapers after getting expelled from Harvard for printing an "anti-establishment editorial" in the university paper. Upon returning to San Francisco, he convinced his parents to give him control of *The San Francisco Inquirer*, a newspaper that "Papa Apperson" obtained through a gambling debt owed to him.

Just like in the movie, Charles headed down that newspaperman road full speed ahead and never looked back. Sure, there were bumps along the way. He sensationalized some stories here and there, making stuff up if need be. He "sort of" started a war. He was a self-obsessed, power-hungry, holier-than-thou, corrupted bastard. There's "evidence" he might have been involved in a "murder." And his kidnapped granddaughter-turned-guerrilla carried on the family tradition of going a bit batshit crazy by wielding semiautomatic rifles and robbing banks. Nothing a Sansome wouldn't do too, when you think about it. Or a Pulitzer, for that matter.

Even at age fifteen, I knew the name Pulitzer stood for something cool. I never would have guessed that the award was named after a man, Joseph Pulitzer, who, like Holden Caulfield with a gun, klutzily tried to shoot and kill a man in retaliation for an insult. He missed. The man laughed. Pulitzer refocused his passion by aiming it into newspaper ink. I didn't understand why, but for some reason, these newspaperman morals made much more sense to me than the shootings, stabbings, or other improvised attempts to maim or kill happening at my school.

I continued to flip through the pages while walking down four full blocks to the Apperson Building off Market Fucking Street. At about a dozen stories high, it wasn't as tall and imposing as I thought it would be. But the ornate "A" atop the entrance and the golden gargoyles guarding it gave good clues into his high-maintenance personality. I stared across the city street and thought about how, a hundred years earlier, he stood in the exact spot I was in. Zoning in and out, it occurred to me that I was making eye contact with the statue of a lion outside the first-floor entrance of the building directly across Market Street. It was one of two statuettes of lions situated side-by-side to the words "Sansome Building," spread atop the crest of the San Quentin–esque building that I had visited not long before. I loved that the two competing newspaper publishers had established headquarters directly across the street from one another. I wondered if they had a similar situation set up in heaven or in hell. Boarding the subway with my head buried in the legends of these men's lives, I began to decide whose side I was on.

Chapter 5

It was homecoming season, which meant us dudes were looking for dates. A rainy morning forcing coed PE dodgeball to take place in the gym served as a perfect opportunity. I was gladly eliminated early on from the game by another freshman, Angelo Espinoza, and had scoped out Claire Davies, a pretty-even-in-PE-sweats sophomore. Using my Apperson biography as a prop, I successfully engaged her in conversation, while Angelo tried to do the same.

"Damn, Desi. Too bad your dick ain't as big as that book."

Claire and I did our best to ignore the short and stocky Angelo by talking about how *The Galleon* was not a very newspapery-sounding name. Before I could steer the subject toward Claire's plans for the homecoming dance, Angelo threw a red rubber dodgeball at about fifty-five mph that connected with the side of my reddened face. He then delivered a "yo mama" joke with a punch line that was in no way memorable or funny, yet succeeded in sending me into a temporary fury. Summoning the spirits of Apperson, Pulitzer, and the Sansomes, I stood up, adjusted the sleeves of my blue-and-orange PE sweats and motioned to pick up the big red bouncy ball.

Borrowing a trick from my brother, instead of throwing the ball back, I immediately threw a punch that landed directly between Angelo's upper lip and left nostril. From there, the fight was a rather routine scene, with two sets of arms and legs flailing and wrestling wildly as we both waited for someone to break it up. Neither one of us was necessarily more scared or stronger than the other. I'm pretty sure we had been in the same trick-or-treating group with our older siblings in the not too distant past. Angelo knew my mother was dead. But maybe he had forgotten. As my fury subsided, I began to give him the benefit of the doubt, still attempting to deliver a few key blows to the head and neck area that might encourage onlookers to avoid me next year. Claire, unimpressed, had already left. Seconds later, Coach Webster was escorting us to the vice principal's office. Once seated, Angelo and I stopped flashing the obligatory halfhearted hard looks at one another.

"How long you think we'll get suspended?" he asked.

Of course. This was most likely Angelo's goal all along. He wasn't too lucky with the ladies either. Getting suspended around the time of the homecoming dance would be a good alibi for not finding a date in time.

"I dunno," I said, feeling duped. "I did an interview with Vice Principal Galan, so if we get to talk to her, I bet I can convince her to—"

POP-POP. POP

"*Oh shit!*"

"*What the hell was that?!*"

"Oh, come on. Those were probably just cherry bombs."

"Damn, that was hella close by."

"Everybody calm down and keep quiet, goddammit!"

I don't know who said what. But everyone in the vice principal's office knew that the loud popping sounds outside were not firecrackers. Nobody kept quiet and nobody calmed down. Like any car wreck involving strangers, everyone in that office— faculty included—gravitated toward what they knew would be a bloody scene.

I grabbed a pen and sheet of paper off of the secretary's desk. Angelo stuffed all three colored carbon copies of Mr. Webster's write-ups inside the elastic band of his sweatpants. Near the school's arched adobe entrance, a growing crowd hovered around a student who was sitting with his back against a concrete staircase. He kept a tight clutch on his left leg while leaning back and forth as if attempting a truly agonizing sit-up.

Surrounding the victim were two of his friends and two teachers, both shooing the other pair to get out of the injured young man's way. The lunch bell had just rung. Ignoring Principal Hersey's megaphone plea to disperse, the crowd of students and teachers grew larger. With pen and paper in hand, I inched my way around the crowd and climbed atop the flagpole stand to catch a better view. The sputtering I heard along the way suggested that the injured student's name was Jermaine Haverlock. A senior. This was relatively easy to corroborate since it was also the surname written on the back of his Vasco High football jersey. The pair of teachers eventually won the battle over the pair of Jermaine's friends, convincing them to get out of the way so that a nurse from the Teen Health Center could attend to him.

"Do you think it was Ronnie Choe?" I overheard one girl ask another. "I betchoo it was."

I continued to take notes, thinking for some reason that if I didn't, Maryanne Miller would. I had never met Ronnie Choe, but like most kids on campus, had heard of him. He would have graduated a few years before had he not been expelled for carrying a concealed weapon that he flashed at anyone dumb enough to ask him for his hall pass. Some said it was a knife. Others said it was an Uzi. Hector insisted it was probably just ninja throwing stars and that it all got blown out of proportion.

The story of Ronnie Choe as a suspect continued to take shape as several girls gathered around his little sister, Lillian, who was in my grade. She looked more shook up than the rest of her friends, who shielded her from looking over at Jermaine. After about twenty slow motion minutes passed, someone in the crowd finally snapped us all out of it.

"Damn. Where the fuck's the ambulance at?"

The cops, apparently more familiar with the route, showed up first. Three squad cars and a paddy wagon. Fifteen minutes later when the ambulance arrived, several lingering students chastised the paramedics for taking so long, effectively making it take even longer for them to finally reach Jermaine. After making eye contact with Lillian, Jermaine appeared to look less in pain.

"He looks pissed."

"He looks tough."

"Don't he look like Wesley Snipes?"

These student observations weren't any more or less accurate or meaningful than the comments I heard from faculty members who watched as the ambulance screeched off.

"He'll be fine."

"He's actually really lucky."

"Poor kid."

Indeed.

The poor, pissed-off kid was, luckily, going to be fine.

One of the bullets grazed the back of "his rather muscular calf." Those were the details I picked up on by eavesdropping on a conversation between our principal, Mr. Hersey, and one of the paramedics. Their conversation was cut short by a reporter whom I thought I recognized as the cursing lady who stole my sandwich during that field trip to *The Call* newsroom. They spoke from the center of a short set of stairs that led to the public sidewalk on Cayuga Avenue, where Mr. Hersey's imposing presence attempted to push the reporter back onto the street.

"Mike, I'm going to have to ask *again,*" she said, moving a step forward. "Do you believe this was gang-related or not? Please just answer the goddamn question. That way I won't have to keep asking."

It was her, all right.

"Again. All that I can confirm for you, Miss…?"

"Mike, we've been through this before, and my name is still Maureen."

"Miss Maureen…is that a seventeen-year-old student attending Vasco High suffered serious but non-life-threatening injuries from an incident that we are continuing to investigate with the police. Now, I'm going to have to ask you to please—"

"Vasco has the highest violence, drop-out, and syphilis rates and the lowest test scores in the city's school district. Pretending that these problems don't exist is not going to help you solve them. People need to know what is going on here, Mike. Do you realize that you're only bullshitting yourself?"

Mr. Hersey's arrogant eyes squinted with disdain. The principal folded his arms across his chest, lifted his head, and literally looked down at the reporter.

"Mike, saying nothing is not going to help save your job when the board votes to close down this school at the next budget meeting."

"Miss Maureen, if you have any further questions, I'm sure Sgt. Alexander will be happy to answer them for you. Now, if you'll excuse me."

Maureen walked across the street where several students had decided to eat their lunches, despite the growing rain. As I followed, she stopped and turned her head toward me.

"Look. I'm trying to work here. It's not polite to listen in other people's conversations, you know?

"Sorry. It's just that…well, I'm a reporter, too. With the school paper."

"Aha! Well, in that case. It would be stupid of you not to listen in on other people's conversations, wouldn't it? Good for you, kid. What's your name?"

"Desi."

"Nice to meet you, Desi. I'm Maureen. How would you like to write this story for me for *The Call*? At this rate, it probably won't be more than a few sentences long."

"His name is Jermaine Haverlock," I said, reading from my raindrop-stained notes. "He's a senior on the football team. And the basketball team, I think. Pretty popular guy. Uhhh. He's lucky to have thick calf muscles. Ummm. I think he's dating a Korean girl named Lillian. She's a freshman. So I think everyone thinks her older brother, Ronnie Choe, shot him, which makes sense because everyone knows he used to come to school with an Uzi. And… Let's see. I wouldn't doubt that Ronnie is in a gang, but no, even though Mr. Hersey would be the last person to know, I don't think this was gang-related."

Maureen hesitated for a moment. Then, out of polite obligation, began taking notes.

"You know," said Maureen, talking while writing, "Unless I get to talk to the parents and police, I'm not sure I can use any of this. But that's helpful stuff, Desi. Thanks."

"No problem! Hey. I think you owe me a sandwich."

Maureen let out an embarrassed laugh, like a person does when they're not sure they completely understood a joke.

"Is that right? You expect to get paid with food? Well then, I guess you really are a newspaper reporter, aren't you?"

Her attention became instantly redirected toward two police officers walking back to the last SFPD patrol car on the scene.

"Hey," I asked, as we both walked in that direction. "What was all that about Vasco closing down?"

"Desi, you were a big help," she said, advancing toward the officers. "But look. I gotta go talk to these cops before they leave. And then I got to run back down to the newsroom and work on another story for tomorrow. I tell you what. Why don't you send me a copy of your story when it comes out in your school paper? Or if you want a tour of the newsroom sometime, call the main number and ask to leave a message for Maureen."

Chapter 6

The bell rang, signaling the end of lunch. Instead of going to history class, I ran in the direction of the empty *Galleon* newsroom and began writing a story about the school shooting. Miss Lars didn't have a fifth period class, and always spent that hour on her power walk workout around the indoor basketball courts, so I knew I'd have the space to myself. I wrote down as many of the observations from the past hour as possible, and then used our newsroom's phonebooks to get the addresses and phone numbers for Jermaine and Ronnie. Maybe I'd go to Jermaine's house, or Ronnie's. Well, on second thought, maybe not Ronnie's house.

I found three Haverlocks listed in the phonebooks. One was on Persia Avenue—about a twenty-minute walk from Vasco. During the beginning of basketball season I had photocopied a list of all the players' numbers and home addresses, borrowed from Coach Webster's binder while he was off flirting with the volleyball coach. I kept that sheet, along with a few other similarly acquired documents, in a folder labeled "Desi's Math Homework" in my cubbyhole. Yes, Vasco had among the highest violence rates of any high school in the country, but for some reason we weren't too tough to still call our storage spaces "cubbies." It was like we were all still longing to be in elementary school. I found a Haverlock on Coach Webster's list. Only it wasn't Jermaine.

HAVERLOCK, HERMAN (JUNIOR VARSITY).

CENTER. SIX-ONE. SOLID JUMP SHOT. HOTHEAD.

NEEDS: WORK ON PIVUTTS.

IMPROVE DECISION MAKING IN HIGH STRESS SITUATIONS.

821 PERSIA AVE. 415-615-3554.

MOM: CYNTHIA. FATHER: HARMOND.

BROTHER: JERMAINE (VARSITY).

WITH SEVEN INCREASINGLY NERVOUS minutes left before Miss Lars might show up and start interrogating me, I decided against sifting through the thirty or so Choe listings in the phonebook, figuring Ronnie was probably busy avoiding visits from others. Grabbing someone else's umbrella along the way, I bolted out of the *Galleon* newsroom door just as the rain turned to hail. From the corner of my eye I saw Miss Lars about a dozen yards away, Reebok-ing it back toward her classroom door. Using a lesson planner to protect her shoulder-length brown hair from the icy pellets and through her thick, fog-filled burgundy eyeglasses, she gestured an instruction of some kind toward me. I covered my face with the umbrella I secretly hoped was hers.

Picking up my pace in rhythm with the pounding hail, I exited campus through Onondaga Avenue. I looked up at the street sign and thought about how a few weeks before we learned in Mr. Jones'

California history class that Onondaga was the name for a Native American tribe. It meant "people of the hills." They were involved in some kind of big peacekeeping proposition. This fascinated me, in part because Onondaga Avenue was as flat as it was boring— except of course for the weekly fistfights that broke out at the bus stops before and after school.

I suggested to Miss Lars that we do a series of stories on the histories of all the different street names around Vasco High School. She thought the idea was "cute" but that we needed to stick to her agenda and curriculum of assignments. The relentless rain continued to fall, and I began walking faster with its pace, stomping through puddles, kicking at garbage and leftover lunchtime litter along the way. I was overcome by a sudden and overwhelming sense of anger and hatred for Miss Lars.

The only thing that eased my fury was the thought that maybe this was how real reporters feel about their editors. That's how it always seemed in the movies, anyway. Perhaps this was all part of my process in my movie. But those guys always get the stories out and get their way in the end. Somehow I knew for certain that no matter how hard I worked, Miss Lars—or Mr. Hersey for that matter—would never let me publish it in *The Galleon*. Now I hated Mr. Hersey too.

"No," I thought to myself. "I don't hate him. I *fucking* hate him. I fucking hate him and his Ward Cleaver haircut and I fucking hate Miss Lars and her stupid fucking gold stars." The hate inside of me was as destructive as it was undeniable. I yearned to find a way to let it out. I couldn't understand why, but I also began feeling an equally deep sense of empathy for Ronnie Choe.

As far as I knew, he was an absolute asshole and would probably shoot me in my skinny calf just for the fun of it. I imagined his honest and earnest father coming from Korea twenty years ago or so and washing dishes at a fancy Nob Hill hotel restaurant. I pictured him getting scolded and disrespected by the manager the way my father always told me happened to him at the Mark Hopkins Hotel when he first arrived in San Francisco back in 1962. The Asian cooks would always find a way to get my father to calm down or laugh it off. They'd distract him by sending him home with free food or expensive silverware that would then make its way back to our family in Chile.

I wondered if our fathers might have worked together. I wondered if Ronnie was ever friends with my brother Hector, or whether they had ever been on opposite sides of a brawl. If they had, I doubt they would have remembered it. Just like they wouldn't have remembered that they were probably standing next to one another fifteen years ago, both learning to speak English by singing "Rudolph the Red-Nosed Reindeer" at the same elementary school assembly before Christmas vacation.

When the rain finally stopped I looked up at the Ocean Avenue street sign. I had walked in the opposite direction of Jermaine and Herman's house on Persia Avenue, which is where I thought I was supposed to be going. I continued north on Ocean Avenue, passing defunct train tracks, empty playgrounds, and illegally parked cars with smashed windows; this all led to the freeway overcrossing, not far from where my family lived.

That was the last place I wanted to go. Starving, but with no money, I considered stealing something from one of the Latin American fruit stands that spilled onto the sidewalk. Indecisive, ashamed, and exhausted, I finally sat down on a bench below an awning outside a small pizzeria. With the back of my head pressed up against the storefront window that divided the restaurant from a cigar shop, I sat and watched people get on and off the city streetcars, waiting for someone to either recognize me or until the pizzeria manager told me to go away. A half hour passed and neither one of those scenarios had played out. I forced the issue by sprawling out on the bench and attempting to fall asleep.

"Ain't you Hector's little brother? Damn, little man. You look like you is through for the day."

I instinctively snapped back the way I had learned to do with the worst of my older brother's friends.

"Shut up, man. I ain't that much littler than you, man." He was about three inches taller and, at five-foot-five, I still had about as many years to catch up.

"I'm just playing with you, homey. You've got yourself a little bit of temper there. And I guess you do look like you've had a fucked-up day, now, don't you?"

I took a closer look to see if I could recognize him as one of the usual suspects that would take over my family's basement, where Hector hung out to lift weights or drink and smoke while my father was at work. He had a San Francisco Giants baseball cap on, positioned slightly sideways. He wore a matching black-and-orange Adidas track suit, with a thick gold chain wrapped around the fully zipped collar. Instead of an umbrella, he was carrying what looked like an old and possibly broken record player wrapped in a see-through plastic trash bag.

"You know my brother?"

"Everybody knows Hector the Protector."

He placed the record player next to me on the bench in order to attend to a smudge on his very expensive looking hi-top sneakers. Three visible cigarette burns were grouped below his knuckles.

"Are you Filipino or Latino?"

This was an attempt to better determine the nature of his relationship with my brother. He laughed and continued to attend to his other shoe, where there was no smudge.

"Damn. Now, that's an interesting question. Well, if you must know, I'm half Filipino. Half Korean."

As he carefully and methodically tied each shoe I could make out the letters "RC" dangling from the middle of his gold necklace. I froze in fear.

"So, to answer your real question, no, I didn't exactly roll *with* your brother. But it's cool. None of that shit matters no more."

He straightened up and suddenly appeared especially taller.

"So. What the fuck happened at Vas today?"

"Are you Ronnie Choe?"

"I prefer to be called the Chosen One."

"Wait a minute. You didn't shoot nobody, did you?"

"No. Not today. Not tomorrow. Not I, son. Not I, said the fly one."

"How come everybody keeps saying you shot Jermaine?"

"Lemme tell you something, little man. People will believe what they want to believe. I choose to believe in me, little de Leon."

"How did you recognize *me*?"

"You in my little sister's grade, ain't you? Sometimes I'll be looking through her school yearbooks. Reminds me of all the shit that don't matter no more. Shit trips me out how you can tell someone's headed for a fucked-up life just by their last name or the stupid hard look on their face. Damn. You look exactly like your brother. But I take it you don't act too much like him, now do you? You in the chess club or some shit like that?"

"School paper."

"That's right. Good for you, little man. Good for you. You gonna be on the news someday?"

"Yeah, I guess so. Well, I dunno." I put my next thought on hold before deciding to fire away. "Actually. I'm working on a story for the school paper about how *you* shot Jermaine Haverlock. Can I interview you or something like that?"

Ronnie took a moment to decide whether this was funny. He gave his final verdict with a smile and a sigh.

"Awright. That's cool. But only if you talk about how I'm the flyest turntablist that barely ever went to Vas."

I followed Ronnie Choe into the tiny pizza place. The bells on the door banged against the glass, announcing that customers had entered and that our destiny-planned interview had begun. The college kid behind the counter put down his Kerouac paperback to take our order.

"You know, I think the cops might be looking for you."

"They so hella stupid. They was all over my mom's house, going through my room and shit. They tried to pretend they couldn't understand her English when she told them I was *at an appointment with my parole officer down by eight-fifty Bryant the whole time.* My parole officer even drove me to the Ingleside station to back it up. They thought I was turning myself in. So stupid. No apologies. Nothing."

"Man."

I had no idea what to ask next.

Ronnie ordered two slices for me, and two for him. "It's like I told you, little man. People will always be believing what they want to believe."

"What about your sister? I heard she was going out with Jermaine or something like that."

"Little man, I've made enough mistakes in my life to know that ain't nobody gonna figure you out but you. I mean, I got her back if it's an emergency or some shit like that. Hey, I tell all my little sisters, when it comes down to it. In this world, you come in on your own…"

He paused to avoid speaking with his mouth full.

"And then you leave on your own."

Feeling more confident talking to him as a reporter, and in some weird way as a friend, I went against the grain of the good vibe by asking a very, very stupid question.

"So. Who do you think shot Jermaine?"

Ronnie dropped his pizza on the paper plate and slammed his fist against the counter.

"Now how the hell am I supposed to know?"

He wiped his mouth with a napkin.

"Look. I ain't been near that school in like five years. I wouldn't be surprised if that dumbass probably shot hisself by accident. Probably him and his friends trying to show off they's gat or some stupid shit like that."

He took another bite as if it were a reward for not losing his temper.

"But hey. That ain't no none of my business anyhow, now is it?"

Our conversational interview lasted for about forty-five more minutes. It wasn't until the very end that Ronnie pointed out how I hadn't taken a single note. I told Ronnie that my tape recorder ran out of batteries, but that I'd remember the important things he'd said, the most significant of which was that he didn't shoot Jermaine. We walked out onto Ocean Avenue back toward the Balboa Park train station.

• • •

THE EARLY EVENING SKY grew into wintered darkness as we crisscrossed along shortcuts between unyielding cars and busses, ignoring the flashing red hands telling us when and where to stop. The headlights and streetlamps gave a shimmering feeling to the street, as if our chosen jaywalked pathway was somehow safer or smarter than using the traditional sidewalks.

It was probably too dark for anyone to notice, but I secretly hoped someone from my school would see me walking with Ronnie Choe. Ronnie was on his way to a club somewhere downtown, south of Market, where he said he could get me in, even though it was twenty-one and older only. He had been a regular DJ there for six months, and planned to do the same in New York because he was a finalist in some kind of turntable competition. Ronnie talked about how he had applied for his passport the week before and that he was saving up for a flight to London. Stopping in the narrow pedestrian walkway in the middle of a freeway overcrossing, he placed headphones over my ears.

"Check this out, little man."

I listened to the repeating piano riff played over a simple drumbeat, with a woman's voice singing something very sweet and catchy about not hiding from the truth. The Chosen One rapped aggressively in-between her verses, giving the song an unexpected but beautiful balance. Even with the freeway sounds of cars driving by below, I could hear what he wanted me, and soon, the rest of the world, to hear. The song came to an end. Ronnie appeared equal parts strong and vulnerable as he waited for my reaction without asking for it.

"This is nice, man. It's got tenderness. But it's also got teeth, you know?"

"Exactly! My man! Damn. Little Desi. Tenderness with teeth! See. You get it, man!"

We said little else as we walked another quarter mile to the train station on Geneva Avenue that would take him toward downtown and me to I still didn't know where.

"Hey, Ronnie. I mean Chosen One," I said as he inserted his ticket into the turnstile. "I've been meaning to ask you. Did your dad ever wash dishes at the Mark Hopkins Hotel?"

Ronnie appeared half-aggravated, half-amused.

"Desmond de Leon," he said, as his chosen train approached. "I don't know what it is, but something tells me you just a little bit loco in the coco."

Chapter 7

My brother loved me more than I loved him.

"*Mira*," our father would tell us, breaking up wrestling fights. "I don't care if you like each other or not. But you'd better love one another. *Siempre somos familia, carajo!*"

Sometimes it seemed like my widowed father was trying to convince himself of this, particularly when it came to dealing with Hector. Our father had limited parenting energy after our mother was killed by a hit-and-run driver in 1982—a week before my seventh birthday. Overnight, Hector and I were awarded Artful Dodger lifestyles and could more or less come and go as we pleased. My brother was seven years older than me, and I can never remember a time when he wasn't getting into some kind of trouble. It started with shoplifting at the Stop-N-Go liquor store around the corner from our house on Joost Avenue. I was with him the first time he got caught. Menthol cigarettes. They weren't for him, he told my father, which technically speaking was the truth.

Hector was constantly trying to impress the older kids in the neighborhood who spent days and nights hanging out front of the twenty-four-hour liquor and sandwich store. That first time he got caught stealing, I was five and Hector around twelve. It wasn't long before she died. Our mother had sent us there to buy some milk and eggs, and told us to use the change to buy a little candy or a small toy. She must not have gone down by herself in years, because if she had, she'd have known it was the most convenient place in our immediate neighborhood for kids to get into some kind of trouble. She had known Hassan, the Armenian owner, for years—but mostly by phone, from when she'd call in an order for us to pick up.

On our way in Hector felt obliged to confront the older kids in some way, usually by challenging the biggest and therefore drunkest one to a "cap off" where they'd outdo one another with insults until one or the other took the words too far. Hector's bark actually was just as strong as his bite, which meant that Hector might eventually take the place of the biggest and therefore drunkest dude in the parking lot.

But at twelve, Hector still had further years of initiation yet to undergo. Hassan always kept our mother's order in a bag in the walk-in closet where, being the only employee, he would occasionally go, leaving the counter unattended for about seventeen seconds. Hector had his cigarette-stealing time clock worked down to nine seconds. Flat. Kool Menthol Lights had become the cigarette of choice for the neighborhood kids because those happened to be the closest to the unlocked portion of the glass window behind the register. My theory is that Hassan eventually caught on when his stock of Kools ran out in a neighborhood that was traditionally Marlboro Country.

I was sifting through a box of baseball cards when an enraged Hassan emerged from behind a rack of Hostess CupCakes to grab Hector by the throat. When Hector punched Hassan in the stomach, Hassan's Soviet-trained military might collapsed Hector facedown into the tile floor. Hector's heavyweight soul fought back for every second that Hassan spoke by phone with my mother, as the storekeeper's knee remained planted firmly in his back. The biggest and drunkest kid out front watched and laughed. The rest of what I remember from that incident is being back home waiting for Hector's crying and my father's Chileno cursing to end. When it did, I went to console Hector, only to find him smiling through his tears as he held up a pack of Kools like some kind of tobacco trophy.

Through the years, the tension between my father and Hector increased. Hector would argue that my father had a similarly aggressive and problematic history, and point to my father's many knife scars that dated to childhood fights around the docks of Valparaiso, where he was often found stealing cargo from ships. My father emphasized that the difference was that he only ever fought and stole for himself. And to survive. This was the premise of a never-ending argument that continued as Hector graduated from petty theft to grand larceny to assaults with deadly weapons with intention to inflict serious injury.

These memories came back to me as I walked down Geneva Avenue, passing several scenes of crimes and misdemeanors that Hector always insisted he was either innocent of, or at the very least, had not instigated. Thanks to an overcrowded county jail and a recent serious girlfriend, Hector was making somewhat of a comeback around this time. In-between jobs that apparently didn't bother with background checks, he spent the late evenings as a limo driver, bouncer at a club, and security guard at concerts. Hector liked to be around as many people for as long and as late as possible. During the days, he lifted weights or lounged around the rented house of his older girlfriend. I was pretty sure she lived somewhere off Geneva Avenue and in the direction of where I was headed, which I had finally decided was the Haverlock family home on Persia Avenue.

According to most San Francisco maps, the Haverlock house is in the Excelsior District. According to my mental map the Haverlocks lived in Cleveland. That's the name of the nearest elementary school, which had its playground directly across the street from the Haverlock home. Unlike the other side of the city, where folks are proud to point out that they live in North Beach, Russian Hill, or Pacific Heights, people around these unromantic Southern sections of San Francisco don't always want their neighborhood to be so easily identified.

My family's house on Joost Avenue was about a mile and a half away from the Haverlock's. Some of our neighbors claimed it as belonging to the more clean-and-friendly sounding Glen Park. Some saw it as the more realistic Balboa Park. Others stretched the geographic truth to place us in the more glamorous-sounding but absurdly incorrect Diamond Heights. I, my brother, and everyone else whose earliest memories began sometime in the seventies called it Sunnyside, because that's the name of the elementary school we went to. Around the first year of junior high school when kids from these ambiguously bordered neighborhoods came together to establish where they were from, the simplest thing to do was say:

"Yeah. I went to <u>Name of Elementary School Here</u>," with emphasis on past tense, as in, "I'm one day closer to getting the hell out of here."

Most of the kids I knew who went to Cleveland were either Filipino or Latino, with maybe a few Vietnamese, Korean, or

Chinese in-between. Most of the black kids we'd meet in junior high were from the other side of the freeway in the Bayview–Hunters Point district, where they most definitely could immediately pinpoint the precise name and location of the neighborhood that they did or did not live in. Being skeptical and cautious of people who looked different than you made practical and survivalist sense to my father. But he always insisted that he was not a racist, and he openly raised my brother and me to not be either. In his own way.

"*Mijo*," he'd say, from behind the wheel of his Buick Riviera, while watching and waiting at a stoplight for a black person to cross the street. "There are two kinds of *los negros*. The ones who have jobs and minds his business. And the ones who do not. And *es lo mismo con los Mexicanos…los Salvadoreños…los Filipinos…y…los Chilenos.*"

"What about *los gringos*?" I'd ask.

My father never knew how to answer that question. He would only ever laugh.

Approaching the 800 block of freshly puddled Persia Avenue, I wondered if Jermaine and his family would laugh or yell at me for asking to interview him about the shooting. Out around the driveway, several Cadillac-sized sedans were double-parked with their headlights still on. A few teens assembled around the front steps, where Vasco High–colored balloons were attached to the railing. Jermaine sat in the dazed center of attention.

"Hey, Jermaine. I'm Desmond de Leon. I don't mean to bother you, but I'm writing a story about the shooting for *The Galleon*—I mean the school paper. Is it cool if I ask you some questions about what happened?"

Jermaine fiddled with a string attached to a bouquet of raindrop-stained balloons at the top of the steps and stared out at the basketball courts across the street.

"Yeah. I know who you are."

That this popular senior (who would undoubtedly become more popular by tomorrow) knew who I was caught me off guard.

"Look, dude," said his brother, Herman, "Jermaine ain't got no comment."

"Herm. Leave him alone. He's cool. This is the dude who wrote all that cool stuff about you when you hit fifty against Washington."

"Which game against Washington? We ain't even played Washington yet. I don't remember no story like that."

Neither did I.

"*Herm.* This is the dude who *will* write that story when you hit fifty against Washington. So there ain't no reason you can't be cool. Quit being a fool."

An older woman's voice from inside the white clapboard house called out with instructions for the younger boys to put jackets on. They ran up the stairs in the direction of the front door, while the two older guys went over to check out one of the sleek sedans.

"Hey, Jermaine. I just want to make sure I clear up all the rumors and spread the truth, you know?"

"That's cool, man. There ain't much to know. I got shot. It hurt hella bad. Bullets is no fun. But I'm gonna be all right. That's all people really need to know."

"Do you know who shot you?"

"Yeah," he said, looking at me quite intently in the eye. "I know who shot me. But *like I said*, I'm gonna be all right. And that's all people need to know."

I considered ending the interview then and there based on the fact that getting this far was a victory in itself. But the newspaperman voices in my head urged me on.

"It wasn't Ronnie Choe who shot you, right?"

I was just as surprised by my question as Jermaine and Herman appeared to be. Jermaine shook his head back and forth and let out a mock laugh of disgust, as if he couldn't believe that I had disrespected his earlier peace offering of allowing himself to acknowledge that he even knew who I was.

"Yo, dude. Jermaine ain't got no comment about no Ronnie Ching-Chong-Choe." Herman appeared more agitated than Jermaine, who was back to staring out at the empty basketball courts across the street.

"That's cool, man. You don't have to answer if you don't want. Just part of my job to ask, you know."

"Job? The school pays you to do this shit?" asked Herman.

"Well no. They don't pay me. But if I want to do a good—"

"If you ain't getting paid, then it ain't your *job* to be asking no motherfucking questions."

Sensing the interview-ending buzzer, I prepared to launch a half-court question toward Jermaine.

"Hey, Jermaine. Did you, uh. You know. Sort of. Kinda. Accidentally. You know…shoot yourself? Or something like that?"

Jermaine snapped out of his daydream daze and cocked his head in my direction.

"Who the fuck told you that stupid shit?"

Both brothers appeared equally eager for an answer. Their combined anxiety gave me a sudden sense of strength.

"Ronnie Choe."

A longer, sleeker, and much more classic Cadillac drove up, braking abruptly and honking a get-the-hell-out-of-the-way message to the two older guys standing nearby. With the engine still running, the driver's side door opened up and out stepped a tall and lean forty-five-year-old looking hybrid of Jermaine and Herman. He wore a brown beret with a matching MUNI subway operator uniform.

"Get your damn jalopy out of my driveway," he shouted to the two older guys, who had already nervously begun to do so.

Herman attempted to make a discrete exit toward the backyard while Jermaine went back to staring in the direction of Cleveland.

"Herman Haverlock, you ain't going nowhere."

The man carefully parked his car in the driveway. He did so without closing the driver's side door until completely stepping back out of the vehicle. The steel bottoms of his leather boots clacked against the concrete as he and Herman both walked back in my direction.

"And who the hell is this?"

"Pardon me, sir. I'm a reporter with the school paper writing a story on the—"

"A reporter? Where's your notebook?"

It was a fair point.

Like with my Ronnie Choe interview, I hadn't thought about actually writing anything down. And I still had no batteries for my tape recorder. I patted down my pockets and pulled out a scrunched up napkin from the pizzeria. It would have to do. But something was still missing. A pen. It likely fell out of the hole in my pant pocket and was probably somewhere in a gutter near Hector's girlfriend's house on Geneva Avenue.

"Sorry, sir. I must've dropped my pen."

Staring at his two sons the entire time, Mr. Haverlock reached into his leather vest, pulled out a pen and handed it to me.

"This is good," he said, apparently to all of us. "I could use a reporter's help. We need to get the real story of what happened here today. And that's exactly what we're going to do."

Audibly clicking the plastic pen open, I took my first note:

...the real story...what hll hopned...?!?

"I told you, dad," said Herman. "It was..."

"It was a *lie* you told me back there in that hospital. If I didn't have to run back to my line so damn fast I would've caught you in that lie then. But I caught you now, son."

Napkin/notebook:

Dad...lie...cot u son,...!

"This wasn't no Oriental gangster thug who done this, now was it? You shot your own brother and you did it with *my* gun! Now how you gonna take another man's gun and then go and shoot his own son with it? What is *wrong* with you boy?"

Napkin/notebook:

holy shit.

"Dad. We shouldn't be talking about this in front of Desmond. If this dude writes his story it's going to get Herm expelled and he won't get no scholarship."

"Expelled?! How's about I expel you both out of my house? Po-lice come embarrass me at my work to tell me they found my gun—my daddy's Smith & Wesson no less—in a *garbage can* across the street from your school? You think I'm so dumb I ain't gonna find this out? No-no-no. Mr. Desmond the reporter needs to write this story. We ain't got no need to cover up no nothing in this Haverlock house."

"But, Dad. We was going to buy you another gun to replace it. We was just showing it off to get some other kids to back off Jermaine," said Herman, breaking into tears.

"We?" Jermaine's eyes also began to well up.

"Another gun? Son, you need another *brain*. You just lucky the detective was kind enough to wait 'til my shift was done before he come to question me."

Embarrassed to see Jermaine and Herman crying, I clicked the pen to the closed position, which made a noise loud enough to catch Mr. Haverlock's attention.

"Why aren't you writing this down, Mr. Desmond the reporter?"

"I'm sorry, sir. It just seems like this is more of a family matter now. Kind of private. You know what I mean?"

Tense seconds of my stomach-noise-over-silence passed.

"You two. Get in the car. Now."

"The car? But what about my leg?"

"I give a good goddamn about your leg the way you give a damn about my good name."

"Where…you taking…us…Dad?" said Herman, crying harder with each hyperventilated word. Herman helped Jermaine into the front seat and then slowly made his way into the back.

"To the po-lice station. You gonna tell them every damn detail about this ridiculous mess you created. You gonna answer every one of their questions, and you going to clear up the good name of Mr. Harmon Haverlock that I worked my whole damn life to make proud."

Walking toward the driver's seat of his Cadillac, Mr. Haverlock stopped and looked at me.

"Mr. Desmond the reporter. You need a ride?"

"No, sir. I'm not far away at all."

"What street you live on?"

"Joost."

"Listen," he said, pulling out a bus pass from his pocket and handing it to me. "The twenty-nine should be right there on that corner in about two minutes. I think I can see it from here. Jump on that. Tell Guillermo that Mr. H. says hello. Get off at San Jose Avenue by the Balboa station. Cross them there K tracks and look for either the thirty-six or the forty-three. I can't remember if the thirty-six is running this time of night. You'll have to forgive me. My mind is somewhere else at the moment and a bit preoccupied, you could say. But either the thirty-six or the forty-three should take you close enough to Joost."

"Thank you, sir. I'm sorry for all of your troubles today."

"Oh, I know how to take care of trouble, Mr. Desmond the reporter." He sat down in the front seat to insert the keys back into the ignition, pulling down the window to continue the conversation while backing out of the driveway onto Persia Avenue. "You just send me a copy of that story of yours when you're done."

Boarding the twenty-nine, I said hello from Mr. H. to Guillermo, who made no indication of whether he heard or understood what I said. The lights were bright in the back of the empty bus, giving the fluorescent effect of an office space. I unfolded my notebook/napkin and read over the four or five scribbled lines. Not having many notes wasn't going to be a problem. This had by far been the most unforgettable day of my fifteen-year-old life. Using Mr. Haverlock's unreturned pen, I took the extended time on the twenty-nine to write down a few more descriptive lines. The San Francisco Giants black-and-orange colors of Ronnie's Adidas sneakers that I had never seen in any department store before. I wrote down "my daddy's Smith & Wesson, no less," and I wrote down that at least one person had already signed their name on Jermaine's protective leg bandage. I wasn't sure why any of these details were important to me, but I wrote them all down nonetheless.

Guillermo shouted out "San Jose Avenue" before I had a chance to pull the rubbery rope sagging above my bus window. I said "Gracias, Guillermo" as I exited through the back of the bus. I crossed the empty K tracks and never found out if the thirty-six was running at that time of night as I walked the rest of the half mile or so home instead. I entered through a side door to the basement, where Hector's car was long gone for the night. I could hear my father snoring from the master bedroom as I changed into an extra pair of PE sweats. Then I went to bed and dreamed of kissing Claire Davies.

Chapter 8

The next morning I narrowed down my introduction to either
Ronnie Choe did not shoot Jermaine Haverlock.
OR
Herman Haverlock accidentally shot his brother, Jermaine.

I made my choice in-between bathroom breaks when I overheard faculty members insist that police suspected Ronnie Choe to be the shooter and that he had already been arrested. I waited until the end of the day to hand it in to Miss Lars. She frowned as she read the first sentence, *Ronnie Choe did not shoot Jermaine Haverlock,* which surely would have been sufficient enough for her to come to a quick editorial judgment.

"Thank you very much, Desmond." She placed the story in the top right drawer of her desk. "I will read this tonight and then maybe, if there is time, we can go over it together tomorrow. Thank you."

Without saying another word, I walked over to my cubbyhole, where Claire Davies had placed the journalism history books that I had forgotten in the gym during my fistfight with Angelo. Grabbing the books, I walked toward Gilbert Stortz, *The Galleon* sports editor, who was inspecting his pages.

Gilbert was the only absolute towheaded kid that I knew of at Vasco High. It must've been like being the only black or Asian kid at a suburban school. Gilbert didn't have very many close friends, nor did he particularly want any. Come to think of it, neither did I. Gilbert let his guard down with me in seventh grade, when I invited him to a Giants game at Candlestick Park. My brother had been working there as a stadium concessionaire for a while and would occasionally be paid for overtime in the form of extra tickets. Gilbert always said he wouldn't go because he was an Oakland Athletics fan. But we both knew the real reason was that Gilbert's parents wouldn't allow him to hang out with guys who had mulatto-sounding last names. But the gesture was enough to finally earn his trust.

I offered Gilbert a Jose Canseco rookie baseball card that Hector had acquired during a short stint of cleaning residential homes while an apprentice for Mr. Rug Doctor. In exchange, Gilbert (the only student Miss Lars allowed in the newsroom without adult supervision) would leave one of the classroom windows unlocked for me to climb in after school. He agreed. With about two hours to kill, I went to the school library and began production work on a special "EXTRA" edition of *The Galleon*.

Finding a functioning photocopier was often the biggest challenge of the student newspaper production process at Vasco. No toner. No paper. Copier jams because a student forgot to take off Miss Lars' paperclip. Those were the sorts of things that could mean the school might not get its student paper until the following week. Because Vasco often couldn't afford to replace toner, photos did not look so sharp when printed in *The Galleon*. To compensate, Miss Lars insisted we use the collection of clipart saved from her abandoned minor in graphic design. She had a thing for horses and so headlines were often phrased as such:

VOLLEYBALL TEAM GALLOPS TO VICTORY

STUDENTS BACK IN SADDLE FOR NEW SCHOOL YEAR

and my personal favorite:

PRINCIPAL HERSEY ALLOWS

(HORSE OUT OF BARN PHOTO HERE)

The latter headline must have given Miss Lars a bit of the trots. She shrugged it off when I pointed it out to her the morning I discovered it in *The Galleon*. I vowed to keep the horseshit out my story.

EXTRA EDITION

THE GALLEON

VASCO SCHOOL SHOOTING
WAS ACCIDENTAL

Victim expected to recover. Suspect not whom you'd suspect.

By Desmond de Leon

of *The Galleon Staff*

Ronnie Choe did not shoot Jermaine Haverlock...

There were several photographs of the Haverlock brothers in the library's school yearbook shelf. Most were sports team portraits. Finding a photograph of Ronnie Choe wasn't so easy. Since he was about my brother's age, I knew he would have attended Vasco roughly between eighty-one and eighty-seven. None of those yearbooks included portraits of Ronnie Choe. I wondered if that was because he had dropped out of school or if he was just cutting class on picture day so that no one could look back at the yearbooks and make guesses as to what happened to his life. Before giving up, I looked in one last place. The chess club.

And there he was. 1984. Ronnie, the chosen chess player, captured in pensive mode, planning his attack, hat to the side, chin resting firmly on fist. The photo caption didn't identify who he was or what grade he was in. But unlike the rest of us, it wouldn't have mattered. Ronnie Choe always looked cool.

At 6:45 p.m., I scoped out the teacher's parking lot from the dark, lampless hallway outside the library. I saw Miss Lars climb into her green Volvo station wagon, complete with KQED bumper sticker in the middle of the back window. After watching Barb Lars drive off into the night, I made my way back across to the *Galleon* newsroom on the other side of campus. I climbed through the window that Gilbert had left unlocked and made it inside. On the first week of class I had noticed that Miss Lars hid an extra key to the copier room in the back of the bottom drawer of the unlocked metal file cabinet next to her desk. (Those are the kinds of burglary skills you can't help but pick up when you have an older brother like Hector.)

That night I made 500 copies of my EXTRA edition. It took about forty-five meditative minutes to insert each EXTRA into 499 copies of *The Galleon*. For Miss Lars' copy, which I placed on her desk, I inserted nothing. I liked the idea of her being the last to know.

Walking to school the next morning, I fantasized over the details of what was sure to be my hero's welcome. All of the cool kids would give me high-fives in the hallway. Mr. Burritt, my first period anti-establishment philosophy teacher, would sneak a smile as he read my name out in roll call. Claire Davies would leave a love letter in my locker. Whether these scenarios would play out precisely as I hoped, I didn't know. But I was certain that something good would result from my unbending purpose.

But as I entered campus and made my way to first period class, no one offered any high-fives. There was no love letter in my locker. And Mr. Burritt didn't even bother to take attendance.

Mr. Burritt wrote down main talking points of the chapters of a book few of us had read. Christina Vallejo, sitting near the front of the class, had a copy of *The Galleon* sticking out of her backpack, apparently for later reading. Gerald Irving, sitting in the far back, also had a copy. I watched him open it and flick the folded copy of the EXTRA aside, as if it were an unsolicited coupon. Folding the EXTRAs so that the words enclosed upon themselves was not a great marketing ploy, I then realized. Mr. Burritt lectured on about *The Iliad* while I burned inside with anxiety.

"Christina," said Mr. Burritt. She was the smartest in our class, but often pretended not to be. "Can you tell the class the story of Deiphobus?"

"I guess. He was like, the brother of Hector, right? And he got all caught up in some shit—sorry—I mean trouble. And then I think he got killed. But I'm not exactly sure how he died. His enemies did something. I'm not sure. That part was kind of complicated."

Larry, a campus security guard, stormed in and handed Mr. Burritt a note.

"Desi?" He sounded surprised. There was no secret smile. "Desmond. Gather your things and follow Larry."

Grabbing my backpack and slowly walking toward Larry at the classroom door, I didn't look at any of the expressions on the other students' faces. But I could feel them. It wasn't disdain and it wasn't pity. Just curiosity. Larry grabbed hold of my underdeveloped bicep as he escorted me to Mr. Hersey's office. I fantasized about kicking Larry in the knee and running off into the direction of downtown, where I would be reminded that my coming problems would someday soon be deemed trivial.

•••

"MR. HERSEY, SIR," SAID Larry, positioning my back against the frame of the principal's opened door. "I have Mr. Dee-Lee-On here for you."

Mr. Hersey wrote expeditiously with one hand while casually motioning with the other to allow me in. Larry nudged me forward without entering, and closed the door behind him.

"Desmond," he said, continuing to write with a shiny silver pen that had a digital clock embedded near the tip. "I don't suppose your father makes a lot of money?"

"He does all right, I guess. He's a longshoreman, so, you know, they've got a pretty strong union and…" I stopped talking upon realizing that the question was rhetorical.

"Longshoreman, huh? Too bad he's not a lawyer. Because there's a good chance you're going to need one."

"Why would I need a lawyer?"

"Listen up, little cub reporter boy. When one of the attorneys representing any of the persons mentioned in this here newspaper story of yours calls my office, shall I forward the messages to your father?"

Principal Hersey stopped writing to look me in the eye.

"Or would a representative at his *pretty strong union* like to return the call for him?"

"Why would anyone sue me?"

"How about slander?"

"You mean libel? Slander is when someone speaks someth— "

"You can work those smart-ass details out with…a Mr. Harmon Haverlock…who has already left two angry messages with my secretary today."

"But he's the one who said he wanted me to write it."

"Desmond. You're suspended. For two weeks. After that, I'll have a discussion with the superintendent, and he'll decide whether or not to expel you, which has already been my recommendation."

"*Expel* me? You're going to kick me out of school? For what? I didn't shoot anybody!"

"Let's see. How about for..." Mr. Hersey put on his reading glasses and picked up the essay he had been working on, "...breaking and entering into a classroom after hours... stealing school property...slandering...excuse me...*committing libel* against an innocent minor..."

"The guy brought a gun to school. You don't think the students have a right to know what really happened?"

"But wait. There's more...cutting an average of four classes a week...getting in an aggressive fistfight with one...Angelo Espinoza...stealing a stack of referrals from the vice principal's office...and arguing defiantly with your principal," he said, fine-tuning an addendum.

I aimed a defeated stare at Mr. Hersey's spotless carpet.

"You have one hour to gather your belongings from your locker. Your teachers have been notified of your suspension. I've also spoken to your father. He'll be here to pick you up. Meet Larry at the attendance office. Larry will escort you to your father's vehicle."

Realizing that Mr. Hersey had actually spoken to Hector was what kept me from crying.

"You know something, Desmond," said Mr. Hersey, standing up and opening his office door for me to leave, "I thought about being a journalist. Even took a couple reporter classes at UCLA. Two classes is how long it took me to figure out it was a complete waste of time. The pay is lousy. And journalists, especially the newspaper ones, are all a bunch of self-important, sanctimonious blowhards. So come to think of it, Desmond, you might have found your calling after all. Now get out."

•••

I APPROACHED MISS LARS after emptying out my cubby.

From the up-and-down movement of her shoulder blades, I could tell that Miss Lars was quietly crying. She placed the chalk down on the board railing and shuffled her way toward the entrance to a corner where fewer students could see her. I followed.

"Miss Lars? What's wrong?"

Miss Lars pulled out already used sheets of tissue from her knit cardigan pocket.

"You made a fool of me, Desmond. *Again.*"

"Again?"

The rest of the students took advantage of the opportunity to speak freely and loudly. A few had copies of my story in their hands and were showing it to one another.

"Do you have any idea how many times I've had to go to bat for you?"

"What are you talking about?"

"Every day, one of your other teachers asks why I enable you to skip their classes. They accuse me of enabling you to be a bad student. I've always told them that they're wrong. That you're just focusing on your passion. But now, I'm the fool. I told you yesterday that we would go over your story today."

"But you acted like you didn't even want to read it.

"Of course I read it. I even showed it to my husband. We both agreed that what you did was very brave. But being brave doesn't give you a license to undermine authority."

I was at a discombobulated loss for words. To begin with, I couldn't contemplate the revelation that Miss Lars was married. I had always imagined her as a lonely lady reading cheap supermarket romance novels, living in a stuffy one-bedroom apartment building in depressing Daly City. I could have sworn she was a closeted lesbian. I wondered what her husband looked like.

I thought about apologizing, but didn't know how or if I could do so with sincerity. She turned her back in disdain. I left Mrs. Lars' classroom with a debilitating sense of shame that pressed down on both of my shoulders. The thing I learned that day about shame is that it has to be the most unproductive and destructive of all human emotions. Anger, for instance, can make you feel powerful. Sure, that sense of strength might only last for a few moments. But it feels good while it lasts. Sadness can make you feel complete, especially after a thorough and true weeping washes away a cycle of grief. But all that shame ever does is constantly crush down on your ribs so that nothing can protect or stop the suffocation of your soul. Still in a daze, I made my way toward the front entrance of Vasco, where I knew Hector would be parked. Jamal Condon spotted me and shouted out across a hallway.

"Damn, Desi. I hate to be you right now. Jermaine and Herman are going to whup your ass for reals, man."

Ignoring Jamal was a challenge, thanks to that damn bright yellow crayon outfit he was wearing again. I kept walking and could see Larry from the corner of my eye, which I covered up with a pair of my father's aviator sunglasses from the sixties. Staring toward Cayuga Avenue, I saw my brother's primer-painted Impala. I had never been happier to see Hector than at that moment. I was desperate to latch onto any thought that would keep me from crying in front of anyone.

Were those new rims? Looks like Hector got rid of that dent from his parking lot hit-and-run accident the other day.

Just before reaching the top of the final steps leading to the black metal gates that divided Vasco High from where my most-likely-inebriated older brother was parked, someone ran up from behind and grabbed my hand.

"Hey, Desmond. Wow! That was *crazy* what you did."

It was Claire Davies.

"Oh. You saw that? Yeah, I guess it was kind of crazy." I was glad that I had sunglasses on because I couldn't remember if I had been crying. Claire and I stood there in a nervous moment of silence in which I realized there was little left to lose.

"Claire. Do you want to go to the homecoming dance with me next Saturday?"

"Sure."

"Well, I can't take you."

"Ummm. Oh-*kay*."

"No, I really want to. But I just got suspended for two weeks and I'm not allowed on campus starting pretty much…right…now."

Larry made his way toward us.

"That's too bad. Are you in a lot of trouble with your parents?"

"Nah," I lied. "They'll understand. Hey. What do you say we go to some other high school's homecoming dance next Saturday instead?"

"Yeah! That sounds even better."

"I guess this is the part where I am supposed to ask you for your phone number, right?"

"You already have it."

"I do?"

"I wrote it down in that history book of yours."

I considered telling Claire Davies that I was in love with her and that maybe we should get married next Saturday instead. Larry was fast approaching. Claire smiled, quickly kissed me on the cheek, and ran off toward her class.

As Larry's sweaty palm grabbed a hold of my arm and escorted me through the final fifteen feet to Cayuga Avenue, I thought about how strange it is to feel ashamed of something you're proud of.

Chapter 9

I have only one non-quotidian memory of mother. It was around Christmas 1981—three months before she was killed by a hit-and-run driver at a crosswalk a few blocks from our house. I was almost six years old and Hector about thirteen. My brother and I were sitting around the living room record player while my mother was playing an out-of-tune nylon string guitar along to her favorite forty-five-rpm records. These songs symbolized my parents' new life in San Francisco that began when they emigrated from Chile in the early sixties. Her collection included all of the usual pop star suspects—*Los Beatles, Los Rolling Stones, Los Kinks*—but with more of an emphasis on the acoustic protest spirits of *El Bob Dylan, La Joan Baez,* and the like. Her all-time favorite was *El Grupo Peter, Paul & Mary,* and her all-time favorite song was their version of "If I Had a Hammer." She played this song last and did so over and over throughout the night, singing each verse with the loudest part of her soul, proudly out of key, in her uninhibited Chilean accent. For the last verse she'd stop her out-of-sync guitar strumming and raise her delicate nail-polished fist in the air to illustrate emphasis.

"*It's dee ha-more uh jus-teece! It's dee bell uh free-eee-ee-dom!*"

We asked our mother what the song was about.

"Fighting."

"Fighting who?"

"*Los bad guys.*"

"Who are the bad guys?"

"*Mira, mijos,*" she said, explaining the rest in Spanish. "In every story, every song and every land, there are good people. And then there are bad people. But..."

She turned the record player down and put her arms around our necks, bringing us closer together to whisper a very important secret.

"There is also a third group. It's a much bigger group. It's *alllllll* of the people who don't let people know if they are the bad guy or the good guy."

She paused to let that sink in, and then turned the record player's volume all the way back up.

"Those are the people you need to be very careful around. You don't need to be afraid of the bad guys, *mijos,*" she said, as if to do so would be quite comical. "Because at least you know who they are."

She then went back to singing about hammers and bells.

My father strived to be a moral person. He never hid the sins of his scrappy childhood departure from the seaside shanties of Valparaiso. He didn't deny the debauchery days of his brief but scandalous soccer-star twenties. After he finally made it into the comfortable New World life of his thirties, complete with woman, home, and children, he made a point to never put any of it into jeopardy. Outside of "accidentally" taking home the occasional bottle of Johnnie Walker Black Label Scotch whiskey from the container ships down at the wharf, my father had long ago left life's gambling table. While indulging in his lonely Saturday night Scotch and 7 Ups, my father would point out that other longshoreman, most of them Irish, had a tendency to open the cases of Scotch, take one sip and then smash the rest of the perfectly good bottles against the sides of the ship. "Saving" the rest of the Scotch from the Irish was the right thing to do, my father rationalized. And if that didn't put his conscience to rest, it would always be good material for confession.

The odds were good that I would not have to confess anything about the suspension to my father. Hector and I were fairly certain that Mr. Hersey was bluffing about expelling me. My brother knew all the ins and outs of how best to hide report cards and impersonate parents on the phone. He could have easily pursued a career in forgery. So long as there were no visits or calls from the police, the FBI, or the Haverlock's attorney, I was temporarily in the clear. To be on the safe side, on Monday morning I woke up and went to school anyway. Maryanne Miller's school, that is.

•••

THERE WAS NO SECURITY guard to stop and question me when I first set foot onto Union High's campus. I walked the three miles (uphill both ways) from my house, arriving in the early nine o'clock hour while classes were supposedly in session. Students walked freely about the campus, holding nonchalant conversations without any grown-ups warning them to get a move on. Other kids did classwork together in the halls, with a relaxed entitlement that I could not comprehend.

The Union High newsroom was easy to find, thanks to the graffiti-free campus signs. The most interesting thing about *Union's* newsroom was that it was an actual newsroom. The spacious work area was used solely for putting out the school's newspaper, *The Union*, and unlike at Vasco, was not shared with a speech and debate or creative writing class. Other than a curmudgeonly elderly man in the back, it was empty. There were more computers in the Union High newsroom than even the maximum number of *Galleon* student reporters who ever showed up on the same day. The walls were decorated with fancy plaques and national awards that I had never heard of. Next to the wall of trophies were portraits of "notable Union alumni"—famous authors, actors, musicians, and politicians whose names meant nothing to me. Back at Vasco, I think we had that guy from The Grateful Dead. Only problem was that he dropped out. I'm pretty sure we had a couple of athletes who turned pro, including one my brother said he knew—a pitcher for the Oakland Athletics. Of course, Hector got to know him after the guy's career ended due to a drug problem. Mr. Burritt told stories about one of his favorite students from the late fifties "whom everyone used to call 'The Cigar.'" Last my philosophy teacher had heard, "The Cigar" was on the FBI's most wanted list. Another wall in the *Union's* newsroom was devoted to portrait shots of every student newspaper staff dating all the way back to 1898. I scoured over nearly a century of faces in hopes of finding one that might look like me.

"Looking for me? I'm right there…there…and there."

Maryanne pointed out pictures of herself as a freshman, sophomore, and junior on the *Union* staff. I hadn't recognized her when she walked in. She had cut her long red hair into a short, full-bodied perm that bordered around the bottoms of her dangling shell-shaped earrings. Her conservative white blouse and black, shell-patterned knee-length skirt made it difficult to point out what clique of kids she might best be identified with. She could have easily passed for an attractive substitute teacher or some kind of corporate working-woman visiting her old campus to share career advice with students.

"So, you're a senior?"

"Yes, thank *God*." She plopped down a purse that doubled as a backpack. "Don't get me wrong. I love Union. My sisters went here, my parents met here, and my grandparents did too and all that. But I am *so* ready to get out of here. Out of this freakin' fog, you know what I mean?"

Maryanne seemed worried she may have misused the word freakin'.

"Yeah, sure. So, did you already apply for colleges and all that?"

I couldn't tell if Maryanne scoffed or smiled. They tended to look the same.

"Georgetown. Columbia. Northwestern. Harvard. Oh, and UCLA. Just in case."

"Cool," I said, pretending to be familiar with the ones that didn't have Final Four–caliber basketball teams. Union journalism students made their way into the newsroom and began logging on to computers. Others, with cameras around their necks, entered the separate glass photo lab that I hadn't noticed until then.

"Jody! Jody! Don't ignore me. I can see you. Do you have that op-ed piece on why students cheat on tests?"

Jody waved a sheet of paper and slapped it onto a large desk in the center of the newsroom.

"It's about time, Jody."

"So. Maryanne. Are you the editor or something?" I asked.

We walked toward the large desk where Jody placed her story.

"Editor-in-chief. Yes. But believe me, Desmond, it's not as fun as it sounds. Hey. The last Union-Vasco game? I didn't see you. What brings you here today?"

She sat down at the editor-in-chief's desk, equipped with a telephone and—

"Fax machine? Jesus Christ! You guys have your own fax machine? I don't even think our principal has one of these."

Maryanne sorted through faxed pages, which had logos from the likes of the San Francisco and Oakland Police Departments.

"Desmond? You're dodging the question, aren't you?"

"Nah. I just got a lot of shit going on in my life right now, you know?"

"Let me guess. You still want some help applying for the *Call* and *Inquirer* high school reporting internships, right?"

"Well, yeah. I guess so. If that's cool."

"I'd be happy to help you. But there's just one problem. The application deadline was Friday. I'm so sorry, Desmond."

"That's cool."

"*That's cool?!* You're not giving up just like that, are you?"

"I guess…I dunno," I said, jumbled up. "You just said it was a problem."

"Then solve it, Desmond. Turn in your application anyway! If they tell you it's late, then tell them you're turning it in early for next summer. Desmond, Desmond, Desmond. Don't you know that you don't get what you don't ask for?"

"I guess you're right. But there's one other problem I'm dealing with right now."

Our conversation was interrupted by a public address announcement about the crew team's last shuttle departing for rowing practice at Lake Merced.

"I got suspended on Friday."

"*You* got suspended *at Vasco*? What for? Don't you have to like at least stab someone to get suspended from Vasco?"

"I got a two-week suspension for printing this in the school paper without permission."

I pulled out a crinkled copy of my EXTRA story and handed it to her. Maryanne's eyes widened, and her posture appeared to look more like that of a fellow student's. I hoped that meant that she was impressed.

"Hmph. Well. That's an interesting way to get suspended. Shit. Who knows? Maybe this'll actually help you get an internship. Or maybe not. Look, you'll still need a letter of recommendation from your principal and your journalism advisor. So I don't know. I guess it depends on whether or not they're the ones who suspended you, right?"

She handed the EXTRA back without reading the entire thing, then opened a desk drawer and pulled out a bright yellow folder labeled INTERNSHIP.

"Here. These are the instructions. Desmond, the only thing you really need to remember is that it all comes down to your personal essay. What's your last name?"

"De Leon."

"That means you're Hispanic, right? You don't look very Hispanic. I would have guessed Jewish."

"My parents are from Chile. My dad's got mostly Mapuche Indian blood. But my mom's side comes from Irish descendants who emigrated to South Am—"

"Well. Definitely play up the Indian dad blood stuff. Tell them he fought his way out of the favelas or whatever it is they call them down there. Ixnay on the Irish part. Unless you need a good reason to explain whatever it is that possessed you to write your own rogue story or whatever. I can *totally* see *The Inquirer* loving that and *The Call* hating it. But you never know. Just don't lie about your grades, because believe me, they *will* check on that. I know a guy who got screwed because of that. I might've had a little something to do with helping him get caught. But hey. It's all about due diligence, right?"

"Thanks, man. I mean, Maryanne. I can see why they made you the editor. You're really good at giving directions, you know? Hey, is it cool if I use one of these computers?"

"Sure. Use the computers, the photocopiers, whatever you need. Just put the folder back in my desk when you're done."

"Thanks. But shouldn't I explain to him that I'll be working in here today?" I asked, pointing to the old-timer possibly sleeping in the corner.

"Who? Mr. Goddard? The retired editor from *The Bulletin* that hasn't existed in like forever? Puh-leeease. He'll be drunk by lunchtime if he isn't already. He's harmless enough, though. He'll probably just take a nap in the back, when he isn't out smoking or trying to flirt with the volunteer moms."

"Ha! That's hella cool. He actually worked at *The Bulletin*? He must be like a real old-school newspaperman, right?"

"*Newspaperman*? Are you freakin' kidding me? Good Lord! What century were you born in, Desmond? Look. Whatever you do, don't write anything about being a 'newspaperman,'" she said, ending that thought in a rather convincing "retard" accent. Maryanne wrote "Desmond" on a visitor sticker and placed it on my shirt. She took off her earrings, grabbed the gym bag beneath the editor-in-chief desk, and made her way toward the hallway. Before exiting, she stopped, turned around, and noticed the Apperson biography that I had pulled out of my backpack.

"Step into the nineties, Desmond. The nineteen-nineties."

•••

BESIDES FILLING OUT FORMS with questions that I felt inclined to lie about—grade point average, extracurricular club memberships, academic awards—the rest of the internship application involved writing a 500-word essay stating why I was the best candidate. The last step would be to include a sample of writing clips along with a permission slip signed by a parent. With the crinkled copy of the EXTRA story in my pocket and a forgery apprenticeship from hours of watching Hector, I could have this completed by the end of lunchtime, head downtown, and turn it in the same day. The only problem would be overcoming my fascination with Mr. Goddard, the old-school San Francisco newspaperman.

That he spoke with a Scottish accent made him all the more mesmerizing. The feeling did not appear to be mutual. Twice I tried to strike up a conversation with him, but chickened out after seeing him scold other students for placing soda cans too close to their computers or for chewing gum while typing. For the hell of it, I placed the copy of my Apperson biography in plain sight, in hopes that it might catch his attention. Less than two sentences into my essay he had fallen into my trap. Or I had fallen into his, depending on one's perspective.

"Is that nae the Chief staring back at me there?"

"Oh. Hi. This? Yeah. It's just a book I've been reading." I hoped I didn't sound too coy. "I'm Desmond, by the way."

"I know who ye are boy. It's ma job to know who is in here. So ye can take yer wee stew-pid sticker off now, Desi boy."

"So. Did you know this dude...I mean Mr. George W. Apperson?"

"Aye. Signed many of me paychecks, didn't he now? And yer correk, surr. He did dress like a bit of a dude too, I must say."

Mr. Millard Goddard proceeded to tell me his life's story. He was seventy-seven years old and had been born on the East End of Glasgow. In 1928, if he remembered the year correctly, he and his older brother, William, ran away from an orphanage and stowed away on a ship from Liverpool to America. After arriving in San Francisco by way of hobo train, the two brothers were hired as street-shouting delivery boys for what was then *The San Francisco Bulletin*. Millard got a gig as a copyboy in the newsroom, where he became hooked on the fast-paced lifestyle of chasing San Francisco stories. He was officially hired as a reporter during the city's waterfront strike.

It was July 5, 1934. The reporter responsible for covering the strike that day had passed out drunk and so Millard instinctively grabbed a notebook from the unconscious man's coat pocket and headed down to the wharf. There, Millard was the first to discover the body of a Mr. Howard S. Sperry, a longshoreman who was murdered on what would forever be remembered as San Francisco's "Bloody Thursday." The events of the day sparked the longshoremen's now historic union strike. I interrupted to say I knew of the spot, as it was memorialized with paint, which I often walked by while accompanying my father to pick up his paycheck.

Mr. Goddard was not crazy about my interrupting his Celtic-spirited storytelling. He acknowledged that it was a fair anecdote by nodding his head and taking a sip from a brown-bagged bottle of something. Millard went on to say he reported on the trials of labor leader Harry Bridges, the end of the Great Depression, the beginning of World War II, the opening of the Golden Gate Bridge, and the closing of Alcatraz Federal Prison. He had been all of these things—reporter, editor, photographer, columnist, cartoonist, delivery, and copyboy—in-between side jobs as an ambulance driver, pilot, occasional bartender, and self-published novelist. That the dates didn't always seem to add up and the accomplishments sounded a bit exaggerated mattered little to me. These memories might not have all been part of his story, but they were clearly part of somebody's. Millard was just doing his part to keep them all alive.

"What am I most proud of?" Mr. Goddard asked, interviewing himself. I couldn't tell for sure, since just about every other sentence in his Scottish accent sounded like a question to me. Mr. Goddard took another sip.

"Ehhh… Probably most proud to have been part of a group that secretly met in the bathroom, passing out a petition to unionize our newspapers, while knowing full well that it'd be much to the chagrin of that there Chief of yours. He could've been walking by on the other side of the bathroom wall at any time."

Forty-five long years of stories had passed in three very fast hours and I hadn't written a single word beyond two meaningless sentences. Mr. Goddard leaned over to read what I had completed on the computer screen.

"What's this then?"

"'I believe I could be a good candidate for the San Francisco Newspaper Agency's reporting internship?!' 'Although my grades are not as good as they should be, I have always worked especially hard for the school paper?!'… No! No! *No!* Desi. This is terrible. No one will fall for this phony, fake pile of shite. Okay. You type. I'll dictate. We've got fifteen minutes before I take my afternoon break."

Mr. Goddard literally rolled up his sleeves and screwed closed the cap to the bottle of what I would now recognize as Cutty Sark.

"What's your name?"

"Desi."

"No! Your full name, son. What's your *byline*?"

"Desmond de Leon."

"Jesus Christ! That's a beautiful alliteration. Much better than mine even. Okay. Repeat after me. My name is Desmond de Leon and…"

"Wait. You want me to repeat it or you want me to write it?"

"Both, boy! Both! You'll never know you have a good lede unless you say it out loud and hear it for yourself, boy! For chrissake, Desmond. Have they taught you nothing?

"My name is Desmond de Leon..." Mr. Goddard continued, *"and I am the best candidate for this newspaperman..."*

"internship."

Mr. Goddard was either unable or unwilling to hide his disdain for the word "internship." He dulled the pain with another Cutty Sark sip then continued dictating.

"If you don't believe me..."

"then just take a look at my..."

"grade point average."

"Period. End of sentence. New paragraph."

"There you will see that..."

"I have no time for mathematics..."

"I have no time for sciences..."

"I have some time for history and literature..."

"And I dedicate ALL of my time..."

"to writing..."

"newspaper..."

"stories."

"Period. End of sentence. New paragraph."

"Enclosed is a copy of my..."

"You have written a story, haven't you, Desi?"

"Yeah, yeah, yeah."

"What's it about?"

"Well, I guess you could say it's about what really happened during a school shooting."

"Oh, that's beautiful, Desmond! Just beautiful! Och! You're going to get into this thing, Desi. I know it. I can feel it now! Now where were we?

"Enclosed is a copy of my best newspaper story."

"Period. End of sentence. Last paragraph."

"I look forward to hearing from you..."

"Signed. Desmond de Leon."

Mr. Goddard rolled down his sleeves, pulled the bottle back out of his pocket, and took one more sip.

"That's it?"

"Aye. That's it. What the fook else is there to say, son?"

"I dunno, Mr. Goddard. It's just that…"

"It's just that what? Spit it out, son. What is it you feel this desperate need to blab on about?"

"It's just that, I dunno if I really am the best candidate, you know. I mean. I think I am. At least I hope I am. But doesn't that come across, as you know…a little conceited?"

"Jesus Christ, Desmond! Do you not understand? Man's faith *is* his fortune! If you want to be the best candidate then you have to believe you're the best candidate. Now, do you believe it to be true or not? Do you truly want this thing or not?"

"Okay, fine. Yes! Yes, I do!"

"Then just remember one thing, Mr. Desmond day Lay Fookin ON. You are…whatever…you say you are! Now print this g'damn thing out and turn it in. *Today.* And now, if you'll excuse me, sonny jim, it's time for my afternoon break."

Mr. Goddard walked toward the empty photographer's darkroom, where there happened to be a couch.

"Thanks, Mr. Goddard."

Before he could close the darkroom door, I asked one last question.

"Hey. Mr. Goddard. Can I, uh…have a sip of that before I go?"

"Absolutely not! It's not my business to baptize you, son. For that, you're on your own."

Embarrassed by my disrespectful question, I quickly printed out the new and improved personal essay. I gathered my things and, in a daydream daze, made my way downtown to visit the newsrooms of *The San Francisco Call* and *The San Francisco Inquirer.* It was somewhere in the subway tunnel between the Van Ness Avenue and Civic Center stations when it occurred to me that I had already forgotten what Millard Goddard's face looked like.

I could only picture him as Obi-Wan Kenobi.

Chapter 10

For reasons I could never grasp, the *Inquirer* and *Call* divided the same Sansome-family-owned building. These "competing" newsrooms were separated only ceremoniously with different entrances at opposite ends of the same San Quentin–esque building. Meanwhile, the more romantically ornate and newspaper-headquarters-looking Apperson Building across Market Fucking Street, where readers presumed *The Inquirer* was published, was in all actuality rented out to mostly private practicing dentists and lawyers.

That a rival newspaper staff did its business on one side of a Les Nessman masking tape "wall" while the other might be chasing the same stories on the other was not a means of further intensifying any kind of editorial or territorial faceoff. It had to do with what was called the Joint Operating Agreement, which was intended to save newspapers in cities across the nation where people got their news from television and radio and not so much by reading more than one newspaper. It was signed into law as the "Newspaper Preservation Act of 1970" by Richard Nixon, who initially opposed the idea, but conveniently changed his mind when the Apperson Corporation sent the White House a letter accompanied by before and after samples of future presidential endorsements.

In San Francisco, the Apperson Corporation's *Inquirer* was the scrappy, catch-the-late-train-commuter's-eye-in-the-afternoon paper that went well with happy hour, while the Sansome family's *Call* controlled the traditional, straightedge morning cuppa-joe news fix. Modern American newspapers typically reserved Sundays as the showcase edition of the week for its best stories. Not so much in San Francisco. Our Sunday paper consisted of a combined *Call* and *Inquirer* delivered by *Marmaduke's* full-color funny pages folded around the front page.

Standing in the alleyway that divided the two "separate" entrances, I wondered which of these former sworn enemies would have been more pissed off about this shared living arrangement— The Chief or the Sansome brothers? Presuming these ghosts were still somewhere at war with one another, I wanted to dedicate my internship allegiance to the winner of this spiritual standoff. Remembering that they carried guns, I gave the edge to the Sansomes and entered through *The Call*.

A security guard immediately eyed me up and down as if he had spotted an unwelcomed apparition. I directed a gaze toward the powder-blue-painted ceiling that was decorated with strewn-about letters of the alphabet and carvings of stoic-faced lions in the crown-molding corners. The security guard continued to aim his frozen stare at me while going through the reluctant motions of getting up from his swivel seat. Searching for the right words, I zoomed in on a random letter C in the middle of the sky ceiling.

"Little D! What up with you, little Dez-mundo? You back for another newsroom tour? How's the family? How's your pop? How's *Hector*?"

From the moment Cy walked through the front lobby, I knew for certain that the day would end with more than just another tour of the newsroom. I knew this only because I longed it to be true.

"You know this young man?"

"You kidding me? This is Desmond de Leon. He's a big-time newspaperman. He'll be running this place someday, ain't that right, Dez-man?"

Cy set down the bundles of newspapers that he had been carrying on his broad shoulders, and adjusted a back support belt that effectively concealed his gut, which had grown just a little since we last met. I showed him my internship papers.

"I got you, little Dizzle. I got you. Why don't you come on up with me?"

The security guard flicked a sign-in sheet in my direction. With my attention fixated on the bronze eyes glaring back at me from the plaque behind the guard's desk, I signed in as Desmond Charles Sansome. Next to my signature I drew a happy face, complete with nineteenth-century moustache.

It was about four o'clock in the afternoon, and the top floor of the newsroom was very busy. Cyrus spoke the entire time from the elevator to the "wire room," his cramped headquarters where he oversaw the distribution of mail, supplies, timecards, out-of-town newspapers, coffee filters, and the like. I interrupted only to mention that I had been suspended.

"What? Now how you gonna tell me that *you* got suspended at Vasco. For what?"

"For this," I said handing the EXTRA edition to him. "I published it without permission. I was kinda hoping it might help get me the internship. You know? To show that I'm really dedicated and all that. I dunno. Maybe they'll just think I'm crazy."

"Ha!" he said, glancing at it before quickly handing it back. "I tell you what Tele-Dez-mundo. This is Big Cy country! Follow me."

We weaved our way around the bustling newsroom toward the desk of Maureen, the reporter I met at Vasco. She was shouting into a telephone while occasionally writing notes on a piece of paper. When she saw Cy and me walking toward her, she smiled and motioned for us to come over, as if she had been expecting us all along. Cy handed the internship application to Maureen, who appeared to read every line even as she continued with her conversation.

"Fine. Listen. Supervisor. We've been going around in circles for the past fifteen minutes. At this point, I'm going with what the superintendent told me this morning…I know…I know… Listen. It's almost five. If before six-thirty you suddenly feel inspired to actually say something worth printing…you've got my number… but at six-thirty-one, I'm not answering the phone. Got it?"

Maureen hung up without saying goodbye.

"Desi! You'll have to excuse me. I was in the middle of dealing with a professional bullshitter."

"Pardon us, Moe. But my little man Desi here is interested in *The Call*'s reporting internship. He's going to be a big shot in here someday, you know."

Cy always had the loudest voice in the room. To have such in a newsroom was especially difficult to do. My ears burned with embarrassment. A reporter smiled in my direction. Another scowled.

"I know, Cy. We've met. Desi is quite intrepid, isn't he?"

Cy walked back to the supply room, loudly complimenting anyone and everyone along the way. Maureen continued to inspect every inch of the internship application.

"So, Desi. Looks like you missed the deadline and your grade point average is below the requirement, huh?"

"I guess so."

"But I love your explanation here. No time for mathematics. No time for science. This is hilarious."

"Thanks, Maureen. An old newspaperman guy helped me with that."

"Newspaperman? Wow. I haven't heard that word in I don't know how many years. I don't suppose I can be a newspaperman, too?"

"Did you see the EXTRA thing?"

"The what?"

I pulled out the last page. Unlike everyone else whom I had shown it to, Maureen was the only one who read every word of the story before expressing any kind of reaction.

"Holy shit! You did all of this on your own?"

"Yeah. But, uh…Principal Hersey. He wasn't too crazy about it. He kinda. You know. Suspended me for it."

"Well, get used to it. Mike Hersey doesn't like reading anything in any newspaper. I'm sure he'd like to suspend me too, if he could."

Maureen swiveled her chair in the direction of cubicles stationed below a sign that read "Copy Desk" and started shouting at no one in particular.

"Anybody know who handles internship applications?!"

No one answered. Not with words, anyway.

"HELLO?! ANYBODY?! I bet Taylor will know… HEY, TAYLOR?!"

A decidedly fashionable man, wearing jeans and a pastel-colored sport coat with cotton sleeves rolled up in *Miami Vice* manner, answered from a distance that didn't require shouting.

"Yes, Moe. I'm right here. Where I always am. What's up?"

Taylor spoke without ever looking away from his computer screen.

"What do you know about our high school internships? I've got this kid, excuse me—*newspaperman*—here. Says here he's the best candidate. Only problem is he missed the deadline to turn it in."

A crew of copy editors laughed out loud.

"Sure," said Taylor, repositioning a set of reading glasses between his salt-and-pepper receding hairline and reddish Roman nose. "It's through the Newspaper Agency. There's one for *The Inquirer* and one for *The Call*. Which one is he interested in?"

"Both!" I shouted back.

Everyone laughed.

"Talk to Judy Dorland in HR. She's on the second floor."

For just a single moment, he looked away from his computer and over toward me.

"Tell her Taylor gave you an extra couple of days to turn it in."

Maureen's phone rang again. Placing the receiver back between her head and shoulders, she fluttered her hands in shooing motion for me to go away.

"Supervisor? Is that you? What a pleasant surprise."

•••

THE GLASS DOOR TO Judy Dorland's office was wide open, but she wasn't there. I tiptoed in and contemplated sitting in the wooden chair that was situated much like the guest seat in a vice principal's office. Halfway through this decision, Judy Dorland burst through a disguised door that doubled as a wood-paneled wall. It felt like a trap.

"Young man?"

"Whoa!" I said, still suspended in a crouch. "Pardon me. I was told to look for Judy Dorland about turning in my internship application. Hey, wow, is that a secret passageway door or something?"

Judy Dorland's introduction was far too bizarre for me to remember to be intimidated by her angrily penciled eyebrows. It felt like she had been waiting for me on the other side the whole time.

"Young man, the internship deadline was Friday. Looks like you missed it. Try again next year." She closed the wall-door behind her.

I sat down.

"But Taylor, up in the newsroom, he said to tell you he gave me some extra time to turn it in. Is that cool with you?"

"No. That is not *cool* with me. Have a seat."

Judy reached toward a tremendous telephone that took up a quarter of her desk space. She pressed a button amidst a vast speed dial directory.

"City desk, Taylor."

"Hi, Taylor. Did you instruct a Mr...?" Smiling through the telephone, Judy motioned for me to hand over my application paperwork.

"...a Mr. de Leon to take some extra time in turning in his internship application?"

"I did. I liked his spirit. He deserves the extra day. Look. I gotta go. I'm on deadline."

"Thank you, Taylor."

Judy's smile disappeared.

"Have a seat, Desmond. Let's see here. Missed the deadline. Grade point average is below requirement. And...*this* is your personal essay?"

"Uh. Yes. Yes. And Yes."

"Which internship are you better suited for, *The Call*'s or *The Inquirer*'s?"

"Both," I laughed. She didn't. "Which one do you pick the candidates for?"

"Both."

I stopped laughing.

"What's this EXTRA thing?"

"Oh that? That's my best story. At least I'd like to think so. It's also the one that, I, sort of...got suspended for publishing without permission. In fact, that's the reason why I couldn't turn the application in on Friday. Otherwise I would've been on time."

"Suspended? Look, Desmond. I admire your...your *spirit*. But frankly, you are *not* the best candidate for this '*newspaperman*' internship."

Judy apparently hated the word "newspaperman" as much as Mr. Goddard hated the word "internship."

"Desmond. What you need is a reality check. You see that two-foot-tall stack of folders over there?" Judy pointed to that two-foot-tall stack of folders over there. "Those are all internship applications. I can tell you without even looking at them that every one represents a better candidate than you. And the reason is simple. They all meet and respect the basic requirements. Whereupon they were all turned in *on time*. Look, Desmond. It's nothing personal. It's business. It's about being professional. Get your grades up. Write a real essay. Turn your application in on time. And don't get suspended. If you can do all that without barging into my office, maybe you will be the best candidate *next year*. Now, if you want a tour of the newsroom, I'd be happy to—"

"That's okay. I've already done the tour. Thanks for your time, Miss Dorland."

I walked back upstairs to the newsroom to find Cy. Something would work out; I knew this for certain. But I still didn't know why. Back in the cramped wire room, Cy was nowhere to be found. Two phone lines were ringing continually and competitively. In the far back, a man in a polyester suit was kicking and swearing at a large photocopier machine.

"How the fuck does this fucking thing work? Piece of fucking shit," he said, possibly to me. I sat down in Cy's empty chair and wondered whether I should leave or wait for him to return.

"Hey. How've you been? I haven't seen *you* in a while," said the cursing man in a calmer voice.

"Me? I'm fine. Wait. Have we met?"

"Great. Great. Hey. Can you do me a big favor?"

"Yeah. Sure. I mean. Thing is. I don't actually—"

"Great. Great. Hey. So. The automatic stapler on this thing is acting up, right? And I *really* need twenty-five copies of each pile separated and stapled. And they absolutely *have* to be ready *before* our six-thirty election meeting in the news conference room. In other words, no later than fifteen minutes. Umm*kay*?"

"Sure. I'll tell Cy—"

"Great. Great. Hey, thanks! I owe you. *Again.* I know. You guys are the best. See you at six twenty-nine, then. Umm*kay*?"

The man left a complicated yet systematic mess of copies atop the machine. I walked over and began sorting them as best I understood from his instructions. Before I could find a stapler, Cy walked back in.

"Dez-zay! Looks like you making yourself right at home, now aren't you?"

"Man, Cy. I'm sorry. It's just that this guy said he needed me to sort all these papers for him. He said it was urgent. Something about a six-thirty election meeting tonight?"

"Election meeting? Tonight? At six-thirty? What in the *hail*?"

"Yeah. Guy in a tan suit. Beard. Glasses. Real friendly. Except that he kept saying the f-word."

"Edelstein!"

"I guess. I dunno, man. I didn't catch his name. But he sounded real serious about getting these copies right away. I got no problem helping out, if that's cool with you."

"Edelstein! Edelstein!" Cy kept shouting, emphasizing the disbelief at being foiled by this man yet again. Cy began attending to the flashing lights signaling problems and paper jams at all corners of the copier. "I told him ain't nobody going to show up to his six-thirty meeting. Election ain't for another how many months? What is he thinking, messing up my copy machine?"

I moved the papers out of his way and continued sorting. Two, possibly three phone lines began ringing again as Taylor walked into the wire room.

"Hey, Cy," said Taylor, collectedly. "We've got a little problem."

"Damn right we do! The problem's name is Stan Edelstein. Man just *loves* to mess with the rhythm of my workflow, you know?"

Taylor kept calm and I kept sorting.

"Cy. Our night EA in sports just called in sick. The news EA just quit. We've got no one to work the phones and run the proofs or do the sports agate and weather pages."

"Quit? Who quit?"

"Can't really get into that right now. We definitely need you tonight, Cy. There'll be some good OT in it for you, of course."

"Now, how in the hell am I going do sports and news *and* finish with all this Stan Edelstein...*silliness*?"

I stapled the finishing touches on the Stan Edelstein special. Taylor tapped his finger on the door sill while looking over at me.

"How'd it go with Judy and the internship?"

"Terrible. Said I had no chance."

"Hmm. How old are you?"

"Sixteen," I lied, stretching the truth by a few weeks.

"No chance, huh? Well. How would you like a job instead?"

"Like for money?"

"Of course for money. That's why it's called a job."

"Hell, yeah! I mean, yes, sir. I would like that very much, sir."

"Well then, first of all, don't call me sir. Call me Taylor."

He walked over to a wall in the back of the wire room, where several government-looking documents were stapled. I looked over to Cy, who was quietly smiling and giving me a thumbs-up sign.

"I'm not completely certain, but I think the law limits you to only work for about four hours on a school night. Or something along those lines."

"That's not a problem. It's not actually a school night for me."

"Isn't it Monday?"

"Yeah, but I don't have school tomorrow, or for like the next two weeks. I got suspended. So I'm totally available anytime, you know. Anytime."

"Suspended? For what? Actually, that's okay. Never mind. I don't want to know. Let's get through the night and then we can deal with the rest of your scheduling tomorrow. Cy will show you what to do. Now let's get back to putting out a goddamn newspaper."

The rest of that night was a happy and fast-paced blur of a milestone up there with getting laid or drunk for the first time. Since neither of those things had happened to me yet, this was the closest I'd felt to experiencing either. It felt good, even though I didn't really know what I was doing. Cy led the way as we bounced back between the cigarette-smelling sports department, the B.O.-scented printers' back-shop, and the herbal tea–spiced news desk. I helped Cy answer phones, add paper to printers, and conduct nonsensical small talk with those willing to participate, or not. It was the first of many nights when Roberta Zambini, a news copy editor from Queens, would tell me she didn't need "any goddamn fucking faxes on or around my workspace, thank you very fucking much."

Roberta was nowhere near as mean as the back-shop printers, what with their nicotine-tinted beards and wielding of knives used to cut-and-paste each newspaper page together—a job that hadn't existed at just about any other major metropolitan newspaper since the invention of the computer. These Hobbity, drunken-leprechaun-like men loved to hate.

"Don't touch my type, you stupid son-of-a-bitch kid," is usually how they introduced themselves, waving X-Acto knives to illustrate their points.

"Desi, my right-hand man," Cy would say, "whatever you do, just don't go trying to change nobody. Kill it with kindness. That's all you gotta do. It's like they say, 'It's better to be above ground than below.' That's all you gotta know."

• • •

As usual, Cy was right. Nobody showed up to Stan Edelstein's six-thirty election meeting, except for me—on time and with the sorted and stapled paperwork just as he asked. At first I wondered if Stan's feelings were hurt that no one else had come up to his "really important" meeting. It was on that first night of meeting political reporter Stan Edelstein when it became immediately apparent that if anyone was capable of hurting Stan Edelstein's feelings they sure as hell didn't work in a newsroom. Stan went on with his election meeting as planned, highlighting sections from his own notes, writing ideas on a board, and talking aloud to either himself or me during the few times I'd check back to see if there was anything else he needed.

"We're good. Thanks, Desi," he said, alone in the room.

How he figured out my name without ever asking me, I still don't know.

At about a quarter to midnight, with twenty-five phone calls answered, forty-four faxes stapled, an innumerable amount of insults/introductions thrown at me, and three editions of *The Call* ready to be completed later, my first night on the job was over. I asked Cy where in the building we could find the presses so that I could save some souvenir copies. He explained that the presses down in the basement hadn't been used in years. It was all printed offsite, and I'd have to wait until the morning like everyone else to get the latest editions.

•••

BACK HOME, HECTOR WAS long gone for the night, and my father was fast asleep. I tried to sleep too, but lay wide-awake with adrenaline. At 4:00 a.m. I got out of bed. Wearing PE sweats and socks, I walked out on to Joost Avenue and spotted a home-delivered *Call* in an unknown neighbor's driveway across the street.

Picking it up and bringing it back to my room, I placed my stolen *Call* into a protective plastic covering sheet that my brother used for rare vinyl albums back from when he wanted to be a wedding DJ. Before filing it on the shelf next to my binder of my best baseball cards, I labeled the newspaper: "Number One." I knew that this would be the first newspaper of the rest of my life.

Chapter 11

The rest of that week went by so fast that I forgot to call Claire Davies. Since I wasn't welcome at school, I was spending all day at *The Call*. Each morning I camped out at an empty desk in the wire room and pretended to like coffee during abandoned attempts to read every single word in *The Call, Inquirer,* and whatever other local or national newspapers I could find. Mostly it was an effort to meet and make small talk with the other reporters and editors.

The day shift proved to be a much easier crowd to win over than the night crew. If ever any of them needed supplies, or help relaying a piece of interoffice mail, I always obliged, regardless of if it was before my night shift. This drove Cy a little bit crazy, but in the end he admitted he appreciated it more than he appreciated the other day shift editorial assistants who were taking two-hour, two-drink-minimum lunches.

Late Friday afternoon, I finally found the courage to call Claire Davies. The confidence to do so was rooted in money. I had been sitting in the wire room desk sorting through a pile of mail when Taylor came up to me.

"It's payday, Desi. Got to fill out your timecard."

He watched over my shoulder as I slowly wrote in hours worked only for the week's evening shifts. I included time for that Friday night.

"Wait a minute," he said.

I quickly erased that night's hours.

"No, no, no. Keep those hours on there. But what about the rest? You've been coming in early and helping out Cy during the mornings, right? Don't forget to include those hours, too."

"I was just helping out here and there."

"Well, were you working or not?"

"I guess. A little."

"A little? Work is work. Desi, don't *ever* be scared to get paid for your work. Look. Nobody should ever work for free. And nobody should ever work for fear. Understand?"

"Yes, sir! Thanks, boss!"

"Knock it off, Desi. I'm not your boss. I'm your editor. Okay? And hey, quit trying to over-impress everyone by working outside your regular shift. That can be dangerously annoying. Just remember, if you do good work here, the proof is in the paper. The proof is *always* in the paper. Now go make sure Judy Dorland cuts you your check today."

I ran down the stairway, ready to burst through Judy Dorland's secret wall-door. I hadn't seen her all week, but had thought about her many times, worrying that she'd find a way to disqualify me from working for *The Call*. Judy was on the phone when I walked in. She grabbed my timecard without otherwise acknowledging my presence. Rolling her office chair toward a typewriter, she slowly typed away, then un-carefully ripped a check-shaped page out and handed it to me. Before letting go, she hung up the phone, and began her signature salty staring contest.

"Desmond, I want to congratulate you on your new job with *The Call*. Taylor speaks very highly of you. And a lot of people in the newsroom have already commented on how much they enjoy your, your…shall we say…energy."

I attempted to maneuver the check out of her hands, but Judy wouldn't let go. Unflinching, she continued to talk down to me as if I were a child, which technically speaking, I still was.

"But I want you to understand something, Desmond. You will… never…ever…become a reporter here at *The Call*. Not through this job. Do you understand? That is never going to happen. If you want to be a journalist, go to journalism school. Then get an internship. Then get a job. Somewhere else. Allentown, Pennsylvania. Anchorage, Alaska. Anywhere. I don't care. But not here. I don't even want to see your résumé on my desk for at least another ten years. That's just how it's done. Desmond, do you understand?"

It was one of those confrontational moments in life where you don't think of the best comebacks until well afterward. Over the years, I've since thought of many. But that day I said nothing. I slowly finagled the check out of Judy's hand, and glanced at the amount while walking out the door. I planned to spend every penny on Claire Davies.

•••

I CALLED CLAIRE FROM the newsroom. Our conversation was abrupt and awkward, which was the best I could muster considering my inexperience in speaking with very pretty girls. Claire seemed pleasantly surprised, but also expressed a level of irritation over my waiting to call until the night before our date. I apologized and explained that it was a crazy week and gave a couple of other lame excuses rooted in my innate and about-to-bloom guyness. I didn't tell her about the job yet, as I hoped to save that for the moment in the movie where the soundtrack cues my victory of finally getting the girl.

Although I hadn't asked him yet, Hector would be our chauffeur for the evening.

"*Orale! Sopla wey!*" he said the Saturday afternoon I woke him up to ask. "*Te vas a apapachar!* Finally, *wey!*"

Hector always wanted to speak Spanish in our conversations, which I always refused to do. For one thing, he always spoke in Spanglish with a twist of Mexican and Central American slang. This drove our father crazy. Hector's accent was genuine, considering those were the folks he and I grew up with at church, school, and outside the corner Stop-N-Go store. What felt odd was that I spoke Spanish more fluently than Hector did, even though he was older and spent many of his childhood winters in Chile during a time when my parents still routinely visited the old country. By the time I was born, not long after Uncle Lalo came to live with us instead of with General Augusto Pinochet, our parents had decided they'd seen enough of South America.

Hector insisted on taking care of everything for my date with Claire.

"*Caramba, wey.* I got everything you need, bro—the limo, the restaurant reservations, *la tequila*, the rubbers. And you know I get you two in any club you want, *wey!* Strip club, dance club. White boy rock gig. Whatever, yo."

"That's cool, man. You know, I don't think she's going to be all into strip clubs and all that. Least I hope not."

"Hey. You ain't gettin' what you ain't asking for, little bro. If you can grab you some *nalgas o tetas, chingala wey*! If you don't, believe me, yo, someone else will. Yo. I don't mean to be rude, D, but it seem like you ain't got too much experience in that department, no?"

"Come on, man. That's kinda private, you know?"

"I'm just sayin! You a freshman now. At *Vasco*, yo. They practically got a coed class on how to use condoms, yo. What you waiting for? Make it happen."

"Come on, man."

"I'm just sayin'. Yo, I was getting my *chiludo en la panocha* in the sixth grade, bro. For reals. You've gots to get it on while you can, little man. The back of the limo would be perfecto, yo."

"Nah, man. I don't want no limo. What about one of them sorta black cars you're always taking people to the airport in?"

"Lincoln…Town…Car," said Hector, as if he were about to start singing the last verse from "This Little Piggie." "Awright. I see where this night is heading. Keep it all businesslike, with a little mystery at first. Then close the deal. *Asi*, no?"

"Awright, awright. What about that place on Mission? Bruno's? The one with the cool tables in the back corners with the brick walls? Where Mami and Papi used to go out on dates back in the day?"

"Bruno's? Oh hell no. Come on now. You know I'm a marked man in the Mission, bro. Nah. Man. Don't worry. I got you covered. One word, my brother: North Beach," he said, illustrating each syllable by opening and closing his palms.

"Hector. I think that's actually two words."

"Man. Why don't you shut the hell up and let me do my thing?"

"Okay, fine. Sorry."

"Now, let's go to Stonestown and get you some real clothes. Yo, this is gonna be like a fly-by-night operation, know what I'm sayin'?"

•••

WE PULLED UP IN front of Claire's house at 7:15 p.m. Hector insisted we be a little late, as he believed it best to have something ready to talk about before a date starts.

"Yo, tell her we got pulled over. Then she'll know the cops already ran our plates and now we cool for the night."

Judging from the custom three-story Spanish-style home with a view of the Pacific Ocean and her family's gated driveway which Hector double-parked in front of, I didn't think Claire would have heard that excuse before. Nervous and not thinking straight, I used it anyway—on her mom, who answered the door.

"Goodness. I hope everything is okay," she said, holding a glass of white wine.

"Oh yeah. Just a busted taillight. Fix-it ticket, you know. Those things can take forever. That's my brother out there. He's got it all taken care of."

I held up tulips for Claire.

"Please, come in. These are beautiful. And you look so handsome in your...very, very...black clothes. I'm sorry. Your name?"

"Desi."

"Desi! I love it. Like, Desi Arnaz? Ricky Ricardo, right?"

"Exactly."

"*¿Hablas Español?*" she said in a deep, gringo man voice. She spilled a bit of wine without noticing.

"Yeah. I mean, *sí*. My parents are from South America."

"Well. *Encantada*, I'm sure. Victoria! Your little Latin lover is here to see you!" she shouted up the spiral staircase. I double-checked the address in my pocket as a confused girl of about fourteen or so slowly walked toward the bottom step, stopping halfway down.

"I'm sorry, Mrs. Davies. I'm here for Claire."

"Claire? Oh. How funny. Victoria. Please go get your sister. She must still be her room, no doubt listening to that depressing Gothic music."

She took another sip, then led me by the hand into the glitzily furnished house.

"Now, Ricky. Please have a seat in the foyer, and I'll get you a drink. And please, call me Jamie. I haven't been a Davies for about ten years now. Would your brother like to come in?"

"No, that's okay," I said, having a hunch that Hector would end up drinking the night away with Miss Jamie-I'm-Not-a-Davies-Anymore. Three other sisters of varying but not too distant ages walked by, sorta-kinda saying hello.

Jamie went to the kitchen. I gazed out the ceiling-high windows and saw the polished Paloma Avenue street sign glowing white in the night. We lived only one neighborhood, or about a mile, apart. But it felt half a world away. It was a world I could get used to, I thought, while taking my first ever sip of sparkling mineral water from the flute glass Jamie handed me. I loved everything about the house and the way they appeared to live. Fancy furniture without the plastic covers that my father put on everything. Glasses designated for specific type of drinks and not made of dishwasher-melted Tupperware. Views of the Pacific Ocean instead of shoes hanging from telephone wires. Someday I'd buy a house like this. I didn't know how. But I'd find a way. And my first *Call* paycheck was as good a start as any.

"So, Ricky. I mean *Desi*! What's your discipline?"

"You mean, do I have a job? Well, I'm interested in journalism. In fact, I just got hired by *The Call* this week."

"Wow. *The Call!* Good for you. Are you writing?"

"Well, no. Not yet. Just learning the ropes. Doing assistant work."

Jamie was now drinking red wine, as Claire walked down the stairs. She had her hair dyed black in a bob and was wearing a black knee-length skirt with a blouse that opened quite liberally just beneath where her chin would touch her chest. Other than the black low-top Converse sneakers she wore, Claire looked five years older me—which is more like ten in puberty years.

"Claire! Ricky here just a got a job with *The Inquirer*! Isn't that exciting?!"

"*The Call.*"

"I mean *The Call*. Of course." Jamie cursed after spilling a drop of red wine on what I would now recognize as an Eames ottoman.

Claire had already packed an annoyed look for her mother.

"Who's Ricky?"

"I'm sorry. I mean *Desi*."

"Bye, Mom." Claire stood by the front door, motioning for us to go.

"You two have fun tonight. And Desi, make sure you send us a copy of your first article in *The Inquirer*."

Claire slammed the door and I could hear Jamie's muted voice sing out:

"I mean *The Caaall*!"

On the way from her front door to Hector's borrowed car, I knew I had a choice. I could either appear nervous—or not. Probably because I didn't want to look dumb in front of Hector, I chose the latter. Opening the door to the back of the waxed black Lincoln Town Car, I skipped the Hector lies and for the rest of the night stuck to the truth.

"Damn, Claire. You look so incredibly pretty. Are you sure you're a freshman in high school and not college? You look amazing."

The truth immediately set me free. Claire smiled and nervously fixed the side of her hair. She pretended not to have trouble adjusting the back of her skirt to sit-down mode.

"Thanks, Desi. You look really nice, too."

"Please," I said, before closing her door. "Call me Ricky."

Sitting diagonally toward one another with the excited sensation of our knees occasionally touching, Claire dove into her life story. With Hector speeding through yellow lights along the busy thoroughfare of Nineteenth Avenue, I learned that Claire was born in San Francisco too, but hardly knew the city. Her father was an investment banker, she told me, as we turned the corner onto Ocean Avenue. This meant that she spent a lot of time in London and Paris with some summers in Tokyo thrown in, she said as we entered the Great Highway that bordered the Pacific Ocean. During the only awkward moment in which I couldn't think of the next question, I looked out to the Westward sea and tried to visualize what her life was like on the other end.

"So you must have lots of good memories living over that way."

"Not really. All I ever remember is my parents fighting, no matter where we were."

By the edge of Golden Gate Park, her parents were divorced. At the Cliff House, where the ocean highway ended, her father had remarried and her mother was divorced a second time.

"My dad always had this thing for San Francisco. So he bought a house here and lets us live in it when he's not visiting town. He's never here," she said, her eyes cast down with reproach. "My parents always said they'd settle here because this is where they met in college. Obviously that's not going to happen. We're just here temporarily, until my mom figures out whom she'll divorce next. I just think she likes it because it reminds her of my dad. And he probably likes it that he's still supporting her. You know, classic case of those who giveth like to taketh away. It's like they still believe that they'll somehow get back together again in the end. They're so sentimental and weird."

Along the stretch of Geary Boulevard where I was born, I asked a question that I was afraid to hear the answer to.

"Temporary?"

"Yeah. We'll probably end up in LA eventually."

"Oh no. That's horrible. I hate Los Angeles."

"Really? Why?"

"I dunno. I've never actually been. Somehow I just know I've always hated LA. And now I hate it even more."

Claire laughed in Japantown.

Hector backtracked us through the Broadway mansions that make up the Pacific Heights hills where I could imagine Claire and I living together un-divorced.

"I've been meaning to ask you a personal question if that's cool."

"Sure."

"Of all places, how did you end up going to Vasco? Shouldn't you be at like some European diplomat school or something? I know there's gotta be one around here somewhere."

"Yeah, well, I guess you could say Vasco was kind of an accident."

"You know, I've often said the same thing."

"You are too funny," she said moving our knees permanently together. At that point I should have been nervously preoccupied with an uncontrollable body part that at that age I was still trying to get to know myself. Where the confident charm and control came from, I have no idea. With a sense of energetic support and without balking, I casually placed Claire's hand in mine and began reading her palm with the tips of my fingers. I could almost feel Hector smile.

"So. Vasco?"

"Umm, yeah…Vasco," she said, breathing a little differently. "I definitely didn't want to go to the same private school as my sisters. My mom got all pissed off and said 'Fine, go wherever you want.' So I filled out some paperwork for the city and they sent me to Vasco."

"Fate!"

"Fate. I like that." Claire edged her shoulder against mine right at the North Beach corner of Columbus and Broadway. From that point on I cannot recall a single moment where our skin did not touch in one form or another. Even during dinner, we sat side-by-side with either our arms or legs tangled together. We ate at the beautiful hole-in-the-wall Gold Spike restaurant—a choice Hector vehemently protested against. I liked the old-San-Francisco-saloon feel of the Gold Spike. It seemed like the kind of place a teenaged Sansome would take his girl. Over spaghetti and soda I told Claire about my EXTRA story and how the suspension led to my getting a job at *The Call*. Claire was genuinely impressed. Waiting for the check that I insisted paying for, we wrote our names on a napkin and push-pinned it onto the ceiling wall like dozens of others had done during decades of dinner at the Gold Spike. We walked across the street and passed the strip club where Hector was chatting it up with two security guards and a voluptuous woman wearing a hybrid bathing suit/ Dallas Cowboys cheerleader outfit that had been irresponsibly thrown in the dryer.

"The girl gets in free," the lady sang.

Hand in hand, we ran past the cheerleader and her defensive linemen. Turning the corner back onto Broadway, we raced to touch down in the direction of the silver-lit Bay Bridge tower standing in the distance from the end zone of the Embarcadero. We ran out of breath and into each other's arms outside the door of the Green Tortoise Hostel.

"Hey, a hostel. Let's get in here." Claire led us past dirty-bearded college men leaning on backpacks.

"Hostile? What's a hostile? Hey, what time do you gotta be home?"

"Tomorrow." Claire smiled, and bent over to read a floor sign that had the hostel's rates. I was getting nervous. Claire was not.

We read over the rules, which stated something about needing an out of the area ID and a bus or plane ticket as requirements to check in. Claire looked into her purse and saw that she was one for two.

"Wait here." Claire walked over to the check-in counter to speak with a guy who looked like he was in a Grateful Dead cover band. Claire played with her hair as he handed over a key and pointed to a staircase that, as far as I could see, led directly to heaven.

When the Deadhead turned his back, Claire motioned for me to follow.

"He thinks I'm from France. I told him that I left my plane ticket in the last hotel. I can't believe he fell for my ridiculous accent. Must be fate."

This was beginning to feel like a scene from one of those movies I could only watch on the scrambled cable channels while my father was asleep. Classier, of course. But just as and equally confusing.

Once inside the room, the plot unfolded innocently enough. There was an appropriately placed wooden double bunk bed in one corner and a kitchenette area with table and chairs facing the window out to the North Beach nightlife. Claire and I sat in the carpeted middle and talked for several hours with Big Al's and other strip club's shining neon signs providing the only light. Claire had brought a Walkman with a custom-decorated ninety-minute cassette inside. She had filled it with songs she said reminded her of me. I was flattered, but had difficulty not laughing at all of the crazy-sounding band names: Echo & the Bunnymen, The Jesus & Mary Chain, The Velvet Underground, The Stone Roses, Nick Cave & the Bad Seeds, Tom Waits, Mazzy Star. What these odd singers were saying to her about my life I did not know. But from that point forward these ninety minutes of messages would forever provide the soundtrack to my soul.

We listened to the tape over and over while sharing the headphones—the left channel hers, the right channel mine—until well past midnight, when the batteries finally went dead. We stared outside the window where the Broadway clubs and bars approached last calls and whistlers began competing for the attention of taxicabs. We witnessed some couples break up, and listened to overambitious dudes throw up.

"You know what I love about you, Desi?"

"No, what?"

"You're the only person I've ever met who knows exactly what he wants to do with his life, you know that?"

"You think so?"

"Seriously. Kids. Adults. My parents. Teachers. Seems like no one I ever meet is happy with what they're doing or knows for sure if they want to keep doing whatever it is they think they're supposed to be doing. You know what I mean? But you, you know for sure that you want work for a newspaper. And everybody who knows you knows that's exactly what you'll do with the rest of your life. It's like you were born to work for *The Call* or something. I just think that's really cool."

"Well, thanks. I never thought of it that way. Hey, maybe when I die, I'll come back to life as a doctor. That's what my dad wants me to be, anyway. I try and tell him that I always faint at the sight of blood, but he still insists. He doesn't get journalism. He says it can't be a real job if all you do is just read and write all day. Hey, what about you? What are you going to do with your life?"

"Oh, I don't know. I guess I could have a bright future as a stripper around the corner."

"Don't say that!"

"Why? What's so wrong with being a stripper?

"Lots of things, don't you think?"

"Nah. I don't think there's anything wrong with being a stripper or a pimp or whatever. I mean, not if it's the one wrong thing you do with your life that eventually helps you figure out whatever the right thing is. Hey, when are you going to kiss me?"

And the last thing I remember from that night is Claire smiling to sleep as I watched the sun rise in San Francisco.

Chapter 12

That Monday, it wouldn't have been difficult for anyone to notice that there was a little extra pep in my step. But, appearing too cheerful in a newsroom can be quite an aggravating offense. News copy editors in particular did not appreciate my renewed, optimistic outlook on life. They'd glare. They'd swear. And they'd remind me that whatever fax or phone message I carried in my hand, "nobody fucking cares." I continued to kill it with kindness, remembering that the mostly morbid "if it bleeds it ledes" subject matter on which they were concentrating had much to do with them not wanting to turn their frowns upside down. But there's a reason why so many of the best newspaper journalists are always so goddamn grumpy: the happier you are, the more likely you are going to make a mistake.

By the end of the Monday shift, I had forgotten to deliver a message to Taylor from the managing editor about a last-minute story switch. This resulted in a City Hall shake-up story appearing in every Tuesday paper except *The Call*.

Sorry.

On Tuesday, I misplaced the cabinet key to where we locked the keys to the company's fleet of press-pass-license-plated cars. A photographer had to call Triple-A to get to the camera he had left locked in the trunk. The pictures weren't developed in time for deadline. Of course, it turned out that the key was in my jacket pocket the whole time.

Damn.

On Wednesday, after insisting I could edit the scoreboard pages in my sleep, I inadvertently transposed both the horse racing results with the horse racing handicaps and the NBA East standings with the NBA West. I found out about these errors via several sarcastic comments from angry men on the subway the next morning.

Shit.

On Thursday, I had to explain to everyone why the pizzas Taylor asked me to order all had extra onions and anchovies on them. The Brazilian guy I ordered from on the phone was just being polite when he said he understood my stab at Portuguese.

Oops.

By Friday I was just as much of a depressed wreck as the rest of them.

All, except for one Mr. J. Gilbert Clawson.

"Claws," as most called him, was a theater critic. I knew his name from sorting lots and lots of hate mail addressed to him. None of the other dozen or so *Call* critics received even a fraction of the mail that clogged Claws' mailbox every day. Not the pop music guys. Not the fine art critics. Not the book reviewers. Not the many movie critics. Not even all of them put together. And it wasn't exactly fan mail. Several of the senders would take it upon themselves to presume they knew what the mysterious "J" in J. Gilbert Clawson's byline stood for.

Jerk-off

Jackass

Joke of a Writer

Joint Sniffer

They didn't always make sense. But they got their points across quickly enough.

I came into *The Call* early that Friday to borrow a computer and work on my "why I shouldn't be expelled essay" that Mr. Hersey required in the letter that Hector intercepted from our father. Cy asked me to cover the phones while he ran across the street to buy flowers for his mother's birthday.

The phone rang immediately.

"I'm calling about J. Gilbert Clawson's review in the paper today."

The man sounded as if he had a cold, and his tone hinted he was eager to be agitated.

"Certainly, sir," I said, scrambling to find a copy of the features section.

"Have you read the review?" he asked.

"No, sir. Do you have an issue with it? You know, you can always write a letter to the editor."

"You bet your ass I have an issue with it."

"Well, sir, I can always transfer you to Claws, I mean Mr. J. Gilbert."

"Oh, *The Call*'s going to have to do a lot more than just transfer me to Mr. Jim-Dandy Gilbert Clawson."

"Okay, sir. I've got the story in front of me now."

It was accompanied by a very negative theater review rating for the performance of *The Grotto Nymph*.

"Sir, what seems to be the problem?"

"Well, let's start from the beginning, shall we? First, the headline: 'Grotto Nymph, Frankly, Falls Flat.'"

"Well you know, sir, Mr. Clawson doesn't write the headlines."

"Oh that's not all Claws doesn't do, kid."

The man cleared phlegm from his throat, then continued to read, this time with an extra touch of snoot permeating through his snot:

"'In musicals, there are great singers and there are bad singers. And then there's Fred Franks, who is greatly bad. The capacity crowd at the Orpheum Theatre was aghast during Thursday's opening night performance of *The Grotto Nymph* as lead actor Franks sang us all to sleep with, as usual, his abysmally boring voice.'"

The man cleared his throat again.

"I see," I said, feeling an acute need to clear my throat as well. "Did you, ahem, happen to go to this performance too?"

"No. As a matter of fact, I did not."

"Well, then what's the problem?"

"I'm Fred Franks."

Because of a cold that sounded contagious even over the phone, Fred Franks had to bow out of singing for *The Grotto Nymph's* opening night at the Orpheum. In the grand tradition of going on with the show, another singer, Walter Stephenson, filled in for him at the last minute. This couldn't have gone unnoticed by anyone in attendance, as it was announced several times and handwritten in all of the programs. Even if Claws had been late to hear the announcement, didn't pick up or read his program, or sat in the furthest nosebleed seat of the Orpheum, it still would have been near impossible for Claws not to notice the cast change if not for the black-and-white fact that Walter Stephenson was black and Fred Franks was white. Fred Franks was nowhere near the Orpheum Theater that night. And, as it turned out, neither was Claws.

This was not at all what I envisioned for my first *Call* scoop. In deciding whom to break the news to first, I went with Hector's-younger-brother-code and confronted the person presumed guilty so that at the very least he could have a bit of a running start. Placing Fred Franks on hold, I anxiously meandered my way to the features department asking passersby along the way for directions to J. Gilbert Clawson's desk. Their snide comments offered a foreshadowing glimpse of the kind of support Claws could expect from his colleagues. With help from the buckets of unopened mail enveloping his desk, I found Claws.

J. Gilbert Clawson had just set his matching trench coat and hat atop a pillar of mail bins.

"Mr. Clawson?"

"Son, you may call me Claws. I am well aware that everyone else here does."

Claws wouldn't look at me as he spoke, while logging into his computer.

"Okay, Claws. I've got a gentleman on the phone. He'd very much like to speak to you about your review today. He has a bit of a...well...an issue with...a few things. But really just one thing."

"That's quite all right. He can write me a love letter like everyone else."

"Well, Mr. Clawson, I mean, Claws. This is not just anyone else. It's a Mr. Fred Franks calling. I've got him on hold."

"Fred Franks? Is that so? Interesting. No actor has had the nerve to call me after a bad review in at least twenty years. I always knew Fred was a bad singer. I wasn't aware he practiced such bad form. Tell him to leave a message and I will return his call later."

"Look, Claws. It's like this."

It caught Claws by surprise when I walked up to his computer, blocking the only passageway out from his corridor of unanswered correspondence and leaving him no choice but to finally look me in the eye. I lowered my voice to just above whisper even though no one else could hear us.

"Check it out. This dude. Well, he's pretty pissed off, right? But it's not about the bad review. You see, he said he's upset about the, well, you know…*the fake review.*"

"I beg your pardon? Fake?"

"Yeah, well, the thing is, Claws, Franks was sick last night and didn't even make it to the Orpheum. Some other guy filled in at the last minute. Walter Stephenson, who doesn't look anything like Fred Franks, for obvious reasons. You know, on account of Stephenson is a black dude."

Claws said nothing, while his irregular breathing said everything.

"So, basically, this guy wasn't even at the theater last night. And, well, kinda looks like he's saying you weren't either. Now he wants to talk to you and all the editors and have *The Call* run some kind of retraction or correction."

I sat on a stack of unopened press releases.

"So? What the hell do we do now?"

I had never seen someone have a heart attack before. Claws showed every symptom of one—widened eyes, squeezing at the center of his chest, paleness of the skin, gasping for air while sputtering, "Call…ambulance…having…heart…attack!"

J. Gilbert Clawson was no better an actor than Fred Franks. Anyone who saw Claws during the forty-five-minute fiasco could tell that he had faked more than just a review. The peeved paramedics who rushed to the scene eventually gave J. Gilbert Clawson the benefit of the doubt that he might have suffered a panic attack. Watching *The Call* authorities handle the situation served as valuable insight into the political structure of a major metropolitan newspaper. Since I was the one who answered Franks' phone call and spoke to Claws first, the top editors requested I stick around to aid in their investigation. Mostly this meant sitting outside a conference room door where I could hear every word of Claws' interrogation.

The masthead of a newspaper is much like the power structure of the *Star Wars* Death Star. At top is the publisher who, like the Emperor, is rarely spoken of and seen in only the most crucial of scenes. If the Death Star were a newspaper, Darth Vader would be its executive editor. He's the most public figure associated with its overall mission, and while no one knows for sure exactly what he does with his time, everyone involuntarily clutches at their throats when they know they've done something he doesn't like.

Deputy managing editors are the equivalent of those nondescript Death Star Commanders typically seen pacing around Darth Vader's empty office. They look alike. They talk alike. And they all take out their nervous angst on the closest subordinate stormtrooper-reporter or editorial assistant unlucky enough to be walking by. In desperately pleading his case, Claws more or less insisted that he was like the rebel soldier who had infiltrated the misguided and evil Empire's newspaper and was only there to enlighten them to their wrong ways.

"I'm a writer, not a journalist, and I've always said so," cried Claws over and over again. Up through the early afternoon Claws pled ignorance to knowing that there was anything wrong with writing a review for a performance that never happened. "Had Mr. Franks performed last night, every word of mine would have been true and accurate."

"But, *Claws.* He *didn't* perform last night. Your review is *a lie.*"

"My God, sir. Have you never heard of Pablo Picasso? Art is merely a lie that tells the truth! I'm an artist. Not a journalist. I have always said so."

From Darth Vader on down, everyone took a stab at answering the ever-burning question: What was the bigger crime—that

Claws wrote a review knowing it was fake, or faked a review not knowing it was wrong to do so? This editorial chicken-or-the-egg debate continued for hours until one rather shrewd and untiring Death Star Commander finally finagled his way into control. He chose his timing after the other responding editors had skipped lunch and were beginning to show signs of severe low blood sugar.

"You guys need a break," said the sneaky one, softly, as Claws momentarily retreated to the bathroom. "Why don't you guys go grab a bite and let me talk to him for a while?"

The editors acquiesced. The sneaky one stayed inside the conference room, forgetting that I was still seated on the other side of the door that Claws staggered back through.

"Richard! Thank God. I can finally have a moment alone with you. Someone who understands and appreciates me. They keep going on about this ethical journalism nonsense when we all know this newspaper practically sells its editorials every day! What about my artistic integrity? Fred Franks has an absolutely horrid voice. It's not my fault the crowd was lucky enough for him to miss the performance. Richard, please. Tell me you agree. Richard?"

Richard waited to be sure Claws had completely emptied the chaotic contents in his head.

"Listen, Junior."

"Junior?!" I concealed a snorted laugh and wondered what higher punishment could there possibly be than forcing J. Gilbert Clawson to reveal to his readers that the J stood for Junior.

"Allison left you recently, didn't she?"

"Well, we've been separated since last spring. Almost a year. But the divorce finally goes through next month."

"I see. And what about your meds?"

"My what?"

"The meds I'll have my doctor prescribe you for anxiety and depression. I've been suggesting that to you for years now. And how about your mother? She died suddenly and recently, correct?"

"She was ninety-five, so it wasn't entirely surprising. That was last summer. I suppose it wasn't so long ago, now that you've mentioned it."

"You see, Junior? You've had a stressful year. It's understandable. How much vacation time do you have left on the books?"

"I'm not entirely certain. At least three extra weeks rolled over from last year."

"Perfect. I suggest you take all of it at once, beginning with today."

"Will they be paid?"

"Of course. Listen, Junior. I hired you because you're a wonderful writer and a delightful person. But we need you to work on becoming a better reporter. After all, that is part of the job. You understand?"

"Yes. I do. I really don't know what I was thinking, Richard. It won't happen again."

"Of course not. Now you head home. Get some rest. And we'll see each other again in a few weeks. By then, this will all have blown over. I promise."

"What about Fred Franks?"

"Hey, I'm an editor, not a miracle worker. There's not much I can do about Fred Franks' singing."

They both let out hearty laughs.

"I don't know how to thank you, Richard," said Claws, through tears of appreciation.

The jittery editors returned from lunch appearing bloated, and subsequently even more tired than when they left. The effects of their two martinis each had overpowered any potential protest that may have been brewing inside of them from earlier that morning.

"Where the hell did Claws go?" asked one, in what would be his most valiant effort.

"I sent him home. On vacation. For five weeks."

"You what?" asked the shortest and roundest of them all, speaking up for the first time all day.

"Listen. Gentlemen. Let's not make this any bigger of a deal than it needs to be. We'll run a clarification. I'll take care of it."

"You'll take care of it? What the fuck is that supposed to mean, Leech?" asked the thinnest and tallest editor, who I later learned was *The Call*'s not-so-scary-looking Darth Vader.

"What it means, *Michael*, is that we'll be guarding the company from any chance of a lawsuit from Claws and minimizing any further embarrassment for the paper."

"Lawsuit?"

"While you were all out to lunch Claws casually mentioned that he has often felt *discriminated* against lately in the newsroom. He also pointed out that he is the only critic at *The Call* in his sixties."

"Oh, come on. That's gotta be the stupidest shit I've ever heard," said Darth Michael, slamming his skinny fist against something solid-sounding.

"Listen, the louder we are about this, the more public it becomes. If it doesn't die down on its own, we can find another way to kill it. Claws said he wrote the piece in advance as mostly background material and notes from what he remembered from Franks' last performance. He had to take care of some issues with his divorce at the last minute. He missed the performance, but forgot to call and tell us to kill the story that he had filed early. I can write around that and work it into a clarification."

"That is absolute horseshit and you know it, Leech," said the nasal-toned Vader. "How come he didn't mention any of this to us before? What the hell are you doing defending this guy?"

"You know, Mike, I think Leech is right," said the shortest and roundest editor.

"What? Are you kidding me, Janus?" asked Michael.

"Let's just fix what we know we have to fix," said Janus. "Right now, a clarification fixes everything. And if something comes up tomorrow, we'll fix it then. I mean come on, it's not like it was an A1 piece on the mayor or anything. We're just talking about a goddamn theater review on D3."

"Well," said Vader, trying not to yawn through his next words. "What about this Frank...Franklin...or...whatever the fuck's his name? How do we know he isn't gonna start singing to *The Inquirer* or someone else?"

"Don't worry about Fred Franks," said Leech. "I already spoke to him this morning. I've assigned another writer to do a profile on him next month when his other show opens. He says he understands the situation."

"*Understandsthesituation*," said Vader, blowing his nose while quickly repeating Leech's words in an irritated, mocking manner. "Jesus. I don't believe this. Look, I've got a lot of other shit to take care of today."

"I know you do, Mike. You've had a rough week. But, I think you've put out some great papers this week, you know that? You really have. And your leadership really shows. Don't waste any more time on this. Like I said. I'll take care of it."

Janus, Michael, and another drowsy editor all said nothing as they swung open the wooden conference room doors, obliviously passing me by on their way out. I took it as a cue to get ready for my shift, which would start soon. My movement caught the attention of Richard Leech. Leech looked at me with an expression that people have when they've forgotten where they've parked their cars and for a moment fear it may have been stolen.

"Excuse me, are you Desmond?"

"Hi, yes, sorry. I was told to wait outside, but now I've got to go start my shift."

"That's fine. Come inside here for a moment and close the door. Please."

I did so, but instinctively looked for one of Judy Dorland's secret wall-doors in case I'd need to make a Han Solo escape.

"Listen. Desmond. Or do you prefer Desi?"

"Either way is fine."

"Desi, this was a pretty serious situation and I think you handled it well. However. The next time something like this happens, I need you to come to me first. Do you understand?"

It was then that I recognized Richard Leech for who he really was.

He was not only the same person whose backstabbing behavior stood out in that editor's meeting during my junior high school newsroom tour not long before. He was not only the person whom I heard lie and manipulate in multiple manners to the point where I had lost count that day. I recognized Richard Leech as someone I did not like, someone I did not trust, and someone I vowed I would never be like. And as much immediate good I knew it would do me, I could not bring myself to pretend otherwise.

"Desi? Did you hear what I said? I need you to understand what I just said."

As if he were an aggro-drunk uncle taking advantage of temporary disciplinary authority while the parents were away for the weekend, Leech repositioned my chin with his hand, forcing it to face him instead of the carpet. I instinctively whiplashed myself out of his grasp, jumping out of my seat. This startled Leech, who instinctively reached over to open the conference room door.

"Sure. I understand," I said, too afraid to say what I really wanted to say.

Richard delivered a compliment that I do not remember. I was too busy promising myself never to be afraid of him in the future.

Chapter 13

That Saturday, Claire and I went on another date. We went to the movies, paying for only one and sneaking into three others without actually watching any of them. Afterward, we went to her house, where her mother ordered us pizzas and insisted I spend the night—in Claire's room, with door closed and no questions asked. This opened a whole new world for me, which I was happy to visit, yet did not exactly feel at home in. Our slumber party ended awkwardly Sunday morning when I politely declined an offer from Claire's mother to join the all-girl family and their boyfriends for a champagne mimosa brunch.

Instead I spent Sunday preparing for any confrontation with the Haverlocks and wondering if it would be okay to kiss Claire at school. None of these things would matter for long. Vasco High School, as the flyer taped to the campus gate informed us that Monday morning, was about to close down.

•••

I DON'T REMEMBER THERE ever being anywhere near as many students on campus as there were that day. Classes overflowed into standing-room-only sessions where students made demands to save a school which, a few days before, they majored in playing hooky from. The chaotic scene, with petitions passed out at lunch and protests held before and after school, made it difficult to find anyone, including my girlfriend.

According to Maureen's Monday morning *Call* article that I had lifted from the teachers' lounge, the school superintendent proposed closing Vasco as a way to save the city more than one million dollars. Classes would continue through the summer session. Students would transfer to varying schools in the district, with priority choices given to the upperclassmen. Teachers with the least seniority would be laid off. The building would most likely be torn down, the property sold.

While Mrs. Lars was loyal to Mr. Hersey's business-as-usual instructions, several other teachers, including Mr. Burritt, joined in on student protests. Together they made SAVE VASCO signs and wrote catchy slogans like "Close Vasco? Oh Hail No, We Won't Go." Intrigued and inspired by this sudden and unfamiliar school spirit, I didn't know where I fit in. Of course, I didn't want Vasco to close down either. But I still felt betrayed for being expelled for following my heart. Why should I share my soul with it now? This conflict came in handy when I took notes of school scenes from the point of view of someone who wasn't precisely sure where he stood on the matter. I shared these notes with Maureen on Monday. She used some of them in her follow-up story, which earned me my very first tagline credit, printed at the end of the story published in Tuesday's *Call*: "Editorial Assistant Desmond de Leon contributed to this story."

Under normal circumstances this would have been a big thrill, particularly because I knew it was how Mrs. Lars and Mr. Hersey learned that I had been hired by *The Call*. But the taglines that continued each day were buzz-killed by my not being able to find Claire all week. No one answered at her number, and the machine never picked up. There were no further secret messages to be found in my Apperson biography, though I left it in my cubby every day just in case. Her house on Paloma Avenue appeared abruptly vacated. Through the window I could see the furniture still in place, along with a collection of Jamie's lipstick-stained champagne flute glasses of unfinished mimosas. Outside sat a week's worth of never-read *Calls* yellowing in the driveway. I picked them up and placed them in my backpack, dejected over knowing that neither Jamie nor Claire would ever know that my name was in all of them.

Days, weeks, and months passed, and with it grew the momentum to save Vasco High School. Finally, even Mrs. Lars and Mr. Hersey began to participate—in their own ways. Students whom I had never seen in class were showing up at the steps of City Hall, shouting: "Oh Hail No, We Won't Go" through megaphones. Even Ronnie Choe and Hector joined a few of the protests. I continued to stay on the sidelines, reporting on the saving of my school with an impartial notebook and pen. By the end of that summer, we won.

Or they won.

I wasn't sure I wanted to be associated in a group that included Mr. Hersey. But since I was happy enough to be associated with *The Call* in spite of Richard Leech, who was making formal complaints against Maureen's inclusion of my taglines and attempting to stop them, I might as well be happy for my school.

•••

THE FIRST DAY OF my sophomore year, Jamal Condon removed his purple hat in class before any teacher had asked. Anthony Mendoza always recycled his empty Capri Sun drinks instead of throwing them on the grass. Angelo Espinoza wore the proper-colored clothes during PE. No one was cited for wearing curlers or work uniforms in the hallways. Students studied during study hour, ate lunch during lunch hour, and led cheers for Vasco High's Buccaneer football team during pep rallies. Wherever he was, I'm sure Ol' Kenneth Basper, Class of thirty-one, beamed with Vasco pride. This well-behaved buzz lasted all the way on through my graduation in 1993, when Vasco High became a certified California Distinguished School.

Of course, some things never change. I still got into at least one fistfight a year, always breaking even with the other guy by being sure not to break into tears. Over at *The Call*, Judy Dorland and I continued our tradition of me turning in my internship application at the last second and she delivering her "You will never be a reporter here" speech. The only other memorable moment of my high school life came on prom night, just a few weeks before graduation. I didn't go to the dance. (Nobody asked.) I spent that Saturday working an extra editorial assistant night shift, listening to the results of everyone else's prom night by way of the SFPD police scanner while sorting leftover *Call* mail that Cy asked me to handle.

It was the first piece of mail that I ever received at *The Call*. A postcard. From New Zealand. With a crazy-faced Maori guy on the front. It was addressed to:

DESMOND DE LEON, NEWSPAPER REPORTER GUY

```
Dear Desi,
Sorry I never got to say goodbye. Life has
been "hella" :) crazy. I live in Australia.
For now at least. I am visiting New Zealand
for the first time this week. It is so beau-
tiful, and I know you would love it. I think
about you all the time. And I know you are
doing something good. Never Stop.

        Love,
        Claire
```

It had a lipstick-imprinted kiss, which I am unashamed to admit I connected my lips to that evening and many other times since. Claire mailed it to the "*San Francisco Inquirer*," where it hung suspended in the rival paper's dead-letter limbo pile until some unknown entity forwarded it to *The Call*. Claire's misaddressing the postcard only made me fall more in love with her. It meant she cared nothing about the newspaper politics that I was about to dive deeper into. It meant she only cared about me. And that was all I needed to get by. ◻

PART II
The World Is Yours

Chapter 14 ▶

"**I** need a Chicano. Or uh, uh, a Hispanic, or whatever they're calling themselves these days. I need one now!"

It was my day off, but I came into the newsroom that Sunday morning with plans to collect materials from *The Call*'s supply closet in preparation for my first semester, set to begin the next day at San Francisco City College. Pens, pencils, binders, notebooks, erasers. Nobody really kept track. Not even Cy, who was instructed to keep a close eye only on the secret stash of AA and 9-volt batteries people "borrowed" for their Walkmans and home smoke detectors.

The man yelling at no one in particular was Howard G. W. Cutler. Howard was an alcoholic newspaperman, which is sort of like saying he was a tall basketball player. There was a time, albeit a hazy one, when Howard was a top contender for the position of *The Call*'s chief city editor. He often filled those hand-me-down shoes on holiday shifts or when news broke during odd hours or when the regular city editor called in dead. That actually happened in 1962 when the then-artery-clogged city editor Robert England phoned the newsroom from his hospital bed one morning to say that he wasn't going to make it.

Mr. England was a very literal editor.

Howard G. W. Cutler became interim editor by default, as he was often the easiest to reach. While the rest of the newspapermen of his generation took their promotions and subsequent pay raises to big suburban homes across the Bay's bridges, Howard never moved out of the Leavenworth Street apartment where he lived as a busy bachelor (1959), indiscreet husband (1963), and guilt-ridden widower (1985).

Legend has it that during all three of the aforementioned stages of his life, Howard never once stepped foot outside of the city limits of San Francisco. Howard's hobby was drinking whiskey. His favorite hobby shop was the Gold Dust Lounge on Powell Street, conveniently located at the exact halfway point of the thirty-minute walk between the *Call* newsroom and Howard's Leavenworth Street flat.

It's where he started his mornings (Irish coffees). It's where he took his lunch breaks (Jack and Coke). It's where he conducted his interviews (whiskey sours), and it's where he fastened his nightcaps (whiskey old-fashioned). It's where he met his wife (Jackie). It's where he cheated on her (Doris, the cocktail waitress). It's where he received the phone call that Jackie had been killed in a car crash (drunk driver). Often, it was the only place where a qualified assistant city editor could be reached to fill an emergency shift.

Howard happily answered the call, the only stipulation of which was being allowed to finish a last drink before making his way into the newsroom at his own pace. Whether twenty minutes or two hours late, Howard had a knack for never missing anything important. In a way, Howard was proof that there will always be room for an alcoholic in newspaper journalism. There was nothing that even the Zodiac Killer could do that Howard wouldn't be able to report, edit, proofread, and, if it came down to it, even "paginate" all on his own. It's the kind of value that can't be measured by a breathalyzer. Whenever under the deadline gun, Howard G. W. Cutler always got it done.

Right now, all Howard needed was a Chicano or Hispanic, and I was the closest thing to it. It was getting close to 10:30 in the morning, and the weekend general assignment reporter was already an hour late. The only other person in the newsroom was the always punctual and ready to roll *Call* photographer, Grant Montgomery.

"Hey, Desi," said Grant, loading a roll of film into his camera. "Your last name's de Leon, right? That's a Spanish name, isn't it? *¿Hablas Español?* or what?"

"Yeah. Sure. I mean, *sí, señor.*"

"Perfecto."

Grant walked toward Howard, who handed over a press release.

"Desi," said Grant. "How would you like to write your first real newspaper story? *Sí?* Or no?"

"Hell yeah. I mean, *sí, señor!*"

"How old are you, anyways?"

"Almost nineteen."

"*Muy bueno.* Howard, I'll take the kid with me. We'll see what the inmate has to say. Zimmerman always comes in after eleven. He doesn't speak Spanish anyways. So might as well have Zim talk to the victim's family and to the police flaks."

"Fine. File (*cough*) by five p.m. (*cough-grunt*). Thirty inches of copy. No less. No more. (*Cough-pleghm-clearing grunt.*) And keep it clean."

Grant folded the SFPD press release into a paper airplane and flung it my direction. I caught it, grabbed my new City

College notebook, and we made our way down the elevator to Grant's company car parked in a red zone. The press release was three-fourths filled with paragraphs of police blotter. Howard had circled only one. It was the longest paragraph of them all. Too long in fact, that Howard couldn't resist but edit it down to the following highlighted words: Homicide…Sea Cliff. Private residence…Victim: white male. Approximately sixty-five. Officers discovered man DOA in bedroom…8:30 p.m. Multiple stab wounds to chest and neck… Suspect: Approximately twenty-five. Hispanic male. In custody.

I read these words over and over again all the way into Grant's car in hopes of memorizing the basic facts. As soon as I'd finish reading it one time I'd forget something else the second time. My hands shook with adrenaline. I continually checked my pockets to be sure I hadn't dropped or forgotten my notebook and pen. They were still there, but my mind wasn't. My concentration was lost in the repeated netherworld of played-out scenarios, both good and bad. In some of those scattered seconds, I was accepting a Pulitzer for the greatest story ever written by a San Francisco newspaperman. Claire was smiling by my side. During other seconds I was the subject of a police blotter paragraph after Howard had stabbed me to death with his red pen for my being a failure and phony reporter. Claire was crying at my coffin.

"Listen, Desi. Just relax. You're gonna do fine. This is the plan. We're going to the jailhouse. We'll check in with the sergeant. He'll have you fill out an interview request. You'll get thirty minutes to talk to the suspect."

"You mean, with the glass window and phones on both sides?"

"Exactamundo!"

I actually did have experience using that telephone during visits to Hector at the same Bryant Street jailhouse where we were headed. Grant double-parked in front of the steps to the main entrance.

He turned the engine off, placed his press parking permit in the dashboard, and popped the trunk to gather his camera supplies.

"What do you think I should ask him first?"

"Desi, all you gotta do is ask one question."

"One question? What do you mean? Why only one question? What question?"

Grant slammed shut the trunk as if illustrating a suggestion of what I should do with my mouth.

"What happened?" said Grant, spreading his arms out like a baseball umpire giving the safe sign. "How do you say that in Spanish?"

"*¿Que paso?*"

"That's it! See, you got it! *¿Que paso?*! That's *all* we need to know, *amigo*. Just remember one thing, Desi. This guy *wants* to talk. So let him talk. You know what I mean?"

"I think so."

"Everyday, I hafta listen to these blowhard reporters walk all over other people's words. And then they wonder why they don't get the whole fucking story. It's absolutely aggravating. Just remember. It's *his* story. Not yours. Know what I mean?"

"I think so."

"Good. And if this guy gets defensive and stops talking, *don't* ask him another question. Just keep looking at him and keep writing in your notebook. Let *him* get out of the awkward moments on his own. Trust me. He will. They always do. If you let them."

I glanced at the SFPD sheet one last time. All the details were beginning to sink into my memory. Except for one.

"Where's Sea Cliff?" I asked about the mansion-clad neighborhood that I wouldn't get to know for another five or so years. "Are you sure that's really in San Francisco?"

Grant laughed.

"Desi, I don't know what it is, but something tells me you were meant to do this. Now let's go find out *que* fucking *paso.*"

Inside the jailhouse waiting room, a skeptical sergeant handed me a press release with updated details: Miguel Salazar. Age twenty-seven. Native of Nicaragua.

Grant went into the booth first. During the three minutes Grant was with Salazar, I tried not to recognize any mothers or sisters from my neighborhood. For the sake of my mother's spirit I held the SFPD press release in plain sight to emphasize the reason for my visit. You never know who's watching you in moments like these.

Grant busted out of the door with cameras slung around his neck.

"Your turn, Desi. I'll be in the car."

From the moment I walked into the room, and before I could sit on the dirty plastic chair on the safe side of the window, Miguel Salazar burst into laughter. Through the thick window he muttered in Spanish something to the effect of, "You've got to be kidding me."

I sat down. Picked up the mildew-scented phone. Opened my notebook. And looked into the soul of Miguel Salazar's eyes. I watched as his sense of humor drowned into a pool of tears. I politely introduced myself and asked if he was from the capital city of Managua. Outside of Montreal Expos pitcher Dennis Martinez and eating Gallo Pinto dishes at the homes of former church friends, I knew nothing else about Nicaragua. For a fleeting moment, Miguel seemed comforted to hear the name of his hometown.

"*Si, Managua. ¿Y tu? ¿De donde eres?*"

"*San Francisco,*" I said in the Spanish manner that it was originally intended to be pronounced. "*Mis padres son de Chile. Santiago. Valparaiso.*"

"*Ah, Chileno. Pablo Neruda.*"

The small talk ended more abruptly then poetically. So I finally asked.

"*¿Que paso?*"

With Grant's sole question, Miguel took a deep breath, adjusted his posture to allow a confident sitting-up-straight position, and told me who, what, where, when, and why he did what he did.

Miguel, along with his wife, Angela, eleven-year-old son, Miguel Jr., and eight-year-old daughter, Martha, had for the past two years been living in the backyard guesthouse of Dr. Kenneth Millhausen's home on Sea Cliff Avenue. Miguel served as the sprawling mansion's lead landscaper while Angela cooked, cleaned, and babysat the two preteen sons of Dr. Millhausen and his wife, Sandra. It was an arrangement that Miguel and his family were very grateful for, and saw as a blessing from God.

The Millhausens had lived in Nicaragua for a few years. Dr. Millhausen was a political envoy, leading an effort to repair relationships between the United States and Nicaragua following the contra mess left over from the eighties. Dr. Millhausen wasn't a medical doctor. He had a PhD in a subject that Miguel couldn't remember.

Miguel mostly remembered Dr. Millhausen wining and dining members of the newly formed Nicaraguan government who competed for political favors at the US Embassy in Managua. Miguel and Angela worked in security and hospitality, respectively, at the embassy. Dr. Millhausen and his wife took such a liking to the young couple that they offered them extra weekend work at the Millhausen residence near the museum and shopping district of the city. By the end of that summer, Dr. Millhausen and his wife extended an invitation to the Salazars to continue their natural chemistry in California, where they could live as well-paid servants, and, of course, as friends. Dr. Millhausen took care of the passport, work visa, and otherwise red-taped paperwork for the entire Salazar family. He paid for the Salazar family's airfare, with the understanding that it could be paid back through the first few months' work.

Miguel remembers seeing the Golden Gate Bridge for the first time from his new bedroom window, and thinking that this was all good to be true. As Miguel looked down at his Golden Gate Bridge–colored jumpsuit he realized that's exactly what it was.

"*¿Y luego? ¿Que paso?*" I asked during the interview's first awkward pause.

"And then I killed him," Miguel said matter-of-factly, and in English.

For this second awkward pause, I asked nothing. Just as Grant instructed, I continued writing until Miguel had no choice but to continue with his story at his own pace.

When Dr. Millhausen came out from the courtyard to ask Miguel for a favor, Miguel said he instantly had a bad feeling in his stomach. Dr. Millhausen wanted Miguel to drive the pickup truck to the hardware store and load up on firewood, which the doctor desperately needed to help concentrate on writing his speech. Dr. Millhausen would do it himself, were it not for his bad back. When Miguel said he needed to watch over Martha, who was ill, Dr. Millhausen insisted Miguel not worry. He would listen out for her. He suggested Miguel use the leftover change from the firewood to purchase some stronger cold medicine and popsicles to sooth Martha's sore throat. Miguel continued to politely resist the offer until the doctor finally forced the truck keys and a hundred-dollar bill into Miguel's hand, and flashed a look suggesting he'd throw the cost of airfare back into Miguel's face if he couldn't "just do this one little favor."

Miguel made it as far as three blocks before that something in his stomach told him to turn back around and check on Martha. When he did, she was gone from her room. He followed the sounds of his daughter's faint and groggy voice coming from somewhere inside the Millhausen mansion. Miguel entered from the courtyard, passing through the kitchen, where he indiscriminately grabbed a steak knife from the Millhausen's recently sharpened cutlery set. He slipped the knife into his back pocket.

Miguel traced the sound of his daughter's voice to a guest room that he never remembers anyone using before. He quietly opened the door to find the messy, gray-haired Dr. Millhausen alone with a frightened and confused Martha. Miguel did not describe what it was that he saw. But the horrors of it reflected in Miguel's furious facial expressions and right through the thick-paned window. Miguel told Martha to run to her room and lock the door until only he or her mother returned. She did as instructed.

The third and final awkward pause of the interview was also the longest. It ended when I finally had the nerve to ask:

"And then? *¿Que paso?*"

"I killed him. With his own knife. As many times as I could, I killed him," said Miguel in both English and in what sounded like a prepared and well-thought out statement. "I want you to write in your newspaper that I killed this Dr. Millhausen. And I want everyone to understand that I am *proud* to accept the punishment for what I have done."

Miguel began to weep in a manner that men like him tend to do only once or twice in their lives. Out of respect, I averted eye contact, and so noticed knifed abrasions on both of his hands.

"We are all sinners. This I understand," he continued, returning to speaking in Spanish. "The church taught me that you are not as bad as the worst thing you've done in your life. I will die knowing that I can still do better things with my life, even if I spend the rest of my time in a prison. But this doctor. He had to die knowing this bad thing was the *last* thing he would ever do in his life."

Miguel stood up to leave. "Now. Go tell this to your newspaper."

•••

I RELAYED BITS OF Miguel's story to Grant during the five-minute car ride back to *The Call* while Grant repeatedly slapped his palm against the horn and shouted, "Fuck yeah! *Que paso! Que paso! Que paso!*" over and over again. When we returned to the newsroom, Howard was already out to lunch. Grant introduced me to Jason Zimmerman, the weekend day shift reporter. Zim was on the phone speaking to an acquaintance of Dr. Millhausen. Zim placed his hand over the speaking end of the phone and whispered for me to get him a few paragraphs by 4:00 p.m. I looked at the clock. It was barely noon.

Hour after hour passed with my not being able to write a single word. At a quarter after 3:00 p.m., Zim walked into the wire room where I hid behind a computer that nobody ever used. Zim looked at the blank screen and smiled through a wad of chewing tobacco. I offered a meandering assortment of explanations, with Zim spitting into a Pepsi can in-between each one.

"Dez," said Zim in his deliberate, and likely stoned, tone. "What was the most surprising thing the guy said?"

"That's easy. That he was proud to accept the punishment for the crime that he committed."

"Man, Dez, that's wicked." Zim spit into the aluminum can again, and then snagged my notes away from me. "What else?"

I repeated Miguel's story as I remembered it, from the Nicaraguan embassy to the backyard hedges in Sea Cliff to the abandoned hardware store trip through the kitchen and into the guest room.

"That's wicked, bro. Write it exactly the way you just told it to me."

I motioned for him to return my notes, but the gruff, native New Jerseyan refused, using the Pepsi can as a barrier.

"The story. It's not in there. It's up here, bro." Zim tapped the diet tobacco soda can against his own head, then walked back to his desk with my notebook in his hand.

With Zim's advice, I finished within twenty-five minutes. I printed it out and walked over to his desk, just as he hung up the phone. Zim found out that fifteen years before, a woman had filed a sex abuse claim against Dr. Millhausen on behalf of her daughter. The case was settled out of court for an undisclosed amount, Zim's source said. Although there were no news reports about that incident, Rita Sullivan, *The Call* librarian, found the original claim in a public records database.

Sitting side-by-side at Zim's computer, we connected our two halves of the story into one singular San Francisco tragedy. At the top, Zim insisted on putting only my name in the byline. He tagged his name at the end as a contributor. By 5:00 p.m., Howard hadn't returned from his long lunch—something Claudia, the night shift editor, loudly pointed out as she rearranged the desk that they shared on weekends. I introduced myself as the writer responsible for her lead story.

"Sorry, I don't have time right now," said Claudia, turning on the police scanner that Howard always left off. "As usual, I have to deal with all of Howard's leftover shit."

I looked back over at Zim's desk. He was gone for the day, too. I stood at the crossroads of wondering whether I should be the flighty kind of reporter who always disappears when an editor wishes to see him, or the lingering kind of reporter that an editor always wishes would just disappear. There was no in-between, as far as I knew. The main newsroom line began ringing. I answered the phone at the desk where the night editorial assistant was supposed to be.

"Newsroom, this is Desi."

"Who's on the desk?" said an impetuous man's voice on the other end.

"Excuse me?"

"I *said*, who's on the fucking desk tonight? Who's the city editor?"

"I'm sorry, who is this?"

"It's Karl. Now who the fuck are you and why am I still not being transferred to the fucking city editor who you still haven't even fucking told me the goddamn motherfucking name of?"

"Karl Floyd?"

"Yes. That's right. *I'm* Floyd. Now, who the fuck are *you*?"

"It's Desi, man. Karl, why you always gotta pretend you don't know who I am?"

"What? Who the fuck do you think you are?"

"I just told you. Desi."

"Listen to me, Desmond de la fucking little dickhead, I'm on deadline. So unless you transfer me to the on duty city editor right now, I'm gonna have to drive down from Sacramento and deal with your little fucking copyboy ass myself."

"Extension 8811."

"What? Is that the city editor's extension?"

"No. It's mine. Call me when you get here, Karl *Motherfuckering* Floyd!"

I slammed the phone down. I had rehearsed my end of that conversation many times before, because I promised myself I would say something the next time Floyd yelled at me, which he had been doing ever since my first day on the job. Proud, but anxious, I continued answering phone calls from readers with delivery complaints and sorted faxes up until Claudia screamed at no one in particular.

"What. The. Fuck. Is. This. Shit?!"

Somehow, I knew she was talking about me.

"Are you Desmond? Come over here please. Right now."

I walked over to Claudia, whom I had met many times before.

"First of all. Who the fuck are you?"

"Desmond. I'm the night editorial assistant. I don't normally work the weekends."

"You're an EA?"

"Yes."

"What the fuck are you doing writing an A1 news story if you're just an EA?"

"Well, it just so happens that I was the closest thing to a Mexican when Howard was looking for one this morning."

Claudia, who I later learned was Mexican, did not laugh.

"Look, I don't give a shit if you speak Swahili. We can't have EAs writing front-page news stories. This is a major metropolitan newspaper, for Chrissakes. And what's all this shit about *the church taught me you're not as bad as the worst thing you've done in your life*? He's a fucking murder suspect. We're not going to give this guy a fucking platform to brag about being a murderer."

"But, Miguel—I mean the suspect—he said all that because he found Dr. Millhausen, you know…molesting his daughter…basically."

"*Basically?* What the fuck does *basically* molesting his daughter mean? What kind of proof did he have? What did the cops say?"

"I didn't talk to the cops. Zim did, I think. Plus Zim and Rita found out that this doctor was accused of molestation before."

"And it says here that the case was *settled. Out of court.* And now you're telling me to use the newspaper to convict this dead guy, who can't even speak for himself, of being a child molester? Jesus Christ! Dr. Millhaven or whatever the fuck his name is— *he's* the victim! He's the one who is dead. What part of dead don't you understand?"

At that point I understood nothing.

"Look, Desmond. It's not your fault this place is so fucking unorganized. I know you were just trying to help. Look, the three-star early edition is already off the floor. It gets delivered out of the area, but we'll have some copies here tonight, so you can show it to your mother or whomever. But I'm going to have to do some major surgery to this story for the next edition. And I'm going to have to take all your work out. I tell you what. I'll tag your name at the bottom as a contributor. Sorry."

I turned and headed in the dejected direction of wherever my spirit wanted me to hide. Winding my way down the cast-ironed railing steps into *The Call*'s basement, passing through a snack room area, I found an unlocked door at the dead end of a hallway.

I opened the door, revealing a room where piles and piles of newspapers were lined up against the walls, architecturally stacked like a child's pretend fortress. The maze of newspapers continued into a smaller room that had the scattered abandoned belongings of someone else's office. An unplugged microwave was propped atop an empty mini refrigerator. Behind a pillar of boxes labeled "EARTHQUAKE SUPPLIES" was a blue vinyl sofa with a large rip down the middle of its back. At the foot of the damaged sofa was yet another door. This one was missing a doorknob and was closed shut with layers of thick electrical tape. It being the most irresistible door in this newly discovered basement labyrinth, I had to open it.

Inside was a closet-like corridor that opened up to the bowels of *The San Francisco Call*—one of the few sections of the building that had survived the 1906 earthquake. The ceilings were high enough to allow an old printing press to stand tall in a corner, where it apparently had spent decades waiting for someone to remember that it was still there. Noticing the hooks and hangers, I guessed that the closet was where the old *Call* pressmen hung their hats, coats, and gloves—as well as graffiti thoughts. With some penciled in and others carved with a knife, the walls of the closet were like a Jackson Pollock painting of little wisdoms that dated as far back as when the building was built in the late eighteen hundreds.

"*I left my heart attacks in San Francisco.*"

"*Not far from now, not far from here, they'll hide their gold and drink our beer.*"

"*Millions now living have already died.*"

"*SEEDED LION.*"

After spending hours interpreting the mantras, I retreated back to the blue vinyl couch, where I slept through the night with the poetry of pressmen ringing around my head.

Chapter 15

"They call this reporting? Jesus H. Christ!" he screamed, furiously marking up notes on the inside pages of *The Call* and crosschecking them with some sort of sophisticated scorecard. "Well, *whattayaknow*? Edited by one Redfield Janus, of course. Why-my not surprised?"

There was no way for me to surface from the backroom bowels of *The Call* without startling this man, who was built like an NBA point guard.

"Hi," I finally said.

"Jesus Fucking Christ!"

He instinctively went into attack mode by throwing a felt-tip pen at my face, successfully leaving a slash mark of red ink above my upper lip. With his head nearly hitting the low-level ceiling, the man stood up to reveal a T-shirt that read: "I'm 6'8" and **NO**, I don't play basketball."

"Dear Lord! Where did you come from?"

"I was just…actually. I don't really know what I'm doing here. I'm Desmond. Desmond de Leon. I guess I was here pretty late last night."

"Dear Lord! You scared the shit out of me. I thought you were a ghost. I'm Ernest. Ernest Holloway. *Call* archivist."

"Sorry, Ernest. The door was unlocked. I was having a shitty night. Just needed a place to hide away for a bit. I won't do it again."

"Hey, man. You can spend every night down here as far as I'm concerned. Next time, just don't walk through any walls, please."

"Did you know there's a whole other room back here? You wanna see?"

"No, thanks. Hey, wasn't that your name at the bottom of that stabbing story today?"

"You read that?"

"Well, as you can see, I read everything in this godforsaken newspaper. Not by choice. It's my job. Somebody has to archive this ragamuffin newspaper. I tell you what, though. Something doesn't add up with that Dr. Millhausen."

"What do you mean?"

Ernest held up his red-ink-stained edition of that morning's *Call*, letting me read it, but without letting go of his grip on the edge of the paper.

"Homeboy from Nicaragua," he said, pointing to the question marks in his notes. "Living in the back of a nice house like that. With his wife and kids. For two years? He ain't gonna all the sudden go all loco like that unless that doctor did something he shouldn't have been doing. Know what I'm saying?"

Glancing at the five-star copy that Ernest held up like a courtroom exhibit, I grabbed hold of the bottom end and read the first sentence that jumped out at me:

The suspect in custody admitted to the killing and later expressed pride in doing so.

There was no mention of Miguel's motive. Much of the rest of the story was dedicated to the professional accomplishments of Dr. Millhausen. I let go of my half of the paper and proceeded to vent to Ernest about all of the details from the night before. In a ceremony that we would continue for many years to come, Ernest listened to every word, shaking his head in support and saying "Dear Lord," whenever I stopped to catch my breath.

"Well," he finally said, picking up his red marker from the ground to get back to work. "Just make sure Mr. Miguel gets a copy of the three-star. And then move on to the next story."

Excited by this advice, I surprised Ernest with an inappropriate hug in which the side of my head barely reached the middle of his rib cage. I ran out the door and up the stairs to the one place I knew I could find a copy of that morning's three-star edition— Richard Leech's mail bin. Plucking out a copy, I pivoted to make an escape. But I should have known better. There is no escaping from Richard Leech. He was sitting at the computer that I had used to write my story the night before.

"Desi. Just the person I was looking for. There are a number of editors who'd like a chance to speak with you."

I turned around to face Leech. He was printing out versions of my story in the order that the computer had saved them.

"Follow me please."

Leech led us into the same meeting room where J. Gilbert Clawson successfully evaded early retirement some years before. At the room-long conference table sat four other men who were in the wrapping-up stages of a morning meeting. I recognized one of them as the deputy Death Star editor, Redfield Janus.

"I have Desmond de Leon here," said Leech.

"Desi. Please have a seat," said Janus. "There are some things we need to talk to you about. It won't take long."

Janus spoke through a soft, whispery lisp.

"Desi, you've met Karl Floyd?"

Janus gestured toward Floyd. We grunted salutations into one another's direction.

"Desi," said Janus. "Lemme cut to the chase. Karl here tells us he had a rather unpleasant telephone conversation with you last night."

"Yeah. That's for sure. It was definitely unpleasant."

"Desi, believe me. I understand. This is a newsroom. There can be a lot of tension in the air. Tempers flare. We all get a little worked up now and then. That's just the nature of this deadline business. But unfortunately, because of you, Karl missed a very important deadline."

With his legs crossed and the bottom of his well-polished shoe facing me, Leech took rapid notes from the other side of the table.

"Desi, this is the news business. You can't take these things so personally."

"Look, man. I wasn't even supposed to be working last night."

"Well, Desi," said Leech. "What *were* you doing in the newsroom last night?"

"I was just helping out, man."

"Desi," said Janus. "I understand you're eager to learn this business. And I think that's really great. Judy Dorland showed us some of your internship applications from the past. I can see you've got lots of passion for journalism. That's wonderful. We need that. But we also need editorial assistants who transfer phone calls from reporters when they're on deadline. You understand?

"Sure, I understand."

"And Desi," said Leech. "According to your timecards, you've had quite a bit of unauthorized overtime. Can you explain that?"

I sighed and slouched in the chair.

"You see, Desi," said Janus, irritatingly calm. "The company has to cut back on editorial assistant staffing. Richard has, for a few weeks now, been trying to make a case for why we should try to keep you. Frankly, your immature attitude has made the decision for us."

"You're firing me?"

"Involuntary layoff," said Leech.

We were interrupted by a rustling sound from the other side of the conference room. Judy Dorland suddenly appeared through another one of her camouflaged wall-doors. She marched over and handed me a large envelope labeled "severance package."

"The good news," said Leech, "is that we'll keep you on the rehire list. You'll be at the top of this list."

I stood up.

"Judy has already boxed up your belongings," said a smiling Janus. "We're having a courier deliver them to your house. Judy will be escorting you out of the building."

One of the extras not listed in the severance package was the opportunity to walk through that trap door and into the secret human resources labyrinth. Judy led us through the empty publisher's office into a long and narrow hallway where portraits of past *Call* publishers hung from the walls. The eyes of these men were captured in such a way that they stared back at me from every angle, regardless of where I walked. At the end of the hallway were two doors directly across from one another. She opened one that exited into an alleyway I had walked by thousands of times before without ever knowing a hallway was on the other side.

"Good luck," she said, closing the "door" behind her.

Chapter 16

I saw Richard Leech that same evening. Sifting through the City College spring schedule, his name called out to me.

(LEECH, R.) JOUR101. Introductory. 7:00 p.m. M 3 UNITS

Richard may have had the upper hand of knowing the ins and outs of *The Call*, but City College was my home-field advantage. The campus was practically in my family's backyard. It's where I went to preschool while my mother earned her associate's degree. It's where Hector and his friends enrolled and dropped out every few months in-between parole releases. It's where all the boys in my neighborhood hopped the fence to play ghetto-rules football on the fancy Astroturf on which O. J. Simpson used to break rushing records. And it was the one place where I knew to find any trap doors.

I was the first to arrive, and set the San Francisco City College standard by taking a seat in the very far back corner of the auditorium. Because I was a late addition to his class, my name would be at the very end of his attendance sheet. I would use the time to prepare smart-ass comebacks. By 7:15 p.m. the entire auditorium was filled with chatty, uninhibited students. Leech walked in at 7:18 p.m. His entrance was impossible to miss. He set the semester's tone by immediately letting everyone in the overflowing classroom know who was in charge.

"Since we all know full well," said Leech, pausing to erase algebra equations on the chalkboard, "that a quarter of those here in attendance will not be returning after tonight's dinner break... and that another quarter of you will drop out before midterm... and that yet another quarter of you will stubbornly stay in the class even though you have no business being in journalism...and that...God-willing...at least the last quarter of you here actually want to learn about journalism...allow me to begin by telling you all a little more about...myself."

Richard used the entire chalkboard to write three giant letters: DIE.

"That's right. DIE! Deadline. Is. Everything." His voice reached an unstrained level that most could not achieve without a microphone. "Everything must be turned in on time. That includes your presence. I don't care if your printer was out of toner. I don't care if the BART train broke down in the tunnel. I don't care if you had a miscarriage. In my class, you're either on time or you're not. With everything."

Leech continued to tell the class "a little something" about himself.

It began with his childhood days growing up in the newsroom of the *Boston Globe*, where his father and grandfather worked as assistant city editors. After witnessing three fatal heart attacks from reporters working the stressful cops beat, Leech realized hard news wasn't his cup of tea. He'd put in his time of course, covering several murders during internships at the *Staten Island Advance* and *Newark Star-Ledger* while getting his bachelor's degree in English and Comparative Literature at Columbia University. Leech covered sports for a time. This was while doing double-duty as both the *Columbia Daily Spectator*'s editor-in-chief and fill-in sports editor ("after that deadbeat dropped out"). Leech thought he'd hate the assignment, but soon learned to never underestimate the power of a story. This lesson led to a scene-piece on a football game between Columbia and Harvard where he intricately described the moods, faces, and emotions of the fans, players, coaches, alumni, food vendors, and ticket takers. Leech couldn't quite remember who actually won that game and wasn't sure whether the final score even made it into the story. But he remembered winning his first journalism award for writing it.

Leech's trip down memory lane included stops at *The Honolulu Advertiser* (too hot), *The Anchorage Times* (too cold), *The Miami Herald* (too humid), *The Austin American Statesman* (too Texas) and *The Denver Post* (too boring). Leech hitchhiked from Colorado to Berkeley. He had plenty of money to buy a plane or train ticket, but that would have been too easy, he said. After deciding that the Bay Area would henceforth be his home, he enrolled at UC Berkeley and completed a master's degree in journalism, while also working nights as copy editor for *The Call*.

After the dinner break, Leech finally took attendance, asking each prospective student to explain his or her interest in journalism. This was like dessert for Leech. He poked fun at several of the students' baggy clothes, slouched postures, "Ebonics-accents," and "inane last names." By the time he reached the end of the alphabet, at least a dozen students left. The first to go was Seleste Mayson, who did not appreciate Leech's suggestion that her mother go back and spell-check her birth certificate. There were only two minutes left in class when at long last Richard reached my name. Whatever thirty seconds I was allotted to share my calling to newspaper journalism with the class was taken away by the first hint of Leech being caught off cadence.

"Desi?" he finally asked.

"Back here."

"Oh. There you are. Well, what do you know? The great Desmond de Leon. Well. I already know your story."

Leech redirected his attention to the rest of the anxious and already backpack-stuffing students.

"There's still one minute left in class. So here's everyone's homework assignment," he said, writing on the board: "*What I didn't do on my winter vacation—eight hundred words that you didn't say at the holiday dinner table.*"

Richard overtly ignored me as I walked past him through the auditorium door. This passive-aggressive tradition continued for six straight weeks, in which I arrived to every class and turned in each assignment on time. The only communication between the two of us was through the thick red marked notes and corrections that he painted all over my work.

Convoluted crap.

Pretentious prose.

Irritating attempts at alliteration.

And the most common:

No. No. No.

No one else in the class received half this level of critical attention on their assignments. With this in mind, I attempted an experiment. I noticed that Richard was uncharacteristically lenient with the very attractive Kimberlee Whyte, despite her tendency to be late to class and forgetfulness with assignment due dates. On that sixth Monday night class, after Kimberlee arrived several minutes late, Richard took a moment to read aloud an excerpt that he deemed to be "near impeccable." The story was based on an assignment to attend and report on a public court proceeding. This one involved a woman's attempt to halt the parole of her physically abusive husband. Richard read the words with modulated tenderness:

"*Alicia Greene doesn't remember the first time her husband hit her. But she'll never forget the first time she made him stop.*"

"Now *that* is what I call a compelling lede."

Kimberlee raised her hand.

"Yes, Kimee?"

"I'm sorry Mr. Leech, but that's not mine."

"Excuse me?"

"I didn't get around to doing the courthouse assignment. Because of, well…that…*thing*…I told you about."

Discombobulated, Leech flipped over the one-page assignment where on the back I left a handwritten note:

Hi, Richard.

This is Desi. I wrote this story. I put Kimberlee's name at top to see it would have an effect on your grading. I realize this is ob-

noxious. But I could not resist.

Sincerely,

Desmond de Leon.

Leech's Scandinavian skin tone blossomed to match the rosy red tint of his necktie. Viking horns nearly sprouted from his balding-but-still-bright blond hair. He loosened his necktie. Unbuttoned his suit jacket. Took a drink of water.

"Excuse me. My mistake. Looks like this was written by Desi."

Leech sped through the rest of Alicia Greene's tragedy with just a touch more of indifference than when he began it. Afterward he offered a few quick compliments that he spelled out on the board. *Compelling. Concise. Qualified detail.*

These were the nicest things Richard had ever said about me.

"Look, Desi," he said, confronting me after class. "I realize you're trying to prove a point."

"Well? Didn't I?"

"You've proved the point of why you still don't belong in a real newsroom. What you just did is utterly unprofessional and certainly justifies your being fired."

"You mean involuntarily laid off?"

"You see? Why must you insist on always proving that you're right?"

"To show who's wrong, man! Isn't that what journalism is all about, man? To point out when someone's been wronged?"

"Listen...*man!* You need to check your temper at the door. And, no. That's not what journalism is all about."

We both took deep breaths.

"Listen, Desi. I like you."

"Well, Richard, I don't like you."

"I know you don't like me. And, frankly, I really don't care. Yes, I have been grading you on another level than the rest of the class. But that's only because I believe you are at another level."

I kept silent, but didn't hide my interest in hearing what else Richard had to say.

"Look, I'm not just blowing smoke. You obviously have a lot of passion for journalism. Ever think maybe there's a reason why I'm still at *The Call* and you're not? Desi, to some degree, everybody has to put up with bullshit. If they want to get a paycheck."

He had a point. But I was in no mood to concede anything to Richard Leech.

"Desi, how would you like to come back and write for *The Call*?"

"What? You mean my old job?"

"No. As a staff writer. Starting tomorrow."

I took a half step back and looked him over the way one does when considering buying discounted tickets from a scalper.

"Desi, I'm dead serious. Look, there's a lot of drama going on around *The Call* right now. I could really use some solid backup writers to help me out. This could be a great opportunity for you to really get your feet wet and jump in. Sink or swim. This could be it."

I didn't know what to say. Richard straightened his necktie back into place.

"Give it some thought. You don't even have to come down to the newsroom. Just give me a call. You know the extension. Seven-five-seven-four. Just be sure to give me an answer before noon."

•••

There had to be a catch.

Guys like Leech never flat-out deny the existence of such a catch. They disguise it. They hint at it. Sometimes they'll even come out and say it so that it's in such plain sight you just don't notice it at first.

I didn't call Leech that morning. I skipped school and walked from my neighborhood to *The Call*, listening to the songs on Claire Davies' cassette for advice along the way. At around 11:00 a.m. and forty-something blocks later, I reached the edge of *The Call*'s entrance. Deep in lyrical thought and still attempting to translate Leech's coded invitation, I hadn't realized that I entered the epicenter of dozens of angry men and women, banging on pots and pans and shouting obscenities through megaphones directed toward the Call Building. I presumed it was another of the anti-media protests that occurred a few times a year. But these weren't college kids. Some were dressed in suits and ties. One of them was Stan Edelstein. Claudia was there. Cy, Karl Floyd, and Roberta Zambini, the grumpy copy editor, were there too—all looking pissed off yet happy at the same time. Someone grabbed at my arm and began shouting into my ear.

"Desi! Where the hell have you been?"

It was Taylor. We continued to shout back at one another.

"Didn't you hear? I got fired!"

"Fired?"

"Yeah. Leech. He called me into a meeting a few months ago!"

"Leech! I should've known. I swear to God, that guy is the spawn of Satan!"

"Yeah! He told me to come by today. Said he could make me a backup features writer!"

"A what?"

It began to rain. *Taylor* and I looked up toward the sky. We could see the silhouette of Leech looking down at us from the tinted and bulletproof windows of his Market Street side office.

"Backup writer? I can't believe that guy. Look, Desi, that's just a fancy of way of saying *scab*, man! Don't you know what a scab is, Desi? You weren't supposed to be fired, man. You should've been put on an on-call list. I've called your house a hundred times to tell you to come in. But every time I say I'm calling from *The Call*, the guy who answers keeps cursing me out and threatening to kill me, or something. I think it might be your brother. He hangs up every time."

Taylor motioned to hand me a picket sign, but then stopped himself from doing so.

"You know something? I can't tell you what to do. If you want to be a…a…a *backup* writer or whatever it is they're offering to put on your business card…man, that's up to you."

The angry crowd's shouting grew exponentially louder as a group accompanied by security guards huddled past the picketers toward the *Call* entrance. I recognized one of them as Janus and another as my long lost mentor, Maryanne Miller.

"Desi, it's draw-a-line-in-the-sand-time! Which side are you on, son?"

With the rain pounding down into hail, I grabbed the sign from Taylor and aimed it like a pistol in the direction of Richard Leech's silhouette. I watched Leech's shadow turn around. I stood next to Karl Floyd, who smiled and winked at me as I joined in on the catchy chorus of minor falls and major lifts sung by bull-horned lead singers.

> *We are the union…*
> *the mighty-mighty union…*
> *the workers united…*
> *will never be defeated…*

It was the first and last time I ever heard that song sung at *The Call*.

•••

FOR ELEVEN DAYS AND nights in April of 1994, we marched round-the-clock through the nonstop rain. The entire six blocks surrounding the *Call* and *Inquirer* buildings were patrolled by the likes of snappy jazz writer Happy Hamilton, tobacco-spitting Zim, and potty-mouthed Maureen. Sweat-ringed-shirt-wearing Lester Braun and his young Asian editorial assistant/boyfriend were there too. Even Claws graced us with his eminence. Our counterparts and supposed competition at *The Inquirer* joined us in the picketing, as we were all part of the same guild. Together we shouted obscenities at the Death Star managers coming in and out of the Call Building.

Everyone else, it seemed, was right there along with us. The cops. The firefighters. The mayor. Corner stores across the city refused to sell the spotty scab editions of the papers. When management tried to hand out copies at cafés for free, folks practically spit their coffee at them. They knew what was up. They knew so because guys like Taylor had been planning a way to fight back the entire last year of our contract. They bought billboards in advance. They handed out bumper stickers and buttons at all the bus and BART stations. They went on radio shows vociferously criticizing the *Call* and *Inquirer* management.

Well before the final night of striking ended we all knew the mighty-mighty union would win. Specifically what, I wasn't exactly sure. I never bothered to look that closely at any of the details. When it came to picking a side, I just knew whom I instinctively trusted and whom I didn't. Thanks to the post-strike-shift celebrations at nearby bars and cafés, I was finally won over by the taste of both beer and coffee, and could often be found carrying one in each hand.

On the eleventh and final day, *The Call's* most notable columnist, Herb McCabe, delivered a pep talk. Herb had marched alongside us every day, even though he was in his late eighties, ill with cancer, and had a separate contract from the rest of us. During the only moment of the strike where I can remember the rain stopping, Herb stepped up to a makeshift podium set up directly outside his office at the corner of Third and Market Streets.

"This ain't *their* newspaper," he said, shaking his finger back at the building. "This ain't *my* newspaper and this is ain't *your* newspaper. This is *our* newspaper! And this is San Fran-*goddamn*-ciso's newspaper! And don't you *ever* let them forget it!"

And then the crowd went wild.

Chapter 17

We won. And for a while, it was fun.

I showed up to work the next morning because Taylor told me to do so. He put me on the editorial assistant day shift schedule for the main news section. He'd be working the day shift now too, as an assistant city editor covering San Francisco news. Taylor said he deserved the right to choose the team he wanted around him. Janus, Leech, and Judy did nothing about it. They were too distracted in coming to terms with all of our new union rights. More vacation. More money. Even for the ones who probably didn't deserve it. Didn't matter. We were all one workforce. Sometimes I'd show up to work and be told I could go home with pay. Once because it was my birthday. Another because it was the anniversary of the first day I was ever hired. And yet another because I told Taylor I felt like a day game at Candlestick would help clear my editorial assistant mind. And when it was time to work, we worked.

Many of my days were spent shadowing court reporter Jack Burnside, a beautiful man with ugly habits. Burnside smoked, drank, and did lots of drugs. Just about every morning, he called in sick. And just about every afternoon, he'd show up to work anyway, though never to the newsroom. Burnside's office was based out of City Hall. My job was to run the downtown city blocks back and forth between Burnside and Taylor, delivering legal documents, supplies, out-of-town newspapers and, of course, Burnside's latest excuses for being late. They were as tragic and intriguing as the courtroom dramas he covered. My favorite was when he called in with a venereal disease.

"Desi," he'd whisper in that phone sex line voice of his. "I was walking to the newsroom to finally fill out some of that paperwork Judy keeps calling me about. Honestly, Desi, I was trying to do the right thing. But then I was propositioned by this absolutely gorgeous blonde."

"A hooker?"

"Well, I knew she worked the streets. That wasn't the problem. I just didn't know she was a he."

"Good Lord, Jack."

"I'm telling you, Desi. She was that gorgeous. There was no way of knowing. Until, well, you know…"

"Damn. What'd you do?"

"You know me, Desi. I don't believe in coincidences. Life is a series of synchro-destinies. The universe is always sending us signs. And it's up to us to follow those signs. I figured since I'd gone that far down the road, then it must've been for a reason."

Taylor put up with Burnside's paranoid personality because the hedonist journalist had a knack for catching stories that fell through the cracks of other reporters' beats. Although he was assigned to cover local court cases, this didn't stop Burnside from finding scoops on the mayor's office, the board of supervisors, police and fire department scandals, and only the most bizarre things in-between. Burnside's early knowledge of these events likely had much to do with whom, how, and where he spent his evenings.

"God, he is *so* slimy," Amelia Lee would say after eavesdropping on Burnside's calls-in-sick. Even though Amelia covered the mayor's office at City Hall, where her main desk was, she always made a point to stop by the *Call* offices first. She liked to check in with Taylor and the other editors in person "to keep in tune with newsroom." I'm pretty sure it also had something to do with getting a parking spot to save on her commuting cost from the East Bay. Regardless, I never hesitated to let Amelia know which managers were on vacation so that she knew which spots were safe to take for the day. In exchange for these favors, Amelia, Burnside, and others at *The Call* shared the highlights of their own personal stories and journeys into journalism.

Stan Edelstein and Taylor couldn't remember a time when they didn't know they were meant to be newspaper journalists. Zim graduated from law school and passed the bar, only to realize he detested attorneys and therefore himself. Maureen and Amelia loved the buzz of catching crooked authorities in a lie. Roberta, the grumpy copy editor, loved the buzz of catching the illiteracies of so-called writers. Claws planned to write for *The Call* for "just one more year" before putting the final touches on his six-act play. None of them understood, related to, or, for that matter, particularly cared much about my obsessions with the gun-fighting San Francisco history of the Sansome brothers. Every Halloween I'd show up to the *Call* newsroom dressed as Charles Sansome, only to lose my temper after one too many of my colleagues would ask, "Who the hell is Charles Sansome?"

•••

"Sorry to bother you, Mr. McCabe" I said, dropping off one of Herb's vodka-bottle-shaped boxes of fan mail he often received. This was to be the last conversation I had with Herb during the time between the 1994 strike and his death in 1997.

"So'kay. Come on in, kid. You can put those down with the others," he said, pointing to a bookshelf that housed more booze than books.

"Mr. McCabe, I wanted to let you know how much my Uncle Lalo loved reading your column. He learned to speak English by reading it when he came here from South America."

"South America? You mean, Los Angeles? What about you, kid? Where you from?"

"San Fran-goddamn-cisco, sir!"

"San Fran *what*?"

A vibe in the air suggested the small talk ought wrap up sooner rather than later.

"I just want to say I thought it was real cool what you did and said during the strike."

"What, are you kidding me? I wouldn't have missed that for the world. I tellya what, kid. Just remember one thing: You don't win what you don't fight for."

At first, I took Herb's advice a little too literally. No year would pass without my getting into some kind of altercation with another colleague at *The Call*. The first was with Stan Edelstein.

He started it.

I was sorting photocopies just like he asked.

"No, *no*. **NO!**" said Stan, inspecting the "ill-prepared" collated piles. "What kind of an idiot are you?"

I grabbed Stan's papers and threw them in the garbage. He screamed incoherently at me as I walked out the door. I eventually won this fight when, for the first time in Stan's storied newspaper career, he actually said he was sorry. I also won when Karl Floyd shot himself in the foot by yelling at me when I again refused to transfer his calls if he didn't stop calling me his "little copyboy." When Taylor heard Karl's commotion from the receiver's end of the phone, he picked up the line and told Karl to quit being such an asshole.

Still, these victories felt self-defeating. By 1997, I was twenty-two, and several of the newly hired reporters were around my age. Some were younger. High school interns were writing stories, while I continued to deliver *The Economist* and *Financial Times* to editors who never read them, but insisted they be placed in a visible manner so visitors would believe they were being read. Somewhere on my quest to become a reporter I had taken a very wrong turn.

Zeke Harte was a year younger than me, but miles ahead in that he had completed three reporting internships, the last being with *The Call* the summer before. After his graduating from UC Berkeley and being rehired as a full-time reporter, I was the one assigned to pick up the pizzas and chocolate cake for the newsroom to celebrate his triumphant return.

"Dude," said Zeke, first in line to grab a slice of pizza. "You're, Desi, right? Desmond de Leon?"

"Yeah, man. That's me." I was dubious of getting too buddy-buddy with the guy who had the job I wanted just as I was coming to terms with the reality I might not ever get it. "And according to the frosting on this chocolate cake, you must be Zeke, right? Congratulations, man."

"Thanks. Hey, I heard you got into a fistfight with Karl Floyd when you were like twelve years old or something? Is that true? Man, that guy's such a douchebag."

I didn't bother to correct the facts in Zeke's exaggerated version of the story. I wondered who told him, as I continued to cut his cake into fair-sized pieces before the rest of the editorial vultures descended upon it.

"And didn't you write some jailhouse interview story a few years ago? About that doctor?"

"Yeah, yeah. Doctor Millhausen. He got murdered. By a guy from Nicaragua, Miguel Salazar."

"That's right! Man. That story was incredible."

"You think so? Wait. How is it you remember that story?"

"My parents," he said, in-between bites of pepperoni and cheese. "They knew that doctor and his wife. I grew up in Sebastopol, up in Sonoma County. I was visiting them on break from Cal. I read that story and was totally blown away, man."

"No kidding?"

I grew increasingly skeptical, and wondered if Zeke was in on some kind of practical joke with Karl Floyd or someone else who didn't like me. If he was, I decided that the most honorable response would require slapping Zeke across the face with a piece of pizza. I zoned in on the pie to find the appropriate slice.

"Yeah, man! We get the three-star early edition out there. And then when I got back to Berkeley to reread the story they totally fucked up the five-star version, man. Your name wasn't even on it or something like that. I always wondered who this Desmond de Leon dude was, you know? You're a great writer. How come you're not filing more stories for us?"

I picked up the chosen slice and took a bite.

"You know how it is. Gets all political around here sometimes."

"Yeah, man. I understand."

I had a feeling that he really didn't. I grabbed another piece of pizza and slice of chocolate cake for Taylor and began to walk away before Janus would come tell me to clean up everyone's dirty paper plates.

"Hey, Desi. Can I offer a little advice?"

"Sure, man," I said, ready to aim and fire, depending upon what Zeke was about to say.

"Food," he said.

I took a deep breath.

"Yes, I can see that. I'm the one who picked it up for you."

Zeke took another bite, pointed the remainder of his slice at me, and with his mouth full of mozzarella, said:

"Exactly."

I took a deeper breath.

"What exactly is it you're trying to say, Zeke?"

"Don't pick up food. For anyone. Ever."

"Well, it's not like I have to clean up any of this shit. I always leave before Janus asks me to."

"But you still pick it up and deliver it, right?"

"Yeah, but that's not such a big deal. I don't mind. It's kind of nice to get out of the newsroom sometimes."

"It's still food, man."

"What exactly is your point?"

"My point is," he said in his hushed scoop whisper, "that every time the editors see you delivering food, they see Desmond, the guy who delivers food. And they don't see Desmond, the guy who should be a reporter."

I put down Taylor's chocolate cake, a piece without frosting, just as he liked it, and looked over at Zeke.

"You know something, Zeke Harte? That's some pretty goddamn good advice."

"I know. Somebody gave me that same advice when I was at the *Santa Rosa Press Democrat*."

Chapter 18

I tossed Taylor's slice of chocolate cake into the garbage, and walked over to tell him that I needed to take the rest of the afternoon off as a mental health day. Then I made my official announcement—no more picking up coffee. No more buying bagels for his team and keeping the change. No more ordering steaks at Izzy's on election night and dropping off an extra order for my dad.

It didn't help that Taylor was on deadline when I went down my list of proclamations. Taylor's rolling eyes suggested that the novelty of an aspiring newspaperman was finally beginning to wear off even on him.

In order to catch up with my reporter colleagues, I would first need a drink.

I avoided Morty's, the smoky newspaper bar tucked in an alley just behind the Call Building. That's where everyone gathered to critique the papers, vent about the managing editors, and begin or end newsroom affairs. Morty's is also the place where I vowed to never ever marry anyone I'd met in the newsroom. Never mind the fact that I was still convinced Claire Davies and I would be back together someday; that I hadn't seen or heard from her since that last postcard made little difference. Journalists marrying one another invariably led to bad news. It never ceased to surprise me how often I'd find out that my colleagues had been or planned to be married. Part of what created this oblivion was how the wives tended to hold onto their maiden names. It was as if separate bylines and opposite pages in the company phone directory would somehow help separate marriage and career.

Redfield Janus, for instance, was married to the Home & Garden editor, Janet Wilson. It took me seven years and several hundred voicemail transfers between them before this reality finally dawned on me. The energy between Janet and Janus was no more or less negative than just about everyone else's who waited in line for Janus to finally return a phone call or show up for a scheduled meeting.

Soon after being promoted to managing editor, Janus always made time to meet with Katherine Robinson, The Call's director of public relations. While their job descriptions and day-to-day objectives were near polar opposites, their appearances and personalities were quite similar. Katherine and Janus both spoke with slight lisps. I never once saw Katherine or Janus lose their tempers, even though it was common for others in the same meeting room with them to lose theirs. On the other hand, Janet was twice as skinny and three times as tall as her husband. She was cold around most everyone—especially Janus, who had less patience for Janet than anyone else. I always figured it was because Janus hated the Home & Garden section. In fact, Janus and Janet hated each other.

On my way out to drink in Zeke's advice, I stopped to answer the main newsroom phone line, figuring it would only take a few seconds.

"Newsroom, this is Desi."

"Desi, it's Janus. I need you to do a real big favor for me."

"Sure, Janus. What do you need?"

"Go into my office. I'll call you there on my extension in just a second."

I hung up, entered his unlocked office and answered as instructed.

"Great, Desi. Say, I think I left my wedding ring somewhere on my desk. It's probably in my old *New York Daily News* coffee mug, where I keep my watch and money clip. Do you see it?"

"Sure, I see it."

It was a thick and heavy gold ring with "Mrs. Janet Janus" engraved across the top.

"Fantastic. That's a real relief, pal. Look, I'm in a lunch meeting down here in Silicon Valley right now. Can you do me one more favor, little buddy?"

"Sure."

A woman's faint voice called out from the background.

"Just a second, Desi."

Janus muffled the phone with his palm and then, to continue his conversation with more privacy, placed me on hold. Janus' ever-gentle voice was replaced by the recorded greeting of a clearly Caucasian man listing the many amenities available during "your stay at the Four Seasons Hotel." I could see the hotel's main entrance across the street from Janus' office window.

"Desi? You still there?"

"Yes. I'm here."

"Fantastic. Listen, pal. This'll just take a second. I just need you to put the ring inside the small pocket on the inside of my briefcase. You see it there next to the coat rack?"

"Yes, I see it."

"Fantastic, Desi. Fantastic. Now, if you could just put that ring in the briefcase, we'll be all set. Now, Desi. That ring is very precious to me. And I don't feel comfortable leaving it out in plain sight, you understand?"

"Sure, Janus. I understand."

"Fantastic, Desi. Hey, I owe you one. Later on this week let's have coffee so you can tell me more about all those story ideas of yours that I keep hearing about."

Janus hung up. With his precious metal vows in the palm of my hand, I stared across at the dozens of hotel windows and wondered which one he was calling from. Then Janet walked into Janus' office with her eyes all welled up.

"Hi, Desi. I'll take that, if you don't mind."

I handed her the ring. What else was I supposed to do? Her name was on it.

Janet took the ring and left Janus' office, staring down at the dirty newsroom carpet while she walked away. As soon as Janet left, Jack McCoy, *The Call*'s editorial pages editor, walked into Janus' office. I always liked Jack McCoy. Over the years, while I typed dozens of handwritten letters to the editors into *The Call*'s computer system for him, Jack and I had many debates over the varying subjects of his pages. Legalizing marijuana. Prostitution. The Gulf War. Bill Clinton's cigars. I always offered my personal insights whether Jack asked for them or not.

"You know something, Desi? I really had to scratch my head a lot over that one," Jack would always say, scratching his bearded head. "Let's make a deal. The day I think I know it all is the day I want *you* to force me to retire."

Whenever our discussions went on too long, he'd end them by saying:

"Some days you just gotta go with your gut and then see if your stomach feels the same way tomorrow."

My stomach was queasy when he walked in that day.

"Desi," said Jack, closing Janus' office door behind him. "Have you seen my wife?"

"Who?"

Jack's demeanor remained as neutral as his editorials.

"My wife, Desi. Have you seen my wife?"

"Sorry, Jack. I don't believe I've ever met Mrs. McCoy."

"Sure you have, Desi. Katherine? Robinson? In public relations?"

"Oh, wow! I didn't realize you two were married."

"Well, apparently you're not the only one who didn't realize we were married."

"I'm sorry, Jack. I really had no idea." I tried to excuse myself but Jack's skinny grizzly bear frame blocked the way.

"Lemme level with you, Desi. I'm pretty certain ol' Janus-face here is screwing my wife. As we speak. Now I hate to drag you in the middle of this. But since you're the one here in his office and, well, J-Anus ain't, well, I'm just wondering if you might know where our esteemed managing editor might be."

After momentarily slipping into the gap between thoughts, I blurted out the answer.

"Across the street. Four Seasons Hotel."

"How do you know?"

"Well. Let's just say that the Four Seasons has its own hold music."

"You know something, Desi," he said, patting me on the shoulder as he unblocked the way for me to pass through Janus' glass office. "Something tells me you're one of the good guys around here."

•••

NOW I REALLY DESERVED that drink.

The Gold Dust Lounge. Two-forty-seven Powell Street. One block off Union Square. Established 1933. With its crystal chandeliers, velvet booths, and half-naked nineteenth-century nymphs painted on the ceiling, it's the kind of place where even Charles Sansome and his assassin could momentarily forget their differences over a cheap stiff drink. Sometimes Sam Spade showed up, or at least fellas who looked like him. Two Major League umpires were known to establish their strike zones there with afternoon pitchers of beer before heading to work at Candlestick Park or the Oakland Coliseum. Every Wednesday, the entire crew for the next Lufthansa flight out of San Francisco International Airport would lighten up by downing as many two-dollar glasses of champagne as they could before heading back to their gruff personalities in the unfriendly German airline skies.

And then there was Howard.

I knew Howard G. W. Cutler's story thanks to the tidbits of whispered gossip I collected from colleagues over the years.

Depressed. Widowed. Alcoholic. Crusty. Old. Newspaperman.

Howard had his back to the entrance. When I tapped him on the tweed shoulder he didn't budge. When I said "Hi, Howard," he didn't answer. When I motioned to sit in the barstool directly next to him, he didn't bother to move his tattered and torn leather briefcase that was occupying it.

"I'd like to buy Howard G. W. Cutler a drink," I said to the bartender in a last resort.

"What? Is this a date?" he asked, finally looking over at me.

I moved Howard's briefcase out of the way, sat down and ordered an Irish coffee. The bartender was already busy preparing Howard's next whiskey sour.

"So, Howard. How long have you been coming here?"

"You mean…*do I come here often*?"

The bartender guffawed as he handed us our drinks.

"I'm Desmond. Desmond de—"

"I know who you are."

"You do?"

I was genuinely surprised. In all the years we worked in the same building, I only remembered having two conversations with Howard. Both times I remember him asking, "Who the fuck are you?"

"Sure. We work in the same Gold Dust news bureau, now don't we?"

Howard lifted his glass toward mine.

"So, Howard. You still live out on Leavenworth?"

I knew this bit of personal information from years of distributing Howard's timecards. He looked me over momentarily until apparently figuring this out on his own. He smiled when he sipped.

"Young man, I'm sorry to say, but you're *not* taking me home tonight."

"Sorry. I've had a really weird day. That Janus. Man, he's got no shame, you know?"

"You mean he's still screwing Katherine Robinson?"

"You know about that?"

"Everybody knows that. Hey, that Kat Robinson sure gives new meaning to public relations, now don't she?"

"Everybody knows?"

"Sure. They've been fooling around for, what? At least the past eight months. Everybody knows."

"Man. I just feel real bad for Jack McCoy."

"McCoy? Why on earth would you feel bad for Jack McCoy?"

"Well, he just seems like such a good guy, you know?"

I ordered us another round.

"Oh, Jack McCoy's a good guy, huh? Well, I don't think his ex-wife would agree. Not after she caught Jack screwing Katherine in the back of a company car in the *Call* parking lot."

"What? Are you serious? When did that happen?"

"Oh, I dunno. Five years ago?"

"Wait, Jack was married to somebody else in the newsroom, too?"

"That would be our good friend Claudia. Now, I think you and I can both sympathize with Jack for making that mistake."

Howard offered another silent toast.

"Well, fuckin' A!" I said, shaking my head in naïve disbelief. "What about poor Janet?"

"The Home & Garden editor?"

"Yeah."

"Lesbian. She'll be fine. Probably better off too, once she dumps Janus and stays in the sack with one of her own."

I took a long, hard gulp out of my drink in hopes of getting rid of that empty feeling in my stomach. The kind when one realizes one definitely does not have the world figured out.

"Everybody knows, huh? Wait. What about me? What does everybody know about me?"

"You? Well. Besides the fact that you're a pain in the ass? That you're self-absorbed with a complete lack of self-awareness? Or that you're always trying to prove some stupid fucking point?"

"Yeah. Besides all that."

"I dunno, kid. I really dunno what your problem is."

Howard and I took simultaneous sips as we both considered whether or not it was best to end the conversation right then and there. Without our asking for it, the bartender delivered another round. At least, I don't remember anyone ordering it. It's difficult to remember for sure because, at that point, I was definitely drunk.

"Desi, what are you always so pissed off about all the time anyways? I mean. For God's sake, wake up kid. You're young. You're healthy. You've got a good job. Your boss lets you leave early so you can go buy strange men drinks in the middle of the afternoon. What more do you want?"

"To be a reporter. You know. A real newspaperman."

"Then go!"

A cable car clanked by.

"Report! Write! There's a whole city filled with stories out there. What are you waiting for? You've already written one story, haven't you?"

"Yeah. But, you know. Claudia fucked it all up."

"And what? You don't think the world has a million other dumb-shit editors like Claudia who aren't going to keep fucking things up? I mean, come on. If that's the case, maybe you really are better off picking up donuts for the rest of us."

I didn't know what to say.

"Okay, listen," said Howard. "I know what your problem is."

"What?"

"*Dead Poet's Society.*"

"The movie?"

"Yes, the goddamn movie. You think you're living in a fucking movie. And you're waiting for Robin Fucking Williams to come discover how much of an amazing fucking genius you are or some horseshit like that. Am I right?"

He was right.

"Well, lemme let you in on a little secret."

Howard approached my ear as if to whisper but shouted instead.

"It ain't gonna happen! Don't you get it? If you wanna be a reporter, be a goddamn reporter. If you can't do it at *The Call*, so what? For Chrissakes, you've got the whole goddamn Internet on your side! You can start your own newspaper if you want!"

I sat in stupor, wondering what was more perplexing, that Howard knew of Robin Williams or that Howard G. W. Cutler used the Internet? I silently decided on the latter.

"What? You think I don't know what the fucking Internet is? What, am I too old and crusty to know how to use a computer? Listen, kid. You think you know my story. *But you don't.*"

The Gold Dust Lounge had long since passed last call, but the bartender kept serving Howard and I drinks.

"I don't give a shit about the Internet, Howard," I said, speaking while also crunching on a whiskey-flavored ice cube.

"Well, you should. You'd be doing yourself a big favor getting a job with an Internet company right about now. That's the future, believe me."

"What about *The Call*?"

"What about it?"

"Well, don't you care about its future?"

"Sure, I care about my paycheck. But *The Call*'s a piece of shit newspaper now. Everybody knows that."

"Well, then let's fix it! I mean, come on, Howard. San Francisco's the most beautiful city in the country. So, it should have the most beautiful newspaper, too, shouldn't it?

"Oh, Christ," said Howard, using a plastic red straw to shovel out a cherry from the bottom of his glass. "Desi, you can't really be that thick, can you?"

"I'm dead serious!" I said, pounding my fist against the mahogany bar, at which we were the only two left sitting. "The problem with *The Call* is that there's no real leadership or vision anymore. These editors have all had their heads up their asses for the past hundred years! It's like, the editor has no clothes, you know? And people like you just keep looking the other way, saying, 'Well, that just the way it goes.' *That's* what everybody knows!"

"Oh, give it a rest, will you? What, you really think *The Call* gives half as much of a shit about you? Look, kid, I hate to be the one to break the news to you, but the newspaper business—*it's broken!* And nobody can fix it."

"Well, if Charles Sansome were alive today, I bet you he would fix it."

Howard choked on his cherry. He had to pound on his chest three times with his white-haired fist to finally spit it back into his glass.

"Who?!"

"Charles Sansome. He founded *The Call* in eighteen sixty-five when he was like twelve years old, with his brother and—"

"Yes, I know who he is, Desi."

A more irritated than inebriated Howard staggered down to pick up his briefcase. That day's front page of *The Call* fell out of his coat pocket, landing behind the bar's brass foot-railing.

"Boy, Desi," he said through a yawn. "You sure are one schmaltzy bastard, aren't you?"

I bent down to reach for the fallen *Call* so as to not let anyone accidentally step on it. Howard yanked the newspaper from my hands.

"No, Desi," he said, making his way through the empty Gold Dust Lounge onto glistening Powell Street. "You don't need this. What you need…is a woman."

Chapter 19

Theoretically, I was still living at my father's house on Joost Avenue. But in reality, I was spending every night in *The Call's* basement.

Magdalena, the night janitor, was frightened half to death the first time she saw me emerge from the far back room that she didn't even know existed. Magdalena was mostly afraid that I would tell her supervisor that she was in there to sneak home a couple of books from the excess stash sent by publishing companies, which *Call* book review editors and writers stored and ignored in the archives room.

Magdalena said she couldn't read much English, and was only interested in checking out the cookbooks. I put her at ease each week by leaving a small pile of these in a corner near the recycle bin. She returned the favor by bringing me clean linens and towels from her day job at the Huntington Hotel, as well as leftovers from her twists on newly learned dishes out of the cookbooks.

One night, in-between bites, I suggested that Magdalena write a monthly column for the Food & Wine section. She blushed, and then feigned a laugh as if her feelings were hurt. I kept insisting on the idea—jumping up to stand while eating and explaining that I would help with the translation and everything and that, well, now there was "*No looking back!*" She had to "*At least try*" because, you know...what with all these coincidences that led to our conversation..."The universe must've intended for her to write for *The Call*." The Food & Wine section was in dire need of a non-snooty columnist, so what better way than to add the voice of someone who actually writes about cooking and not themselves? But with each suggestion, Magdalena only grew more chagrined. That's the night I finally learned not to talk with my mouth full.

Magda never asked what I was doing down in the basement to begin with.

I had a similar look-the-other-way arrangement with Pedro, the security guard who worked the graveyard shift. For the first time in his fifteen-year career, Pedro pulled his gun out while on duty. I had the misfortune of being that first target late one night when Pedro discovered me using the shower adjacent to the old pressmen's changing room. I definitely dropped the soap that time. Pedro aimed his piece away from mine only after I convinced him to check the pockets of my corduroys hanging nearby, where a *Call* identification card would confirm my identity. Luckily, it included my full name: DESMOND CARLOS DE LEON (EDITORIAL)

My middle name was also my father's first name and as fate would have it, Pedro knew him. They met while working the docks as longshoremen in the mid-sixties. They had some kind of falling out, but Pedro couldn't remember why.

"Caramba!"—did Pedro have some crazy stories to share about my father.

And "Caramba!" I'd love to hear all about them—just as soon as Pedro put that gun away. Embarrassed that he had been unwittingly using the weapon as a conversational illustrator, Pedro laughed and placed it back into his holster.

From then on, Pedro stopped by at least once during his midnight-hour break to share stories about my father. Sometimes Pedro would partake in a sip of the wine or beer that I kept stocked in the minifridge of my rent-free basement apartment.

"Okay, *mijo. Solo un sip*," Pedro'd always say, without ever questioning what exactly I was doing down there.

Pedro even encouraged me to take free reign of the boiler room innards that connected both the *Call* and *Inquirer* halves of the building.

"*Mijo*, no one ever comes down here. *Solo mi* and you. This is why I nearly kill you."

The area was decorated with piles of abandoned marketing campaign materials dating back to the nineteen-fifties and beyond, all plopped on top of old, scratched-up wooden desks and broken typewriters. Taking up a good chunk of the concrete space was the original newspaper-pressing machine. It still worked, and according to Pedro was checked annually for an emergency run in the event of an earthquake or nuclear war.

"*Mira.* All you has to do is press these *botònes y presto…los* newspapers."

He pressed one of the buttons, and the machine's motors whizzed into action. The startling noise sent a rat scurrying across the floor. Pedro laughed and turned the machine off. He pointed to the last front-page template used by the machine, which had the date April 19, 1906, and the headline:

EARTHQUAKE AND FIRE: SAN FRANCISCO IN RUINS

One night, when it happened to be my birthday, Pedro decided to commemorate the occasion by indulging in a few extra "little sips" of vino. After reaching the bottom of the bottle, an especially giddy Pedro pointed out a peculiar "lockdown" feature of the Call Building.

It could only be accessed inside a windowless and loculus-like storage room that was protected with a thick sliding iron door that had three antique locks dangling from its center. Pedro shuffled to find all three old-fashioned keys amidst the clanking collection attached to his Ben Davis work pants. He unlocked the odd door, and then once inside, hovered his hands over a series of red-and-green buttons labeled "Total Lockdown 1, 2, 3 and 4." Pedro pretended to lift the switches above the buttons, making little bomb explosion noises to illustrate the potential impact of actually doing so.

I leaned my neck in closer to inspect the antiquated contraption.

"No-no-no!" he shouted.

Pedro maneuvered his vast waistline in order to forcefully usher us both outside of the control room. His longshoreman palms slid the iron door closed and, with a touch of panic, his fingers scrambled to rattle all three locks shut. After twice verifying that all was back in order, Pedro let out a deep, Cabernet Sauvignon–scented exhale.

By activating the switches on those four little buttons, he explained, old, massive concrete walls would come crashing down, effectively isolating the printing press half of the boiler room, the publisher's office, and a small section of the main newsroom from the rest of the building and, if need be, the world. Pedro couldn't remember, or for that matter had never heard of a time when the emergency feature was ever used. The fire department never knew what to make of it during their annual inspections, he said.

Pedro's eyes became fixated on a cobweb-covered sign hidden in a crevice above a corner wall. The sign showed a newspaper-ink-drawn illustration of a man's arm. The drawing began at the tip of an index finger and was cut off near the cufflink edge of a nineteenth-century man's dark coat. From my vantage point and memory, the hand pointed to the secret hallway where Judy Dorland once escorted me out of *The Call* and onto the streets of San Francisco.

Once Pedro's gaze had pointed out the suspect area, I could clearly see the indentations of Judy Dorland's trap door that led directly to the publisher's office. When the concrete walls collapsed down, Pedro said, it would be the only way in or out.

"Hey!" I shouted, all agog to examine every inch of these new features of *The Call*. "I bet this had to do with the Sansome family nerves still reeling from when Charles was assassinated here! You know, way back in the eighteen hundreds."

Pedro flashed a skeptical look that security guards are supposed to show at least a once during every shift but that I'd never seen from him before that night.

"*Mijo.* I think you drink little too much *vinito* tonight, no?"

•••

I DEFINITELY HAD HAD too much to drink that afternoon I traded whiskey for wisdom with Howard. Being that drunk so early in the day was the closest I'd ever felt to being a real newspaperman. And it felt awful. We continued the tradition for several months. Howard pretended to get annoyed whenever I showed up, just like he pretended he didn't care whether I picked up his tab

In-between sips he'd reveal tidbits of advice disguised as distant anecdotes from his life.

One night I'd ask Howard to list his top five favorite writers, which he'd then reluctantly narrow down to about a dozen. The next night I'd share my thoughts on his suggested stories by Joseph Mitchell, Gay Talese, Seymour Hersh, Ray Bradbury, A. J. Liebling, John Hersey, Jack Kerouac, Lawrence Ferlinghetti, Ernest Hemingway, Martha Gellhorn—almost all men, I know. That I'd finally gotten him to admit that "sure," he "liked a few broads as writers," probably spoke at the highest volume as to the level of VIP access I was given into Howard's mind, not to mention our livers. One drunken afternoon, Howard opened up about a story that he worked on for years. Something about crack cocaine, the CIA, and Nicaragua. It was a big investigative piece all set to run on the front page. But then Janus all of the sudden killed it and put Howard on the editing desk full-time. No explanation. Whenever I asked Howard more about it, he'd just talk less and drink more.

When I started working in the newsroom, the old-time drinkers were a dime a dozen—with guys stashing cheap bottles of vodka in the bottom drawers of their desks. When "no one was looking," they'd steal a sip. They never understood that you don't have to see a six-dollar gallon of vodka to know it's there. Most of us averted our eyes anyway. Slowly but surely these old-school newspapermen were becoming a dying breed. Through early retirement, encouraged by newly installed security cameras, Judy Dorland had effectively weeded out those who persisted in passing out at their desks. So far, she hadn't checked the basement.

When the other editorial assistants heard about my no-food ultimatum, they were more vocal about it than Taylor. Some came up with nicknames for me. "Desi Doesn't" was my favorite. Sometimes they'd leave half-eaten sandwiches and leftover pizza in my mailbox along with notes that they were more than happy to deliver food to me.

"Sometimes you kinda be acting like your you-know-what don't stank," Cy finally said to me one day.

I made a deal with Cy and the rest of the editorial assistants that I would make up for my no-food clause by handling all of *The Call*'s contest submissions. This was the utmost tedious task, which involved working with the nit-pickiest personality in the entire newsroom: Charlotte N. Stevenson. Although she was a Deputy Death Star Commander, Charlotte's entire job description revolved around selecting and submitting *Call* stories in hopes of winning prestigious journalism awards. Since *The Call* hadn't won a Pulitzer since the twenties, they hired Charlotte N. Stevenson from the *Washington Post*—not because she had written or edited a Pulitzer-winning story, but because she had a knack for knowing which ones to play up the most. Her journalism skills did not involve red editing markers, and had nothing to do with writing paragraphs or polishing prose. The tools of Charlotte N. Stevenson's trade included X-Acto knives, glue sticks, and cardboard matting materials. She had perfected "the science of presentation."

The actual "story of the stories" was often an afterthought. In fact, some of the award submissions were generated before the story would (or even could) be written. In place of actual reported details, Charlotte would include "dummy text." For example:

POWERFUL FOUR-COLUMN PHOTO GOES HERE

MAJOR TRAGEDY HEADLINE GOES HERE

By Writer To Be Announced
Call Staff Writer

It was a dark and stormy night…

Forty inches of Dummy text here.

Forty inches of Dummy text here.

Forty inches of Dummy text here.

I wrote that "dark and stormy night" lede just to see if it would get a laugh out of Charlotte. She never read it. All she cared about was the editorial feng shui of how the stories were submitted.

"The margins, Desi," she often said in her self-amazed voice. "It's all about the margins. Making it easy on the judges' eyes is an absolute must."

And for this, Charlotte N. Stevenson collected a six-figure salary.

Working the contests also involved dealing with Charlotte's new protégé, Maryanne Miller, who constantly nominated one after another of her own stories to the awards queue. She left these in my inbox, with sticky notes that read "per Charlotte N's request."

After the strike ended, Maryanne continued on with *The Call* as a staff writer. For the first few months she had to endure kangaroo court antics from the rest of the striking staff. This involved thinly veiled stabs at her in the Guild's monthly newsletter. But Maryanne didn't subscribe, and whatever picket line was once drawn in the sand eventually disappeared.

So long as I stayed within Charlotte's margins, working with her wasn't so bad. She was gone half the time anyway, off schmoozing with journalism judges at various newspaper contests and ceremonies across the country. The other perk was that the contest room was headquartered near the archives room, next door to my *Call* apartment in the basement. This gave convenient access to *The Call*'s microfiche stories, archived photographs, and city directories from as far back as the eighteen sixties. There were boxes and boxes of editorial planning files that dated to before Charles Sansome's murder. Someone had gone to the trouble of organizing a corner to store these files with a carefully labeled sorting system. The stacks of yellowed news clippings with decades of different font styles kept me captivated for hours on end. Most fascinating were the boxes of handwritten critiques authored by *The Call*'s Sansome brothers.

Night after night I lived vicariously through the lives of past publishers by way of their annotated editions of *The Call*. I spent entire evenings deciphering the cursive praise and complaints elegantly expressed on the disintegrating pages attached to rusty paperclips. I'd sift through the old city directories to look up the names of the editors and writers involved in these hundred-year-old San Francisco stories about social parties, sports results, and shootings in saloons that probably no one else alive knew or cared about, but must've felt like the most important events in the world during that one fleeting period of time.

Using the city directories, I wrote down all the addresses of the Sansome brothers. From their childhood days in the downtown slums to their uptown Victorian mansions, I'd walk by the addresses, knowing that most of these buildings were destroyed in the 1906 earthquake and fire. Still, I hoped to find some evidence of their lingering spirits.

Back in the basement, behind two of the boxes someone else had set aside, I found a typed noted:

DO NOT REMOVE. These files are being organized and archived under the supervision of Howard G. W. Cutler.
                                   —*Fall, 1988.*

Clutching the note, I ran up to Howard's desk, where in his chair sat a pile of unsigned timecards. As I had grown accustomed to doing, I grabbed the timecards and ran over to the Gold Dust Lounge where he could sign them in his real office.

But Howard wasn't there, either. Chuck, the bartender, hadn't seen him all week. I left the saloon to knock on the door of the Leavenworth Street address at the top of his timecard. Lights were flashing all around the outside of Howard's apartment building at the Russian Hill corner of Leavenworth and Union streets. A fire engine. A paramedics unit. And an SFPD patrol car. But the vehicle that told the whole story was the one labeled San Francisco Medical Examiner.

Howard G. W. Cutler was found dead in his apartment from the effects of an apparent self-inflicted gunshot wound to the head. Since he didn't leave a note, the police had to go through the motions of a more thorough investigation. Standing in a dazed stupor with my heavy heart pressed up against the yellow caution tape outside his apartment building, I eavesdropped on the conversations between the cops. Several clues helped the officers come to a quick enough conclusion. Next to Howard's body they found an empty container of prescription painkillers, a half empty bottle of rye whiskey, and a creased photograph of his wife, Jackie.

Outside on the sidewalk, I bowed my head down into a deep sense of shame. It was as if I somehow felt responsible for this death of a newspaperman whose myth I still couldn't resist romanticizing—like some part of me knew all along that this was how Howard would die, and I didn't do anything to stop it. "Of course. Of course," I kept muttering under my breath as I was gradually overcome by an inexplicable sense of contentment.

"This is how Howard's story is supposed to end."

• • •

Back in the newsroom everyone paid respects to Howard G. W. Cutler. They did so in less of the sarcastic manner I had so often heard and more in an insincerely sweet way meant to clear their collective guilty conscience. For Howard's lionized obituary, Janus offered a gushing statement that sounded nothing like the heated arguments Howard often told me he'd always enjoyed having with him. According to the obituary, Howard's sole survivor was his daughter, Janey. I could hardly believe Howard had a daughter. It was among many new clues that surfaced about Howard's real story during the more authentic and unedited eulogies delivered after work at Morty's.

"So. Howard flew the coop. And he did it on his own terms. Good for him," said Happy Hamilton, raising his glass.

"Hear, hear."

"Cheers."

"To Howard G. W. Cutler."

"To Howard."

With that out of the way, the half-dozen aging men at the table finished their sips and waited to see who'd be the first to say what was really on all of their minds.

"Yap. Howard," said Phil Santini, *The Call*'s pop music critic since the early sixties. "Now there lived one reprobate newspaperman."

They nodded their heads in agreement and took another round of synchronized sips.

"Hey," said Happy. "Remember that year when he said he'd only edit while on acid?"

They all laughed their various laughs.

"Wait," I said. "Howard? On acid? Are you guys serious?"

"Oh, yeah," said Santini. "You kidding me? Ol' Howard wasn't nothing if he wasn't a hedonist."

"I once wrote a story about a jazz musician who killed his wife," said Happy. "Howard edited this thing when he was on one of his epic acid trips. And so naturally, he ends up misspelling the name of one of the bandmates of this murderer guy that I interviewed. So now this homicidal maniac is furious. This guy *kills* his wife, yet he's irate at *me* over a fucking typo. So, finally, I told the guy it was Howard who made the mistake. He sent Howard death threats every year at Christmas all the way up until the electric chair."

More laughs and sips all around.

"What about all those or-geeze?" asked the grizzled veteran newsman Nick King, whose beat covered San Francisco's mostly disappearing history. His latest story was Howard's obituary.

"The what?" I asked.

"Orgies, kid. Orgies," said Happy.

That's what I was afraid they meant.

"That's right," said Santini. "Over at that big purple house in Berkeley."

"Howard? In Berkeley?"

"Sure, kid," said Santini. "Back in those days, having sex in Berkeley was as easy as washing your hands. Back when this job meant something. Back when being a reporter with *The Call* could get you laid any night of the week."

"They used to have a ten-dollar potluck thing," said Happy.

"Bring ten bucks. Bring a bowl of potato salad. And bam. You had yourself a whole lotta nice little or-geeze," said Nick, wiping beer foam from his beard.

The gentlemen all looked away from each other momentarily as if to erase certain memories.

"That's how he found out about that daughter of his," Santini finally said. "What was her name again?"

"Janey," said Nick. "He tried. But Jackie wouldn't have anything to do with her."

"Sad," they all said, one after another.

"I tell you what, fellas," said Happy. "We're probably all better off having our obituaries written sooner rather than later. I hear Apperson wants to merge the *Inky* with *The Call* next year. Sell one of the papers off or close it down. I'm sure we'll all be merged out of here soon enough."

"Merger? What merger?"

"I heard Leech talking about the other day, so you never know for sure with him. Don't worry, Desi," said Happy. "You're young. You'll be fine. Well, then again, you're kind of an old soul, aren't you? How come you're always getting in pissing matches with Leech? Sooner or later, you'll learn it's best to ignore him."

The aura of vulnerability at the table was our cue to wrap things up.

"To Howard," said Happy, raising his glass once more.

"To Howard," we all repeated.

Yes indeed. To Howard. My acid-tripping, orgy-loving, deadbeat father and reprobate newspaperman mentor.

Sometimes you think you know somebody's story. But you really don't.

Chapter 20

There were no gun battles when the Apperson Corporation bought out the absentee Sansome heirs and merged its *Inquirer* staff with *The Call* in 2000. Instead, folks went after one another in true passive-aggressive newsroom style. Top editors at the former *Inquirer* would hold meetings that only assistant editors at the former *Inquirer* would attend. And original *Call* top editors would do the same. Janus, Leech, and Judy Dorland were among the few who always showed up to both.

Squabbles and power plays weren't limited to management meetings. Now that all 600 staff members were on the same team there was a sudden sense of competition that didn't seem so heated back when we were supposed to be rival newsrooms. Now, the four reporters covering the same court case started to get a little testy with one another. Writing better stories was not necessarily the way to win these battles.

Jack Burnside continued to do what he did best—catch stories that fell through the cracks. That he continued to do this by waking up some mornings on the public pavement did not impress his new editor, Patty Chilton. Taylor had been reassigned back to the night and weekend city desk, something he was told was temporary. When it came to screening any of Burnside's calls, I was instructed to forward every one of them to Patty. Even when I didn't, she'd find out about his latest ridiculous excuse anyway, since she discovered a telephone feature where she could listen in whenever he or anyone else called. Patty had a similar practice in "reading over the shoulders" of her reporters as they worked on drafts of their stories on computers with spy-editing software. It's not that these eavesdropping features didn't exist before the merger, but there was an unwritten code at the old *Call* where editors wouldn't try and read a reporter's stories until they were...well...written.

Patty, a former *Inquirer* editor, had what she liked to call a more "hands on" approach to editing. This micromanaging style was too much even for Type-A Amelia Lee, who exercised her right to file a bullying grievance against Patty with our guild. Everyone in the newsroom watched closely to see how that would play out. We got our answer when Amelia was reassigned to the sports copy desk— even though she hated sports and was not exactly an apostrophe genius. Amelia responded with a heartfelt resignation letter stating she was reluctantly leaving journalism to join a startup venture. When that dotcom job imploded soon after, people pretended to sympathize with Amelia. In reality, her misfortune made most everyone else a little happier.

Patty repeatedly reprimanded Burnside. She kept a collection of the erotic bastardized haiku poetry that Burnside traditionally began every one of his stories with. It was a practice that served a purpose, and one that Taylor and I always got a kick out of. Sometimes even Amelia would tape one of these prurient pieces of prose to the side of her computer. Before Burnside could concentrate on whatever story he needed to write, he'd begin each draft by blurting out whatever sexy subconscious thoughts were left over in the back of his head from the night before. For example:

By Jack Burnside
Call Staff Writer

barely legal

I asked for proof

chicks with dicks.

A San Francisco Sheriff's deputy pleaded

no contest to charges that he...

That last installment was Patty Chilton's favorite—and mine too, though for very different reasons. It's the one that got Burnside fired. Janus broke the news to him in his office. Seeing Burnside in the newsroom for the first and ultimately last time was odd. Gluing together one of Charlotte N. Stevenson's awards submissions for the same story that got Jack Burnside fired was even odder.

•••

MY WORK SCHEDULE WAS becoming equally peculiar. On Mondays I'd be assigned to take care of the needs of Patty's team. On Tuesdays I was told to cut up more contest submissions for Charlotte. On Wednesday nights I'd be asked to edit the scoreboard pages for sports. On Thursdays it was my job to sort and deliver two newsrooms' worth of mail to people who might not be working there by Friday. When Cy told me Leech was the one responsible for deciding my schedule, I stormed into his office demanding an answer.

"There you are, Desi. I've been looking all over for you," he said, flipping through the pages of rival features sections. "Have a seat. And close the door behind you, please."

Leech tossed a crinkled copy of *The Contra Costa Times* atop his trombone case. An upbeat Richard Leech played the instrument once a year, when his alma mater Cal band marched through *The Call* newsroom the day before the Big Game against Stanford. It was the only day of the year when Richard Leech expressed unguarded traces of happiness and humanity.

I closed the door behind me. As soon as I sat down, it opened again and in came Judy Dorland. I let out a deep sigh.

"Desi," Leech said, as Judy Dorland sat down between us and began taking notes. "Your schedule has been a little weird lately, I know. I've asked Judy here to try and find as many shifts for you as she can so that we can keep you on."

"Since when do you decide my schedule? I don't even work in your department."

"I know. Things are a little weird right now. I volunteered to help out when the EA manager was laid off."

"Who?"

"Old *Inquirer* position. Doesn't exist, as of Monday," Judy said.

"Desi, listen. We've got some bad news," he said. "We're going to have to let you go again."

"Again? But you weren't supposed to let me go last time, remember?"

"This is not exactly my idea of a good time. We can only handle so many EA salaries, and we have to cut the ones with the least seniority."

"Wait, I've been here ten years. How is that I'm the EA with the least seniority?" I peered through Leech's glass office window to see his über-attractive new personal editorial assistant, Kimberlee Whyte, whom I recognized from the City College cafeteria.

"It's not that simple, Desi. Seniority has to go by department. And frankly, no one seems to know for sure what department you're in anymore."

"We do have some good news," said Judy. "Your position is active through November. Since you've worked in so many departments we'd really like for you to be the point person in training all of the old *Inquirer's* editorial assistants on *Call* procedures and computer programs."

I shook my head in disbelief.

"Desi," she said. "Your last day will be November 7. That's election night. Taylor and several other editors specifically requested you be on hand since you've worked so many other elections."

Judy handed me a folder that included the details on my latest termination. I never bothered to look at it. With so many Deputy Death Star Commanders and veteran writers like Burnside and Amelia being axed, there would be no use in getting worked up over a firing that wasn't even set to happen for another six months.

Week after week I showed up to work Leech's whimsical schedule. As much as it irked me to train other people to do jobs that I was being told I wasn't needed to do, I liked the energy of the old *Inquirer* staff. They were a much tighter and scrappier group, with a natural after-work camaraderie that I had never seen in the colder, stiffer *Call* culture. They were like the Latinos of San Francisco journalism, always kissing, hugging, and high-fiving one another after deadline. By comparison, those of us from the old *Call* crew were the more discrete and reserved gringos who hardly ever even shook hands much less engaged in any kind of extracurricular events like the softball games and Friday night movie parties that we were all now getting invited to. I politely declined these invitations, but appreciated them nonetheless.

•••

ON NOVEMBER 7, 2000, we in the newsroom did what most everyone else in the country did that Presidential Election Night. We watched television news. At around 7:30 p.m., the general consensus in *The Call* newsroom was that something wasn't quite right.

With democracy.

For the entirety of the shift, I sat next to the former *Inquirer* and new *Call* foreign news desk editor, Charlie Richards. Charlie, who was about ten years older than I, grew up in Missouri, where he was once a copyboy for *The St. Louis Post Dispatch.* He was the first firm believer in the 2012-end-of-the-world-because-of-the-Mayan-calendar that I'd met.

He blamed this on a chance encounter at a University of Missouri campus coffee shop, where he attempted to flirt with a very pretty girl majoring in anthropology. She refused to give Charlie her phone number, but did insist on passing along some life-changing literature. He threw it on the pile of various religious pamphlets that only the prettiest girls at Mizzou distributed. But the title of this book was too irresistible for Charlie to ignore as it stared back at him from his dirty dorm room's coffee table while he watched the third quarter of a Kansas City Chiefs versus Denver Broncos football game. The score and the book's name were one and the same:

20-12.

By chance, Charlie Richards was also a compulsive gambler. Charlie admitted he had a gambling addiction, but figured he had another twelve years to sort things out. In the meantime, he bet on anything and everything: baseball, basketball, football, horse racing, soccer, and hockey—even though he didn't follow the latter two. And of course, he also bet on elections. That Charlie Richards was responsible for fact-checking a substantial amount of *The Call*'s foreign news coverage made me want to read those pages for the first time.

Charlie filled me in on his handicap as we flipped through the 7:30 p.m. network news updates. The voices on every channel up one side of the dial seemed to contradict the voices down the other.

"Gore wins."

"Bush wins."

"Too close to call."

"What a weird evening we're having here," said Bob Schieffer to Dan Rather.

No kidding.

"Well, the word 'goofy' comes to mind," Rather replied. "That might be a tad strong but I'm not so sure."

"Did he just say *goofy*?" Charlie asked.

"He sure did," I said. "But, man. I can't think of a better word. Can you?"

"Prophecy, man, prophecy!"

"Prophecy?"

"I'm telling you man, this is *it*," said Charlie, clapping his hands together to emphasize *it*. "Chapter *Six*! " Charlie jumped up and down as if his St. Louis Cardinals had just won the World Series.

"Who'd you bet on?"

"Bush, baby!"

"Are you a Republican?"

"Hell, no. I voted for Nader. But I *bet* on Bush. You see, it's a safe bet. If Gore wins, well, I'd be happy to see a Democrat stay in the

White House. I don't have a problem with that. But if Bush wins, then I make money. Either way, I can't lose, man."

"So Bush wins tonight?"

"Well, if I'm interpreting Chapter Six correctly, this isn't going to be sorted out for some time. They'll probably wrap it up just before Christmas, right about the time everybody's doing last-second shopping or some crap like that."

"Are you saying the election is rigged?"

"The fight is fixed, Desi. The fight has always been fixed."

"That's crazy, man. If you really think so, why don't you write a story about it?"

"A story? For who? *The Call?*"

"Yeah. Why not?"

"Pfft! Gimme a break. A rigged US presidential election? No newspaper will go anywhere near a story like this."

"Well then, even more reason for you to write it, right?"

Charlie laughed at first, but then stopped abruptly, out of apparent fear that he may have hurt my feelings.

"I like you, Desmond Quixote. I really do. I wish I could be that idealistic again. But I can't afford to lose my job until at least two-thousand-six. I've budgeted for four years to prep for D-Day, twenty-twelve."

"You really think you'd get fired for writing a story like that? Come on, man, that's ridiculous."

"Maybe if *The New York Times* or *The Wall Street Journal* does some half-assed investigative piece, then *maybe* some other papers will catch on. But that's a big maybe, Desi. As in maybe next year when they find something else to distract us with."

"They?" I rolled my eyes. "Okay, fine. What happens next?"

"Chapter twenty-one, man. Chapter twenty-one."

"But I thought you just said this was Chapter Six. What happened to Chapter Seven?"

"The Book of Revelation. Chapter twenty-one. Verse one. '*I saw a new heaven and new earth, for the first heaven and the first earth had passed away,*'" Charlie catatonically quoted, as we returned to our desks and checked on the results of the Petaluma City Council race.

•••

SEVERAL EDITORS AND REPORTERS remained in the newsroom long after the last deadline had passed. That's something I had never seen before, and it's something I certainly would have known about, since up until then I was spending all of my nights living in the basement of *The Call.* With the heart of the newsroom still pounding along to the irregular beat of that evening's breaking news, I moseyed up and down the rows of desks in the invisible manner that I often did at that time of night. Even Judy Dorland hadn't noticed that I was still in the newsroom, despite the clock indicating that my last day of being a *Call* employee had officially passed. Judy, a former reporter and copy editor, was too busy getting reacquainted with that deadline buzz to notice.

I locked myself in Herb McCabe's old corner office, which, amidst the continuing edit-territorial showdown, nobody had yet had the nerve to claim.

Portraits of Herb in action adorned every corner like an elegant crown molding of a classic San Francisco Victorian living room. There was one with him and Alfred Hitchcock feeding the birds in Union Square. Another had him and Bill Cosby with arms interlocked in uncontrollable laughter. And another had him playing catch with Willie Mays. My favorite showed a private moment of Herb after an obvious hard day's column, legs up on the desk and fingers examining the visual rhythm of every word. In all of them he'd be wearing a classy coat and tie with his fedora hanging somewhere nearby. I longed to live and dress like that in this magical San Francisco that we all knew only existed in Herb's heart and our minds.

That night I adopted his feet-on-the-desk pose and grabbed one of Herb's books from the liquor library, opening to a page at random. It would become my favorite Herb passage of all time. Choosing one is the equivalent of picking a favorite song by The Beatles. Once you decide on one, a melody from another eventually changes your mind again, and so on and so on. But in that mind-altering kind of way, these favorites have a way of choosing themselves for you.

"You keep looking for the magic, and now and then, when the wind and the light are right, and the air smells ocean-clean, a white ship is emerging from the Golden Gate mist into the Bay, and the towers are reflecting the sun's last rays—at a moment like that, you turn to the ghosts and ask, 'Was this the way it was?'

"And there is never an answer..."

In reading the last line of that passage, something fell out from the back half of the book and into my lap.

A joint.

It had been carefully sealed in a small, yellow-and-blue-makes-green plastic baggie. I opened it to confirm that it was indeed of the wacky-tobacky variety. Approximately how long it had been there I could not say. But I was certain that it chose to be found at just the right time. I opened the top middle drawer to Herb's old desk and sifted through the fortuitousness found in most people's unkempt middle drawer. Emergency ketchup packets and teriyaki sauce. Stamps. Pennies. Business cards with long out-of-service phone numbers. Forgotten keys to unidentified doors. Empty Tic Tac containers.

And a book of matches.

The logo was from a San Francisco restaurant that, like Herb's column, was no longer operating. I carefully lit the marijuana cigarette, and, in hopes of resurrecting the spirit of old San Francisco, reread aloud my new favorite Herb passage over and over again. Especially the last part.

"...you turn to the ghosts and ask, ('Was this the way it was?')

And there is never an answer...

And there is never an answer...

And there is never an answer..."

I kept repeating the words in-between hits, until finally there was an answer.

"Christ Almighty, that smells good," he said.

The feet of his glowing aura were nearly touching mine from the other side of the desk where he sat in the same position as I was.

"Damn. This must be some pretty strong shit."

"Oh, you better believe it, kid. You'd expect nothing less from Kesey."

His ghostly hands directed the smoke back toward his direction as he attempted to breathe it all back in.

"Boy, what I wouldn't give to be in your shoes right now, kid."

Having a supernatural conversation of this nature is like sharing the same elevator with your favorite celebrity. Those moments obviously happen for a fateful reason. But say something stupid or overdo the excitement and you're likely to wish it never happened.

"So. Did any of the ghosts ever answer you?"

"Nah. But now that I'm up here they won't leave me alone. Like I can still get their names in the paper, or something. Geez, Louise. All I can say is be careful what you wish for, kid. It can drive you nuts. Absolutely nuts."

"Yeah…Nuts."

On his orders, I kept puffing. And he kept talking.

"You're doing great, kid."

I was unsure whether he was referring to my puffing or my stage in life.

"There's something I've always wanted to ask you. Have the editors who run this place always been such assholes?"

"Ha! Kid, lemme tell you something. Editors…they're like teenagers. Every generation they get just a little more obnoxious. Think they've the got all the answers before they ever ask a single question."

"Yeah! It's like they can never leave anything to the mystery. To the magic."

"Exactly, kid. Magic. See? You get it."

"Well, thanks. But what good does *getting it* do me if it keeps getting me fired? And all I've got to show for it is one story in the three-star?"

"Blech!" he said, waving his arm as if the smell now repulsed him. "Three star? Don't let 'em pollute your mind with any of that crap. Go ahead and let 'em run around and edit with their little stars. It don't mean they can edit what's written in your stars, kid. You follow? Your constellation lies out there somewhere. *That's* where you wanna be."

"Yeah!" I said, looking out the window to see the bright star of the San Francisco sun slowly begin to rise.

And when it finally did he was gone.

Chapter 21

My delinquent older brother had really begun to turn his life around. He finally moved out of our father's house in the late nineties to live with his fiancée and her two kids from another marriage. She was now pregnant with Hector's child. This was bittersweet for my father, whose simple lifelong wish was to raise sons who would not grow up to murder anyone or get a girl pregnant before marriage. Hector was still one for two.

Well, as far as we knew.

Hector the Protector was making his money as fast as the dotcom dickheads who'd taken over our city were spending theirs. Someone had to watch over these venture-vulturing capitalists who thought that the stock-optioned paycheck they clutched in one hand gave them the right to grab any girl's ass with the other. Hector was still running his limo service, which meant that these worldwide weasels would actually pay my brother to take them to and from the same North Beach strip clubs that he would then be more handsomely paid to kick them out of.

It was just after 2:00 a.m. on a Thursday-night-turned-Friday-morning when Hector introduced me to a side of San Francisco that I had never seen before. We had returned from Palo Alto, where we had dropped off about a half-dozen defeated dudes who spent the entire ride arguing over who had squandered the best opportunity to take a stripper home. I was riding shotgun in Hector's Cadillac Escalade stretch limo.

"Dude, I'm telling you," said the group's khaki-clad ringleader, who was sporting a freshly bruised black eye. "She said her name was Savannah and that we could look up her profile on MySpace. I was about to get her last name, but then that fucking bodyguard got between us."

I sat in awe as I watched my brother collect a nightly rate of 1,500 dollars in cash from the same fool he'd elbowed in the face about an hour before. This drunken business genius didn't recognize Hector in his limo driver's suit and was quick to give him another 100 dollars as a tip, along with a "Thanks, bro" fist bump. Overnight, Hector had become my hero. For the first time in my life I felt that I understood him. He insisted that he always understood me. I opened up to him about my frustrations at *The Call* and my crazy clinging notion that I would somehow marry a girl that I hadn't seen since the ninth grade. With the exception of the latter, I think he really did understand me. Why we could never make this emotional connection when we were motherless children and needed each other most, I'll never know.

When we pulled up to the British Airways zone of the international arrivals at San Francisco International Airport, I told my brother I was proud of him. And it didn't feel weird. The same could not be said for the rest of the night.

The gentleman we were there to pick up was precisely that. A gentleman. He was easy to spot as he stood next to the taxi stand with his leather luggage, wearing a dark, fitted suit that'd look sharp and in-style in any decade between 1920 and now.

"Heyyy, there he is," he said in a soft and raspy voice, as he gave Hector a big bear hug and jumped in the middle of the front seat with us.

The gentleman, who appeared to be in his early thirties, looked nothing like a man who'd just disembarked from a twelve-hour flight from London. And he smelled phenomenal. That's not the kind of compliment I would ordinarily give to another man, other than my Old Spice aftershave-faced father. But there was simply no denying it. Whatever smells were left over by the Palo Alto clown crew were now blanketed by this overppowering scent of musky manliness. It smelled…safe.

"Man, I gotta know. What is that you're wearing?"

"I'm sorry? What's that? Oh. I don't wear cologne."

"Mr. Mayor, this is my brother Desi."

"You've got a brother? Heyyy, that's fantastic!" The man gave me a giant bear hug, which I enjoyed much more than I would ever care to admit.

"Mr. Mayor, huh?"

"Yeaahh. Yer brother Hector here, he likes to pump me up."

"Yo Desi, I'm telling you, bro. This man's gonna be president someday. You watch. It's going to be like you heard it here first, know what I'm saying?"

"Easy now, Hector. One thing at a time. I gotta win this seat on the board of supervisors first."

•••

THE "MAYOR" PUT HIS arms around the both of us and gave Hector instructions. There would be two more stops at the airport. One just a few yards up at the Air France arrivals, then a loop over into the domestic terminal at the Continental gate. We picked up two girls at each stop. Each one of the four appeared to be more in love with Mr. Mayor than the next. Yet they seemed to have equally congenial relationships with one another. The only sense of competition was their constant need to compliment the other on who looked the more beautiful. For that contest everyone was a winner—Mr. Mayor included. He climbed through the front seat window partition to the back to greet his girlfriends. Their conversations began casually enough, with reports on the weather and socialite conditions from the varying cities from which they had just arrived.

"London was massive fun."

"Stockholm was an absolute drag. But good to get over with."

"New York was…New York, of course."

"Ha, ha, ha."

"Oh my God. Totally."

I wanted to be irritated with these people. I really did. But there were far too many reasons to be fascinated with them. For starters, Hector had me flip a switch in the front seat that opened an area in the far back that had been closed off to our previous passengers. This area included a large-screen television and a pillow-padded "play and stretch area." Hector asked me to pull out a small cooler underneath my seat. I intended to do so without asking any nosy or judgmental questions, but…

"Wine coolers? For reals?"

"*Heyyy*," said Mr. Mayor, reaching out to grab the six-pack of fruity colored drinks. "All *riiiight*. You brought the wine coolers. Nice. Good times."

Hector pulled a packet of white pills from his coat pocket. He handed one to me and gave the rest to Mr. Mayor, who then distributed these goods to each girl along with their favorite-colored wine cooler.

Halfway reluctant, I swallowed a pill, too. However, I could not in good conscience do so with a daiquiri-flavored bottle of Bartles & Jaymes. Not when there was a bottle of Johnnie Walker Blue Label Scotch whiskey staring at me from the other side of the partition. I asked Mr. Mayor to pass it down, and he happily obliged.

"Blue Label? Isn't this like two hundred bucks a bottle?" I asked Hector.

"Nah, *carnalito*. That shit used to be Blue. But I usually refill it with Red label," said Hector, of the less-than-twenty-dollar variety. "Sometimes I fill it back up with Jim Beam. Nobody notices no difference."

He was right. It really doesn't make a difference, what with that little white pill mixed in for good measure.

Hector opened the sunroof section above as Mr. Mayor and the girls cuddled and caressed in the play area. A large-screen television mounted in the corner of the "car" was showing an Audrey Hepburn movie. The sound was muted and replaced by the music of what I was told was the "space jazz sounds" of Esquivel.

The girls stripped one another down to their underwear, while Mr. Mayor fastened his necktie across his forehead like a bandana. Blue and green neon lights provided limited visibility from inside, while outside it appeared we were headed down the steepest bit of California Street for what I reckoned was now the fourth time. In what order these incidents unfolded I could not say, as I was caught up in becoming acquainted with some sort of motion-sensory time warp. For the next few hours, we were all feeling very much up above the world so bright. Hector, our designated Cadillac star-cruiser pilot, continued to loop us round and round the most random corners of San Francisco.

"Where…

"Are…

"We…

"Going…

"Hector?" I think I finally asked.

"We already there, *carnal*. Just enjoy the ride."

We stopped a couple of times. To fill up on premium unleaded. To use the bathroom. To order a round of Happy Meals. How Hector maneuvered a super-stretch limo past that drive-thru, nobody knows. It's how a man like him truly earns his money. I was a quarter of the way through a Big Mac when I started to come down to dehydrated Earth. Only two of the girls were now in the back with Mr. Mayor, making it much easier for the threesome to have more focused fun with one another. This didn't stop the multi-tasking Mr. Mayor from going through all of the contacts in his cell phone in hopes of recruiting new members to his taskforce.

"Ah, come on, bro, you're missing out, man. It's five in the morning? So what? Awright, bro. I'll catch you later."

When Mr. Mayor thought to ask me to hop in the back, Hector and I simultaneously declined and immediately reached for the button that closed the tinted partition window.

"Man, this is crazy, Hector."

"Oh this ain't nothing, *hermanito*. I'm telling you. This cat is wild. You should see him when he goes all out. Hookers. Cocaine. Bisexual orgies. Crazy. Whenever he has one of his celebrity friends or politician dudes come along for the ride, he just has them wear a mask so nobody recognizes them."

"He's gets it on with dudes too?"

"I'm telling you, Desi. This guy is *all* about equal opportunity. He practices what he preaches, you know. Makes no judgments, you know. He be real genuine like that."

"What's with the car though? I mean, wouldn't this be more comfortable to do in like, you know, a living room or the back of a nightclub?"

"Privacy. Flexibility. Gotta protect that image. Always gotta be on the run. You know how it is. This way it's his own club. His own neighborhood. His own city on wheels."

"What about the cops? Don't they ever pull you over?"

"Sundays."

"What happens on Sundays?"

"Sundays is SFPD discount day in the Hector Mobile, *carnal.*"

We both shook our heads to the Jay-Z beat.

"How'd you end up meeting this guy anyways?"

"Some coke party out in the Marina. Back in the eighties. He comes up to me and is all like (*adopts nerdy voice*), 'Hi. I'm the student body president and valedictorian of Galileo High School. And I owe it all to cocaine.' Right then, I'm like, 'This dude's gonna be somebody.'"

The future president of free-drug America tapped on the partition window. We lowered it just enough for us to hear that gravelly sexy whisper of his.

"Hector, my friend. I believe these ladies are ready to retire to their homes."

Hector closed the partition and sped up. About twenty-five minutes later we were quadruple parked out front of a sprawling home in a neighborhood called Sea Cliff. The girls got out looking exactly as they did when they got in. We drove off without saying goodbye. Three blocks into the coast being clear, we lowered the partition and Mr. Mayor climbed back up front to sit between the two of us. His necktie was back in place as if it had been straightened the whole time. He reached in the back and pulled out a wine-sized bottle of what looked like very, very cheap fruit-flavored wine.

"What's that?"

"Boone's Farm. Strawberry Hill. You never forget your first love." He motioned for me to take a sip. I politely declined. The night sky was beginning to turn to dawn and Mr. Mayor finally popped the question.

"So what kind of work do you do, Desi?"

"Well, I guess you could say I'm a journalist."

Mr. Mayor spit out his most recent swig of pink wine, a good portion of which landed back into the bottle.

"You're a reporter?"

"Well. Sort of."

"With whoooo?!?" his question sang.

"I was with *The Call* for about ten years. Just got laid off. Again."

The politician laughed uncontrollably. He also instinctively closed the bottle and put it away.

"Don't worry, Mr. Mayor. I'm not a real reporter."

"Oh you're a real reporter, all right. I've been avoiding reporters my whole life. Goddamn. You've *got* to be good if you found a way to watch the sun come up with me. I tell you something, though. Let's face it. *I'm* the one who's not really a mayor."

He sounded genuinely vulnerable, trading his Cary Grant image for a Jimmy Stewart one.

"Come on, now. If ever there's a person qualified to be mayor of this city it's got to be you, man. And believe me, you've got my vote."

"Thanks, Desi. I appreciate that. Especially coming from Hector's brother."

The closer we got to his office at City Hall the more composed and focused the future mayor was becoming. The three of us enjoyed a moment of silence as we watched the sun taking control of the eastern sky in the distance. Finally we pulled over in front of the steps of City Hall.

Mr. Mayor opened the door to Hector's ridiculous car and stepped out to breathe in his first taste of fresh San Francisco air in several hours.

Tightening his necktie, our gentleman cleared his throat and began speaking directly into a Sephora-brand compact mirror that he pulled out of his pants pocket.

"Absolutely," he said, with reflecting conviction. "I'm a civil servant. I understand the contours of social change. Big is getting small. Small is getting big. When I am elected, I will continue my commitment to leveling the playing field."

Mr. Mayor closed the mirror and slipped it back into his front pants pocket.

"Good times," he said, staring at the entrance of City Hall. "Good times."

Then he walked away without saying goodbye.

● ● ●

I WENT TO MY father's house on Joost Avenue that same morning with every intention of going straight to my old twin bed to catch up on at least a week's lost sleep. The only foreseeable plans for getting up and out of bed would be to drink and deposit the gallons of water needed to replenish the previous night's dried-up Ecstasy. Slipping into old baggy Vasco High School PE sweats, which more or less still fit, I tripped over a large parcel of mail near the foot of my bed.

It was a sealed box that had a small envelope Scotch-taped to the top middle of it. The return address listed a Berkeley PO Box. Inside the envelope was a note written on flowery stationary.

Dear Mr. De Leon:
My father wanted you to have this.
Sincerely,
Janey Cutler

There was another letter inside the box. This one was sealed with a gold medallion-shaped sticker. The letter was handwritten in very carefully inked cursive.

Attention: Desmond de Leon
Many years ago, when I was a very young man just beginning my career at The Call, I lifted these items. I took them from an unlocked and uncared-for display case that was situated in the back of a rarely used conference room. Although I initially battled with feelings of guilt for doing so, I ultimately decided there was nothing morally wrong with stealing these items when, after the passing of several decades, still no one

appeared to notice that they had gone missing. However, in the ensuing years, I found it extremely difficult to decide exactly what to do with these enclosed items. Write a book? Return them to *The Call*? In truth, I could never bring myself to do either.

And then I met you.

While I am certain that you will continue to be a pain in the ass to many people, it brings me much peace to trust in the belief that you will also find a productive purpose in putting these historical items to use. Precisely what that purpose is, I do not know. But I trust you will know so when that time comes. Now, stop being a pain in the ass and keep writing.

Yours truly,

Howard G. W. Cutler

Inside the Styrofoam-padded package was an assortment of artifacts from the tragic and dramatic life of *Call* co founder Charles Sansome. There were faded and creased photographs from his childhood. There was also a dulled Bowie knife, two 1879 Morgan silver dollars, and a pair of silver cuff links that had a bit of bluish black hint to them, apparently from being unpolished for the past

120 years. A handwritten note from author unknown indicated that the coins, cuff links, and knife were "in the possession of Charles at the time of his death."

With my attention held hostage by the energy of holding these personal effects in my hands, it hadn't registered that my father's home phone had been ringing continuously.

"Desi, you there? Desi?"

It was Taylor's voice coming from the answering machine's speakerphone.

"Listen. This is a message for Desmond Carlos de Leon. I'm calling on behalf of *The Call*. Desi, it's Taylor. I've got some news for you. But look, you've got to come down to the newsroom, and I mean now."

I changed back into my work clothes, placed the silver coins in my coat pocket, and began the long walk from my childhood home back to *The Call*. As the coins in my pocket jingle-jangled, I couldn't keep from wondering what Charles Sansome would think of the direction his newspaper was heading in.

Chapter 22

Armando Attis may or may not have been a good person. But he was definitely a bad editor.

We all knew of Armando's story before the Apperson Corporation brought him over from *The San Antonio News-Express* to be *The Call*'s new Darth Vader Editor. Armando was born, and was believed to have been conceived, somewhere in the South American estuary of Rio de la Plata that connected the capital cities of Buenos Aires and Montevideo. Armando's was a breached birth. According to the captain's log, Armando's feet popped out of the womb in Uruguayan territory, while his head hadn't quite slipped out until the boat his laboring mother was aboard reached the choppier waters of Argentina. This proved symbolic when, as a nineteen-year-old star soccer player with the Uruguayan national team, Armando scored what appeared to be a game-winning goal against rival Argentina. With less than thirty seconds left in the game and the euphoric effects of premature celebration overtaking his concentration, Armando accidentally scored the equalizer against his own team. He had been making postgame victory party plans with his goalie when a last-second midfield shot ricocheted off of his head and into the Argentine goal.

Argentina went on to win in a shootout.

After being cut from the team, Armando spent a year in Miami, studying abroad. And study the broads, he did. He was married before midterms and divorced after final exams, effectively paving a way to US citizenship. Armando was by most accounts an excellent reporter when he began stringing for *The Miami Herald*. His version of an internship involved breaking action-packed stories that included the early battles of Vietnam, the Munich Olympics massacre of 1972, and a soccer stadium stampede in Cairo. Before settling down at *The San Antonio News-Express*, he covered the Bill Clinton White House during the nineties (the infamous cigar, it has been said, had been a gift to the president from Armando).

No one necessarily believed all of these Armando Attis stories. But they knew of them nonetheless. And no one could deny that Armando Attis, with his six-foot-five 200-plus pounds of mostly bicep and pectoral muscle, had a very well-crafted and effective image of journalistic intimidation. Politicians. Terrorists. Drug lords. Supermodels. Armando feared no one.

But there was one thing Armando Attis was deathly afraid of.

A Google search.

The very thought that his well-earned international man of mystery mojo could be tainted with the quick click of a mouse from some vindictive computer geek absolutely mortified him.

Armando spent much of his workday scouring the World Wide Web of blogs, forums, podcasts, videos, and other links that might make even the most passive mention of him and subsequently strain Armando's Achilles image. If any of these references carried negative tones, Armando would add it to a special list kept in a Moleskine notebook.

He was working on such a list when I arrived fifteen minutes early, as politely instructed to do by Armando's friendly executive assistant, James Fraser. "Fraze," like Armando, was one hunk of a man. He had narrowly missed a spot on the US Olympic men's gymnastics team when he sprained an ankle during a skiing vacation. The accident had happened in the ski lodge when he slipped down the steep spiral steps of a cabin while delivering a tray of hot buttered rum drinks to some lady guests. This anecdote is what won Armando over in the interview process for Fraze's job. I learned all about Fraze's hopes and dreams during the approximate two hours and twenty minutes of waiting to meet with Armando.

A full hour had passed before it dawned on me that Armando was in his office the entire time. I had been pacing around in the waiting room adjacent to his office and was told not to leave even for a bathroom break as it could mean missing the rare opportunity to speak with him. His desk was on the opposite side of the wall, which included a window with closed blinds. While getting to know my temporary cell I noticed a small opening in-between the blinds of the window that was big enough to peek through and see Armando's computer screen.

I watched as Armando Yahoo!'d and Googled his life away.

> Armando Attis
> "Armando Attis"
> Armando and Attis
> Attis and Armando
> "Armando Attis" and "Am I hot or not"

There were an infinite number of combinations to look for. Armando kept track of them all by way of web browser bookmarks and the notepad to his side that he occasionally wrote in—dotting the i's and crossing the t's in obvious anger.

Taking a break and tapping four fingers on his desk to make a trotting horse sound, Armando regrouped his attention and Googled:

"Desmond de Leon"

No results were found.

"Hey, uh, Fraze," Armando finally said. "Go ahead and bring in…what's his name again?"

Walking in just a little bit agitated, I wondered how Charles Sansome would handle this meeting.

"Have a seat…uhhh?"

"Desi."

"Ah. Yes. Like Desi Arnaz?"

"Exactly. Hey, is it true you played on the Uruguayan national soccer team? My dad played in Chile back in the day."

"No, no, no," he said, suddenly uninterested in talking about himself. "Rugby. I'm too big for soccer. Not fast enough. That was a long time ago. So. What can I do for you…Desi?"

"Didn't you ask to see me? You know, I've been waiting for two hours. Taylor said something about getting my job back."

"Right. Listen, Desmond. I don't have too much time to talk, so, allow me to cut to the chase here."

He closed his moleskin notebook.

"How long have you been with *The Call*?"

"Oh, I dunno. At least a hundred years." I began scraping Charles' coins together in my pocket.

"Ha! I know what you mean. I feel the same way, and it's only been a couple weeks. Well, here's the deal, Desi. According to your rather extensive human resources file here, you are...how shall we put this? A bit of an angry young man? What's your deal? What is it that you're so angry about?"

"A lot of things, man, a lot of things. I mean, isn't that what journalism is all about?"

"I don't follow."

"Anger," I said, sounding angry. "I think anger is one of the most important elements of journalism, don't you? George W. Apperson. Joseph Pulitzer. The Sansome Brothers. Anger's what drove them, wouldn't you say?"

"The who brothers?"

Feeling spiritually antagonized, I squeezed the antique coins in my pocket until I felt the blood rush to my fingertips.

"Anger is what got me interested in newspapers. Being seven years old and watching my dad argue with the teller at the bank about why he needs to show two forms of identification to withdraw money from his own checking account. And then the manager comes over and they still won't give my dad his money because his name's '*a little too Mulatto sounding*' to have that large of an amount...man, that made me angry. Really pissed me off, you know? So where do people go when they're angry? When they're pissed off? When they've been lied to? Cheated? They turn to the newspaper! They turn to the goddamn...fucking...newspaper, man!"

I let go of Charles' coins and slammed my palm against Armando's desk.

Armando sat with a silent, paralyzed expression. Fraze poked his gorgeous head into the room to see whether or not security should be called. Armando stood up, placed his hands on his rugby-fullback hips, and let out a deep exhale.

"Now...*that's* what I'm talking about!" he finally said, shouting while syncopating the last syllable with fist pounds on the desk. "Yes! I love it! *Carajo*! That's what I've been waiting to *hear*!"

Armando paced back and forth excitedly. I remained seated, and for some stupid reason, still angry. Fraze flashed me a thumbs up from the corner of the doorway.

"All right, Desi. I've got something special in mind for you," he said, still pacing.

"A job?"

"Pfft. A job? This ain't about a job, son. This is about journalism. Journalism of action! And you, Desi. Why, you're just the...the... *goddamn fucking* newspaperman I've been looking for.

•••

HE CALLED IT "ON *The Call*."

My beat was your beef. Potholes. Busted traffic lights. Faded lane dividers. Obscured street signs. Offensive graffiti in public restrooms. Offensive public restrooms. Did I mention potholes?

Whatever was wrong with your neighborhood, Armando and I needed to know. My three little paragraphs were fed almost exclusively off of senior citizen "tipsters" with a little extra time on their hands to do things like read the inside pages of a newspaper. They greeted me like a superhero. I was their friendly neighborhood Call Man, filling their potholed dreams with results, and getting their names in the paper to boot. They even gave me honorary memberships to all of the local Rotary Clubs, where I was expected to lunch at least once a week.

But my enemies were many. Each editorial episode of On The Call featured a new nemesis to be held responsible for all things broken—mostly Bay Area mayors, city managers, school board presidents, and the county boards of supervisors and the like. Boy, did they hate me. Almost as much as the "real" reporters who spewed their vehemence upon me whenever another public official refused to call anyone from our newspaper back after becoming the latest subject of On The Call. Still, no one yelled louder than the On The Call editor, Eric Larkin.

"Goddamnit, de Leon! Not a-fuckin-gain! I said get me the story on the stop sign in San Carlos, not San Bruno. Now clean the shit out of your ears and get me the San Fucking Carlos story!"

"But, Eric. The stop sign in San Carlos has already been fixed. The mayor took care of it right after I called this morning.

"You what?! Goddamnit, de Leon! I told you. Never call until after four. Now why the fuck can't you follow simple fucking instructions?"

There was a covert formula for filling seven days of even the slightest Bay Area blight into the paper. Larkin instructed me never to call the official responsible for the public property in question until there was less than one hour left on the city business clock. By leaving no time for them to respond, we could effectively fill up two days' worth of columns instead of just one: "What's Broken" followed by "Results." We might even stretch it to three "What's Still Broken" if our game of phone tag extended to extra innings. Getting same-day results, Larkin would say, à la Peter Parker's editor, J. Jonah Jameson, Jr. from the *Daily Bugle*, "was fucking up our system."

Larkin also demanded that I ask the city officials' assistants to send us a photograph of their superiors—without mentioning that we would be using it as the Scarlet Letter to accompany a debut in On The Call.

"Tell 'em we're just updating our archives."

"But, Eric. I cannot tell a lie."

"Who the fuck do you think you are, George Fucking Washington?"

After four long years of debating over the same stop signs and potholes, Larkin eventually "fired" me by replacing On The Call reporting exclusively with reader-tipster testimony from over the phone. Everyone agreed it made for much better copy.

Chapter 23

When Hector found out that I was living in the newspaper's basement, he intervened.

"What you be doing playing Dungeons and Dragons down there all day for?" he said, cracking himself up while driving us to North Beach in his giant black GMC Yukon Denali. I sat next to my toddler nephew, who laughed back at me from his car seat.

"I mean that's cool, you know," said Hector, with a trace of guilt. "So long as you ain't got one of them double lives as the Unit Bomber or some shit like that. But yo, *hermanito*. You in your late twenties now. This is prime time."

Hector insisted I spend my evenings in North Beach, because what with so many inebriated female tourists running around, there would be more opportunities for me to "plant my seed." Hector said he had found the perfect apartment for me. I reluctantly agreed to at least check the place out.

The entrance was on Montgomery Street, though I'm still not allowed to say exactly where. Some days the door to this brick building was accessible. Some days it wasn't. This minor inconvenience could be overcome by walking up a half block and around the corner onto Broadway through a strip club that connected to the same building that housed a little studio apartment. Hector knew the owner of the strip club, who also owned the connecting building and not to mention just about every other place in this three-block heart of North Beach. With its paisano-named pasta houses and rickety cappuccino cafés accented with green-white-and-red-striped awnings lining the streets, North Beach has long been identified as the city's Italian neighborhood, with a heritage that dated back to the eighteen hundreds. It being the twenty-first century, my new landlord was, naturally, Chinese.

"Motherfucking Chinese be owning everything around here," Hector said, introducing me to his Chinese friend, who, judging by the self-possessed silence, was not in the least bit insulted. Not that Rocky Li ever said much anyway. His intense glare and every-once-in-a-while smile did most of the communicating for him. The rest could be read in the tattooed words across his sculpted arms and chiseled chest. These skin-deep declarations were written in Cantonese, Mandarin, Yakuza slang, Spanish, Portuguese, and Latin. To the reader, they all shared a single assertion:

"Don't fuck with me."

Those were the first words I heard Rocky Li utter when one of his tenants interrupted us to offer an excuse for being late on the rent. Repeatedly bowing his head and calling Rocky "Mr. Tai-pan," the young man offered a sputtering of explanations insisting he planned to pay all along.

Rocky Li was born about four blocks away in Chinatown, where he learned to speak Chinese. Rocky Li spent his formative years in Hong Kong, where he learned to speak English. He and his family traveled recurrently back and forth between the two cities throughout each year as his parents operated a conglomerate container shipping company.

Their main San Francisco headquarters was in a seemingly tiny trinket shop on Grant Avenue, about a block off of California Street. For the passing tourist, it looked like every other bargaining souvenir stop in Chinatown that sold plastic cable cars and acrylic I ♥ San Francisco coffee cups. Accessing it through the side stairway alley entrance revealed a cavernous loading area where the Li family employed an undercurrent corporation of Chinese laborers. Inside, this team unloaded, unpacked, sorted, and stocked accoutrements of anything-everything. Designer jeans. Nylon backpacks. Cheap jewelry. Expensive jewelry. Porcelain vases. CDs and DVDs. Community college textbooks. Soda cans with names and logos I'd never heard of or seen before. Steak knives. Beer. Fish. The fish I never saw, but could positively confirm its existence among the inventory when I got my first and only glimpse of the Li and Li Trading Company's expansive warehouse.

Hector forewarned me that the visit was my landlord's version of a background check. Rocky Li would gauge my reaction as I helped this Emperor of Randomonia fit boxes of exotic booze and other party goods into the backseat of his biodiesel van. The more questions I asked, the higher my rent would be raised.

"Yo, just keep quiet and keep loading, and everything'll be cool," said Hector, handing me of a case of hair products to load into the Mercedes van.

"Hair mousse? People still use this stuff?"

Rocky Li slammed a box of beer down to the ground and snatched the bottle of hair mousse for men out of my hand.

"Your hair, it's thick," he said, his thumb and middle finger gently exploring the messy bangs that hid most of my forehead.

"A good mousse like this can add some body, but still keep it all in place. This stuff's got all kinds of vitamins and nutrients. Here. Keep it."

He handed back the bottle and returned to the warehouse to load another box of unknown fun.

"Damn, *carnal*," said Hector, poking me in the chest with the same bottle of hair mousse. "You lucky. I think he likes you."

As in he was gay.

This would be only the first chapter in the book of Rocky Li's revelations.

Depending on the time of day and which entrance was used, Rocky Li's big, amorphous brick building served varying purposes. Billiards and video game room. Gambling hall. Asian fusion restaurant. Indoor parking lot. Law offices. Opium den. We dropped the corresponding supplies off in their designated areas before Rocky Li finally led us through a maze of backstage stairs to my new studio apartment, complete with kitchenette, small but still operating brick fireplace, and a futon that had not yet been assembled. It was perfect. From my bedroom window I could just barely see the edge of the bay window of the room Claire and I had shared a decade earlier.

According to the rumors that Hector had overheard, Rocky Li inherited half a neighborhood of San Francisco real estate after either:

A. Winning a to-the-death martial arts competition.

B. Murdering his parents while under the influence of methamphetamines.

C. Retiring from a lucrative career as lead singer of a Hong Kong boy band.

D. All of the above.

The list of conspiracy theories continued to grow most every weeknight, when Rocky Li would pull back velvet drapes in the first-floor backroom of his amalgamated building to unveil a spiral staircase that lead to the original sea level of old town San Francisco. There, amidst dug up Gold Rush and Barbary Coast artifacts displayed above swirling leather love seats and lounge chairs, Rocky Li hosted only the most supercalifragilisticexpialidocious, psychedelic bordello and hors d'oeuvres parties. There, Rocky played hermetic host to an eccentric crew of his favorite exotic dancers, sushi chefs, bartenders, drug dealers, gang leaders, comedians, and musicians for a few hours of private underground fun. There were plenty of drugs and booze to go around, but Rocky Li engaged only with careful moderation. Music was his wine. And his love was electrified by the mostly British and Australian bands he discovered while going to high school in Hong Kong with mostly British and Australian students. After their sold-out shows, Nick Cave and the Bad Seeds, Echo & the Bunnymen, the Jesus and Mary Chain, Depeche Mode, and several others of the imported genre may or may not have visited Rocky Li's big brick building. (Still not supposed to say.)

Rocky Li insisted I be allowed to spontaneously interview assorted band members—a request they felt more obliged to fulfill thanks in large part to either free drugs, drinks, dancing girls, or a combination of the above. Excerpts of these interviews would sometimes make it into *The Call*. To get the mood started, Rocky Li's favorite local bands would fill our subterranean sky with rainclouds of melodic duende. Seventeen Evergreen, The Society of Rockets, Sonny Smith, Bart Davenport, Dora Flood, Goh Nakamura, Rykarda Parasol—and San Francisco's other favorite psychedelic sons and daughters—all sang their hearts out for Rocky Li. In return Rocky Li demanded that he be allowed to grab the microphone to sing along or tell a story at any point during the performance. This was not a bad way to escape the cubicle warfare going on down at *The Call*. On nights when I wasn't in the mood I could just make my way up Rocky Li's secret staircase to my locked room where I would hide from the girls that Hector wanted me to meet.

Alone on my thirtieth birthday and staring out in the direction of the window of the room where we once spent the night together, I decided to track down Claire Davies. I found an email address on a website that promoted her stage acting and dancing career in New York. The artsy photos of her were all purposely out-of-focus dance action shots. But I knew it was her. So I emailed her.

> *Dear Claire,*
> *It's Desmond de Leon from San*
> *Francisco. Vasco High, Class of*
> *ninety-three. I haven't seen you since*
> *1990. But often wonder what became of*
> *you. Congratulations on your theater*
> *career. It would be cool to see you*
> *perform some day.*
> *Your friend from the past,*
> *Desi*

The moment I clicked send, the anxiety began.

"Your friend from the past?"

Why do I always turn emails into Kasey Kasem long-distance dedications?

"*See you perform some day*"?!

Oh no. Does that sound like a sexual connotation? This was why, now in my thirties, I had never had a girlfriend for more than one night.

Moments later, she replied. Just like that.

Dear Desi,

Wow! It's so cool to get your email. I've often thought of you, too, especially whenever San Francisco is shown in a movie. Even though we only got to know each other for a couple of weeks, those were some of the only good memories I have from, shall we say, an unstable time in my life. Not that I've got my life figured out now! But anyways. Thanks for the kinds words about my website. It hasn't been updated in like forever. Unfortunately I'm not dancing or acting professionally. I travel with a theater company as a makeup artist. I've been promised to get a part soon. But you know how it is. When people meet you as the makeup artist they always see you as the makeup artist. Not a bad thing. Just don't want it to be the only thing. Anyways. My theater company is about to go on tour. We'll be all over—to Japan, Australia, and South America. (Isn't that where your family is from??) San Francisco is on the schedule.

```
Would  be  great  to  meet  up  when  I'm  there.

Been  back  a  couple  times  for  work.  Thought

to  call  you.  Wish  I  did!  By  the  way,  I  also

have  a  kid.  Ruben.  Beautiful  five-year-old

boy.  Best  part  of  the  job,  he  gets  to  come

with  me  on  tour.  They  provide  daycare  and

everything.  Going  through  a  divorce.  Long

story.  Will  send  a  postcard  to  San  Francisco

Inquirer  again.  Please  promise  to  keep  in

touch!
```

Love, Claire

I was unsure of exactly what to call this occasion. But I had to do something. I drove by Claire's old house on Paloma Avenue, which I sometime used to visit on the anniversaries of our first date. I guess it had been a while since I last did. The house had become somewhat of an eyesore, with neglected landscaping, a weathered roof, and chipped paint. But it was still beautiful. And it was for sale.

$975,000.

Hector knew this guy, David, who had done some time at Folsom State Prison. After serving his sentence, David discovered a love for the real estate business and really turned his life around. Hector gave me his number and within minutes, David pulled up to Claire's old driveway in a nineties burgundy Cadillac DeVille. Using a code on his phone, on which he continued to have a conversation while introducing himself to me, David opened the lockbox. With my convicted-felon-turned-real-estate-agent we walked through the door that I had last passed through as a teenager.

The inside was in worse shape than the outside. It still looked beautiful to me. The asking price was out of my salary's reach, but David insisted there was no harm in making an offer. I had a decent down payment to make thanks to living rent-free in *The Call* basement for so many years. I had an excellent credit score too, according to David, who, by the way, also happened to be a mortgage broker and could easily lock me into a temporary and adjustable interest-only rate payment. A month later, the house was mine.

Sure. Buying a house as a way to celebrate an email response might have been jumping the gun.

But it had to be done.

Chapter 24

After the last year of our Guild contract, layoff season was in full swing and all of the weirdoes were coming out of the woodworks. Critics, columnists, and other writers who traditionally worked at home in their pajamas and only sporadically showed up to the newsroom to turn in past-due timecards were now making weekly and even daily appearances. Most of these characters had secret deals with Leech and Janus that allowed them special privileges of carte blanche scheduling in exchange for one or two "really amazing" stories a month.

Unaccustomed to the eight-hour schedule and everyday workplace etiquette, many of these odd individuals would get through the day by cutting their toenails, trimming their nose hairs, and falling asleep at their desks. Others felt the sudden need to catch up on a lost decade's worth of office space small talk. When at the end of the month they were still writing only one or two "really amazing" stories, it was finally decided it would be for the greater good that they all go back to writing and reporting from the privacy of their own bedrooms and bathrooms.

The Call's weekend news shift was affectionately referred to as the "if-the-shit-hits-the-fan shift." It even rotated like a fan, with a pool of reluctant reporters scheduled to work a series of Saturdays or Sundays for one month out of the year. The Great 1906 Earthquake and Fire of San Francisco happened on a Wednesday. The 1989 Loma Prieta quake and Bay Bridge collapse fell on a Tuesday. Nuclear wars, terrorist attacks, and other newsworthy events were not allowed to happen on Saturday or Sunday, simply because *Call* editors had always willed it to be that that way. To shake things up, and to find me a new beat after being fired from "On The Call," Armando assigned Zeke Harte and I to be the only regular weekend reporters.

On that first Sunday shift, the rotating editor called in sick after she was told she was being laid off at the end of the month anyway. Janus filled in. Janus, along with Leech and Judy Dorland, were the only three *Call* managers who had not been replaced by former *Inquirer* editors of the same rank. Janus began by assigning me an obituary. While reading over the details, I noticed Maureen in the corner of my eye. Maureen lived a balanced-enough life to know better than to ever go near *The Call* on the weekends. Something was wrong.

"Hey, Desi. Come help me move some boxes down to my car."

"No! Say it ain't so, Moe."

"Didn't you hear? I got married," said Maureen, waving her shiny ring finger. "But then I got fired."

Maureen was glowing.

"Congratulations! Wait. What?"

Maureen was the lead reporter covering the gay and lesbian community that had lined up outside City Hall to take up the newly elected Mr. Mayor on his proclamation authorizing same-sex marriage licenses in San Francisco. After writing these stories, an inspired Maureen shouted out to nearby newsroom neighbors that she was taking off the rest the month off to marry the love of her life.

Upon hearing the news, Leech immediately set up a closed door meeting with Armando and Janus. As Maureen was booking a flight for her honeymoon with her wife, Leech called her into "a quick little meeting," where it was decided that Maureen's actions constituted a conflict of interest and that she should be removed from her position. Following an unpaid two-week suspension, which Leech suggested be implemented in place of her upcoming vacation, Maureen would be reassigned to the sports desk as a night copy editor. Maureen told Leech to "stick the suspension papers up his ass." And then she quit.

"Desi," she said, "How long have you been here now?"

"I dunno. Sometimes I can't remember a time when I wasn't."

I carried a box to the elevator door and pushed the down button.

"I admire you, Desi," said Maureen, beaming with love. "I don't know how you can last so long in a place like this without going crazy. But, hey. You'll be fine. Watch. Someday soon, you'll be running this place. I just know it. Listen. I gotta go. But I'll call you when I get back from the honeymoon."

We hugged just as the elevator door opened. Janus, who was coming up as Maureen was on her way down, cleared his throat and brusquely motioned his arms in mock maître d' manner to hold the elevator door open for Maureen to leave. As the door closed behind Maureen, Janus pulled a rolled-up stack of papers from his coat pocket and handed it to me without uttering a word.

It was an obituary assignment. I looked down at the name.

Michael Hersey. Longtime San Francisco school principal at Vasco High School and Board of Education administrator.

My heart sank into a sea of culpability as I read the details of how my high school principal and one-time nemesis had succumbed to colon cancer at the age of seventy-eight. I called the family contact number hoping to get an answering machine where I could leave a message that might never be returned.

Mr. Hersey's wife of forty-two years answered on the first ring. Her voice was shaky but strong. I politely introduced myself and offered condolences. She was very happy to hear that *The Call* elected to assign a news obituary on her husband, saying she knew how much that would have meant to him. I assured her that it was our honor to do so and we then proceeded to go over all of the things that Mr. Hersey did and didn't do with his life.

Mrs. Hersey recalled the first kiss she shared with her husband. How they celebrated at a restaurant near Fisherman's Wharf the day he got hired for his first teaching job, and how they went back to the same restaurant for his retirement dinner five years ago. The restaurant was gone of course ("typical of San Francisco these days"). They settled on one with a similar feeling, right across the street. The more she talked about her husband's life, the better Mrs. Hersey felt, and consequently, the worse I did. In the spirit of full disclosure, I told Mrs. Hersey about my connection to her husband.

"That's wonderful!" she said, inhaling with delight. "I can't tell you how happy that makes me! One of his own students? Becoming a reporter at *The San Francisco Call*! Oh, I tell you, Michael would have been so proud of you."

"Well thank you, Mrs. Hersey. But, to tell you the truth, I wasn't exactly one of Mr. Hersey's favorite students. I was a bit of a troublemaker in high school."

"Nonsense! Mike was proud of all his students. Let me tell you something, son. There's a reason you're the one writing my husband's obituary. I just know it. I don't know if it's the work of the Lord or if it's Mike's spirit up in heaven or what. All I know is that you were chosen for a reason."

"Well thank you, Mrs. Hersey. I'd really like to believe that's true."

"No. Thank *you*. And you better believe it's true. We're all connected, son. In ways we just can't even begin to imagine."

I wrote Mr. Hersey's obituary and handed it in to Janus, wondering how he and I would feel about writing one another's obituary. For some reason I hated Janus more than I hated Leech. With Leech, at least you knew whom you were dealing with. But the lisping Janus had a gentle, golly-gee-willikers way about him. He also had this high-pitched Pillsbury Doughboy laugh that he inappropriately resorted to during awkward moments. Maureen mentioned counting three of these laughs during her last meeting with Janus.

"That was fast. Thanks so much, Desi," he said softly, looking over the Hersey obit. "Hey, how you doing, anyway? Are you hanging in there? I know these are tough times. It's a real tragedy to see Maureen leave the paper."

I nodded silently as Janus handed over another assignment, this one of particularly high news value. An off-duty San Francisco police officer had been gunned down in Oakland the night before. The police officer was with his partner at the time of the shooting, which occurred at a private house party. The circumstances of the shooting were vague and the identities of the police officers even vaguer, as their names had not yet been released. Considering the less-than-proactive relationships between *The Call* and the San Francisco and Oakland police departments, it was unlikely that anyone from either would be returning any calls. The only information that the press officer told Zeke was that the wounded policeman remained in an unnamed local hospital, where his condition was listed as critical. Zeke noted that the press officer momentarily slipped up, mentioning that the wounded officer's

262 • *Delfin Vigil*

partner was not doing interviews as he was back at his home in Nap–ahem, north of the city, saying private prayers with his family.

Nap–ahem.

Zeke had compiled a list of the names of all the police officers he had interviewed over the years at the scenes of shootings, stabbings, St. Patrick's Day parades, and the like. Using the six-year-long list, we were able to narrow it down to two officers who resided forty-five miles away in the town of Nap-uh. One was Sgt. Isaac Roche, a traffic director nearing retirement. The other was Officer Oscar Hayes, a homicide inspector assigned to the gang task force. Since Zeke was heading to the hospitals, Janus handed me the two Napa addresses where I was instructed to go knock on the doors. If I'd found the right one, I'd ask for an interview.

The driveway and surrounding area of Officer Hayes' home was packed with poorly parked vehicles as if abandoned in an emotional rush. There were bouquets of flowers and sympathy cards left on the front porch. When I knocked on the door, nobody answered. It was clear that there were people inside the Hayes residence, but even clearer that they were not in the mood to speak to any strangers. I went back to my car to describe all of this to Janus over the phone.

"Great, Desi. That's just great. Now, I want you to give it about twenty minutes. Then I want you to go back and knock on the door again. And I want you to knock just a *little* bit louder this time. Okay?"

This did not seem okay with me. But I said okay anyway.

After twenty minutes passed I walked from my car to the Hayes family home and knocked just a *little* bit louder. An angry baritone being stomped toward the door and shouted through the peephole.

"Who is it?!?"

"I'm with *The Call*. I was hoping to ask Officer Hayes a couple quick questions, if that's okay."

Two children, around the ages of seven and nine, shoved curtains aside to have a look.

"Not interested!" the angry being shouted back. "Please leave. Now."

I waved a wave of understanding in the direction of the angry children and walked back to my car to call Janus.

"Great work, Desi," Janus giggled. "That's just great. Now what I want you to do is this. I want you to give it about another twenty minutes. And then I want you to go back and knock on the door again. And this time I want you to knock even louder."

"Are you serious?"

"What do you mean am I serious?" Janus was not sounding at all like his genteel self. "Where are you parked by the way? In front of the house I hope."

"I parked around the corner."

"Desi, listen to me now. I want you to move your car and park it directly in front of the officer's home."

"But the parking spots in front of the house are already taken."

"Then I want you to park next to their cars. If they ask you to move, you can strike up a conversation then."

"Man, Janus. I dunno."

"What do you mean *you dunno*? Listen, Desi. This is not a request. This is a direct order."

"Hey look, man, I didn't join the army. I'm telling you, Janus, this'll just make every cop in the city even more pissed off at the paper. Even their kids are giving me the evil eye."

"I understand how you feel, Desi," Janus said, back to his calm self. "You're a good person. But to be perfectly frank, Desi, you're not a very good reporter. Any minute now, there's gonna be a brigade of television reporters tailgating outside Officer Hayes's house. Now, you were the first to get there. Are you telling me you find it acceptable to leave now and be the last to get the news?"

"I thought we were the only ones who knew the partner's name."

"I just posted an update online describing the partner's house on Fern Drive in the Alta Heights neighborhood of Napa. Described the bouquets and sympathy cards on the porch just as you mentioned them. I put your name at the top of the story. This *is* your story, Desi. Now, I want you to go after it. I want you attack it. No mercy. And I want an update in one hour."

I was furious. I was embarrassed. And I was stuck. Janus was right. The Botox crews would be showing up any minute. As soon as my pep talk with Janus ended, I got a call from Doug the radio reporter, who had read my "story" and wanted a friendly heads up on whether it was worth his time to drive all the way out to Napa.

Radio reporters are one of the bravest and most dedicated breed of journalists. What sets them apart from newspaper reporters is what they do when news breaks on their day off. If, for example, a moderate earthquake shakes a few things off the living room shelves, the first thing most off-duty newspaper reporters will do is turn off their cell phones so that no editor can reach them. The first thing an off-duty radio reporter will do is grab their cell phones to talk live on the air and describe every moment of the tremor, terrifying or not. I always admired this dedication. But I never quite related. It was while talking to Doug the radio reporter when it occurred to me that Janus was right. I was not a very good reporter. With this new revelation, I disobeyed Janus' orders by closing my notebook and walking back to the company car.

Approaching the Bay Bridge, Zeke called with updates. Though it hadn't yet been announced, the wounded officer was now believed to be dead. Zeke suspected that the officer might have died the night before, but that both police departments were withholding the information in case the suspect didn't realize he was now a cop killer. The plan was for Zeke to follow the police pursuit of the suspect. Zeke suggested I knock on the door of the wounded and possibly deceased police officer's family home. Zeke read his name.

"Haverlock. Officer Jermaine Haverlock. He's got a few connections in the city, one address on—"

I gasped, and narrowly avoided crashing into the tollgate.

"Persia Avenue," I said, as angry horns blared back at me.

"Yeah. How'd you know?"

"I think I went to high school with him."

"Oh, man. Sorry to hear about that."

"Me too. Hey, go find the shooter. Hopefully you didn't go to high school with him."

Those are the kinds of inappropriate jokes you learn to make when you know you're about to document the worst moments of another person's life.

Chapter 25

The Haverlock house hadn't changed much. Balloons and flowers were all over the front steps. Several cars were awkwardly parked in and around the driveway, including Mr. Haverlock's still classic and stillwaxed Cadillac. This time everyone was inside. The door was open and though I knocked quietly, the noise was disagreeably louder than the soft-sounding conversations occurring in the connecting living room. I recognized Herman as he slowly arose from the couch to the doorway.

"Can I help you?"

"Herman?"

"Yes?"

"My name's Desi. I don't know if you remember me. We went to Vasco together."

Herman stood in a dizzying daze.

"I'm real sorry about what happened to Jermaine," I said, not knowing whether Herman's brother was dead, but then again somehow knowing that he was. "I'm a reporter with *The Call*. And I'm working on a story about what happened."

An older man approached.

"Who the hell is this?"

"Mr. Haverlock? I'm real sorry to disturb your family during this time. It's just that I'm a reporter with *The Call* and I've been assigned to write—"

"Hold up." He took a closer look at me the way that city bus drivers do when they think they've recognized a former fare evader. "Yeah, I remember you. You the young man who wrote that story on my boys for the school paper?"

"Yes sir, that's me. I'm Desmond. And I apologize for that. I can assure you that this story will go through more proper channels. I was just hoping to ask a couple quick questions. If it's not a good time, I understand."

He placed his hand on my shoulder.

"No, no, no, no, no. Don't you go apologizing for *nothing*. Young man, you here for a reason. You here to tell my son's story. Now come inside and have a seat. Herm, please get Mr. Desmond the reporter here a glass of water. We gonna be talking for a little while."

Jermaine did die the night before. Both police departments suggested that the Haverlock family not speak to the press.

"Last night I asked the Lord for a sign on how we can get going on starting the healing process," said Mr. Haverlock, standing next to the fireplace mantel where Jermaine's graduation portraits from Vasco and the SFPD Academy hung from above. "Then today, you coming knocking on my door. Now you know I don't believe in no such things as coincidences, Mr. Desmond the reporter."

I felt equal parts freaked out and flattered by this paranormal responsibility. Mr. Haverlock apparently picked up on my self-centered energy.

"Now the Lord may have chosen you, but don't be letting that get to your head now. You need to be keeping your focus, Mr. Desmond the reporter. You know you spelled my name wrong in that story of yours?"

"I did?"

"Yes, Mr. Desmond the reporter, you did. You wrote Harmond. With a D. It's Harmon. You know. Like Harmon Killebrew? You have heard of Harmon Killebrew, haven't you?"

"Of course. Minnesota Twins. They called him Harmon the Killer because he could really murder a pitch...I mean...I'm so sorry about that, Mr. Haverlock. It must've been a typo."

"I called your principal for a correction. Nobody called me back. I tell you what though, Mr. Desmond the reporter, you can't be making no mistakes in this here story, you understand?"

"I understand. I'll get it right this time. I promise."

While the rest of the relatives, including Jermaine's still-in-shock mother, retired to the kitchen and backyard, Herman and Harmon reminisced about a loved one's lost life.

Jermaine and Herman learned their lesson the infamous day they stole their daddy's Smith & Wesson. That night at the police station the brothers bonded with the investigating officer. As part of their punishment, Mr. Haverlock had his sons accompany the officer on a ride-along where they got a glimpse of the glorified life ahead of them were they not to shape up. One night in the patrol car ride was plenty for Herman. Jermaine volunteered to go on another ride-along and then another. After high school he became a cadet and soon after rose in the ranks of the San Francisco Police

Department from foot patrol to homicide inspector. He chose the gang taskforce because he wanted to help kids in the manner that his mentor cop had helped him.

Herman stayed out of trouble too, winning a couple of City College basketball tournaments. He got a degree in hotel management and worked as the director of sales at the Fairmont Hotel on Nob Hill.

The brothers' lives remained closely intertwined. They did everything together. They were the best men in one another's weddings. They were the godfathers of one another's children. They went on family cruises to the Caribbean together. They went to church together. They went in on 49ers season tickets together. They worked out at the gym together. And they were together when Jermaine was killed.

Some mutual friends in East Oakland had invited them over for a barbecue and to play softball at a nearby park. Jermaine got into a confrontation with some teenage thugs. There were three of them. They were camped out in the bleachers, cracking jokes and heckling the players while sipping on bottles of beer. It was no big deal at first. But it got worse the closer the kids got to the final fortieth ounce. Eventually, the oldest, biggest, and loudest one started smashing the bottles against the backstop fence post, pretending to be swinging at a baseball. Glass flew everywhere. Jermaine confronted the kids and told them they needed to clean up the mess and leave. The leader threw a punch at Jermaine. But he was so far drunk that Jermaine actually caught the boy's punch with the palm of his own hand and held onto it for a few seconds until the boy fell to his knees. Jermaine looked just like the Terminator or something, Herman said. Everybody had laughed. Including the other two delinquents.

The "leader" ran off. The other two stayed behind. They apologized and cleaned up the mess. Jermaine was next up at bat, and hit a ball over the fence. It was all good. The brothers went back to the friend's house across the street to eat, listen to music, and relax.

The shooter must have come into the backyard through the side gate. Came right up to Jermaine and shot him in the back. Two bullets. They saw the drunken teenager run out of the backyard into the street, where somebody in a car was waiting for him. They heard the car peel out as it took off. Everybody was in such shock that nobody had the presence of mind to chase after him or to get the license plate number. Herman held his brother's head as the rest of Jermaine's body lay bloodied on the ground.

The only positive thing that Herman could think of was that Jermaine's two kids were out of town with his mother. Jermaine and his wife were temporarily separated, but Herman didn't want to talk about that. In fact, they didn't want to talk about it all anymore.

I apologized for asking so many questions. Mr. Haverlock and Herman walked me out to the company car parked across the street.

"There's a damn good reason you're the one writing my son's story, Mr. Desmond the reporter. We don't have to understand how or why. But I believe the Lord Jesus Christ connects us all together with his spirit. Now, I hope you believe that, too."

I didn't know what the hell to believe anymore. One minute Janus tells me I'm a terrible reporter. Next thing I know, God is my editor. Back in the newsroom Janus had already left and Claudia had taken over. I wrote my part of the shooting story and turned it in within forty-five minutes. I stayed at *The Call* well into the evening to reread every edited version to ensure there weren't any Harmonds or other errors. The one mistake I did make was reading the online comments when the stories were posted on *The Call*'s web site that evening.

"Serves him right. What did he expect would happen at a bbq in East Oakland. Duh." —Redd Dyper

"Leaves behind two kids who live with their mother? Hmm. Guess we know why they live with their mother. And I suppose we're supposed to believe that Officer Haverlock didn't have any alcohol in his system when he hit that homerun, right?"
—PrestoChango

"SFPD officer involved in a shooting where he wasn't actually the shooter? Karma, anyone?"
—AndRKissed

For Mr. Hersey, there was just one comment:

"So a middle aged white guy dies of colon cancer. That's front-page news? Thanks Call. Now I remember why I read the New York Times.
—FranklyMisterShankly

I went up to *The Call* roof, as it was nearing nine o'clock in the evening and the city sun had not yet set. It's often cold in San Francisco during July. That night it felt as hot as it would be anywhere else in Middle America's summer. I pressed my back down against the concrete floor and stared up at the sky, wondering if the spirits of Mr. Hersey, Jermaine, the Lord Jesus Christ, or Charles Sansome had already read metaphysical copies of the stories I had just written. I tried to fall asleep but could not. I had an overwhelming sensation that somebody up there was messing with my mind. ◻

PART III
Do Not Go Quietly
Unto Your Grave

Chapter 26 ▶

Lilah Dee was neither a good editor nor a good person. She was a necessary evil.

Lilah had been recruited to *The Call* by Armando, whose international man of mystery mojo had inexplicably begun to wear off. In place of the intimidated silence that usually permeated the room whenever Armando walked in, newly promoted marketing and advertising managers—most of them young, new to journalism, and unfamiliar with Armando's legacy—would openly and irreverently question his ideas while simultaneously tweeting and facebooking thinly-veiled criticisms from their smartphones.

Appalled and aghast, Armando continued to look for answers by soul-searching himself on the Internet. When that didn't work, he directed editorial dart-throwing crusades against the homeless…illegal immigrants…the fire department…Barry

Bonds…housecat-eating mountain lions…and other growing groups of those who had long since canceled their subscriptions to *The Call*.

Armando connected with Lila Dee through LinkedIn. Lilah had sent Armando an invitation to join the business-related social network as a way of forwarding her résumé. According to Lilah Dee's profile, her skills and qualifications sprung from a DVD she had checked out from the library called "The Secret Law of Attraction." The premise of this self-help film was that one could attract absolutely anything desired from the universe—material or spiritual—simply by believing that one had already received it. Putting the philosophy into practice, Lilah Dee listed an extensive work experience section on her profile, highlighting positions as publisher and executive editor of a myriad of magazines, blogs, and other "multi-medium channels." That these news organizations turned out to be complete fabrications were minor details to Armando, who became absolutely mesmerized with LinkedIn, Lilah Dee, and "The Secret Law of Attraction." Armando invited Lilah Dee to *The Call*, where the first order of business was for her to set him up with LinkedIn, Twitter, Facebook, and MySpace accounts. So impressed, Armando hired Lila Dee on the spot, naming her *The Call's* new "Executive Associate Publisher and Editorial Consultant at Large."

"Man, I just don't get it," said Armando's executive assistant, Fraze, recounting the details of Lilah's interview, while we stood in line for coffee. "The paper is in the worst shape it has ever been in. *The Call* is losing more than a million bucks a week. Apperson executives are calling every day. They're livid with him. But Armando's never been happier. It's just crazy, man."

During their first meeting, Armando expressed concern to Lilah Dee that his social networking profiles would look empty since most of his closest friends and colleagues were retired and offline.

"She kept telling him some crap, like '*Your wish is my command*,'" said Fraze, imitating Lilah Dee's voice as if it were a high-pitched, sex-starved nymphomaniac's dialogue from a porn script obviously written by a man.

She showed Armando how to use the company's email address book to invite select colleagues to get LinkedIn, friend him on Facebook, and follow him on Twitter. Fraze overheard Lilah instruct Armando to pick a number of friends and followers he wished to have and then keep his attention on that number, so that he would be certain to attract it. That first week, Armando reached only half of this number. After Armando showed these disappointing early results to Lilah Dee, she apparently synched up several of Armando's nonresponsive invitees with a surprise layoff list that was announced to *The Call* the following week. Within ten days, Armando shouted out in amazement that he now had exactly ten times the number of friends and followers he had initially imagined.

Despite her protracted job title, Lilah Dee's mission as Executive Associate Publisher and Editorial Consultant at Large was to attenuate what she saw as "a rather wordy newspaper." She named her redesign campaign: "Quick Mix."

Every Friday afternoon during the month of August, about forty of us gathered in a conference room for mandatory workshops where Lilah began by taking attendance and handing out stapled packets and worksheets. Once we all had our copies in hand, Lilah assigned each of us an individual paragraph to read aloud to "the class."

These passages were part of a pamphlet in progress authored by Lilah for a purpose she called: "Quick! Mix! Saving the American Newspaper."

Janus led off the exercise by reading the first installment with extra vigor:

"*What is Quick Mix? Quick Mix offers the professional newspaper journalist the luxury of a bottomless toolbox to write simple stories that are mixed quickly for the eyes of the experienced newspaper reader and quickly mixed for the lifestyle of the yet-to-be-converted crowd of newspaper readers.*"

"Very good! Thank you, Redfield," said Lilah, uncannily similar to Fraze's sexy impression. Leech's paragraph was up next. He had to take a deep breath in order to match the enthusiasm of Janus.

"Okay. Here we go.

"*Is Quick Mix the new catchphrase for 'nut 'graph'? YES. If by 'nut 'graph,' one intends to immediately tell the reader it is okay to invest a few extra seconds in-between the reader's several sips of a double vanilla latte with soy milk.*"

"That's a joke, folks," Lilah interrupted. "It's okay to laugh."

While most of us wondered if it was okay not to laugh, Leech continued.

"*But the answer is also NO,*" read Leech, with another deep breath. "*No, if by 'nut 'graph,' one intends to believe that the reader truly and automatically cares about the content and subject of the said story. One must first convince the reader that they should care. This is rarely done with words. It is almost always done with a quick mix of photographs, charts, graphics, and lots and lots of color.*"

Stan Edelstein was up next. Stan sped into his paragraph the way one reads the terms and conditions of a car loan application, throwing his arms in the air to emphasize that confusion was the cause of his pauses.

"*Whataresomethings…I can do…inorderto reprogram my mind… What the f–?…tothinkQuickMix? One: Train your eyes to*—Fuck it. I'm sorry, Lilah. I can't do this." Stan slammed the pamphlet onto the table that we were all circled around, Romper Room-style.

"I beg your pardon?"

"Come on, Red," he said, looking over at Janus. "What's with these third-grade exercises? Look, I've got two stories due today. And a column that needs to be done by tomorrow."

"You're free to leave at any time, Mr. Edelstein," said Lilah, writing something down in her lesson planner.

"Actually," said Janus. "This is a mandatory class. We all need to be here for this, Stan."

Stan gathered his things and left anyway. Karl Floyd tossed his worksheets aside and stood up to leave, too. Attempting to break the awkward tension, Lilah agreed to put the readings on hold for another day and instead went into a PowerPoint presentation with images of *People* magazine juxtaposed next to *The Wall Street Journal* and a hypothetical *Call* placed in the middle, next to a giant question mark.

After the presentation, a younger reporter in the back offered her thoughts.

"Fortunately, I grew up being taught to love newspapers," she said. "But, I have to admit. These days, even I don't have time to read it the way I used to. So I really like the idea of a Quick Mix."

"Oh...my God! Thank *youuuuu!*" said Lilah, who sounded as if she were struggling to deliver her words in-between bouts of multiple orgasms. She also ended her every thought with an inflection in the high-pitched interrogative mood, as if she wasn't sure she believed in anything she was actually saying. She sounded a lot like Chandler, from *Friends.*

"Could you *be* any braver for admitting that? Oh...my God. Wow. Can you *see* how that's the kind of honesty that's actually going help us *save this place*? I'm sorry? What's your *name again*?"

"Maryanne. My name is Maryanne Miller."

Lilah wrote something down in her lesson planner. After a quick Law of Attraction group meditation exercise where we were all instructed to envision endless clicks and positive comments for the online versions of our stories, class was finally dismissed. A week later, Stan Edelstein and Karl Floyd both lost their livelihoods in the next round of layoffs. Less than a month later, Maryanne Miller was promoted to a Deputy Death Star Commander position.

Working together, Judy Dorland and Maryanne Miller took an hour out of their day to drop in at each department of the newsroom to take "attendance and work appearance" reports for Lilah Dee. This, according to the page Maryanne forgot in the copier that I used after her, included spreadsheets on everything from those who called in sick, to workers with wrinkles or stains on their shirts, to the numbers of likes, friends, and followers on *Call* employees' social media profiles.

It was as obnoxious as it was effective.

Chapter 27

I may or may not have been a good reporter. But I was definitely a horrible homeowner. My house payments had nearly quadrupled and the family that I was renting the place to had grown to hate me. Everything imaginable had gone wrong. The plumbing burst. There was mold in the baby's room. Termites. Roof rats. Carpenter bee nests. I placed all of these problems on a Home Depot credit card. No interest. No payments. No worries. David assured me that I could soon refinance, pull cash out, and come out more than on top. Hopefully by then Claire might finally call or write back. I never did get that second postcard.

On nights when I wasn't sleeping in the *Call* basement, Rocky Li allowed me to live rent-free in the big brick building on Montgomery Street. He had become the closest thing that I'd ever had to a best friend. Rocky Li adopted me as his fashion and makeover protégé. Before meeting him, I had zero fashion awareness. Now I was wearing only clothes that were designed by his friends in Hong Kong, New York, or London. I purchased all of these dark clothes with credit cards. No interest. No payments. No worries. Rocky Li restyled my hair at least once a week, usually the night before one of his super crazy dance music parties. In the process I became more concerned than ever with my appearance. Hector pointed this out as he noticed me checking out my reflection from the sides of parked cars or by borrowing his limo's rearview mirror to make hair fixes. The investment into my appearance did little to pay off in the dividends of finally having a girlfriend for more than one night. I was still waiting for Claire. If it took another fifteen years, so be it. Just so long as Rocky Li made me look cool on the day she'd finally show up.

On an afternoon when Rocky Li was lifting weights in his big brick building's private gym, I told him all about my synchronistic experiences with Principal Hersey and the Haverlocks. I confided in Rocky that ever since that supernatural Sunday night reporting shift, I had been having a recurring dream about my mother. Every time I awoke from one of these dreams I would remember vivid details. The scent of her hair from when she held me close to her neck after Hector made me cry. The sound of her silver bracelets clanking together next to my ear when she caressed my scalp with her painted fingernails. Sometimes I would dream that she was at my funeral. These memories were comforting, but also confusing.

Rocky dropped his dumbbells and immediately motioned for me to follow him.

We jumped into his black Lotus Elise roadster and drove four blocks, parking in a loading zone on Grant Avenue near the corner of Pacific. After instructing the boutique shop owner to watch over his car, Rocky Li walked us a block up Pacific just short of Stockton. We entered a brown tenement building above a drugstore. Some of the residents hid as soon as they saw Rocky Li. He ignored them, leading us up the stairway to the building's roof, where a very pretty woman in her forties tended to the most spectacular rooftop garden I had ever seen. It was so beautiful that I at first didn't notice the near 360-degree views that stretched from the Golden Gate Bridge to the Bay Bridge all the way through San Francisco's skyscrapers.

"Hi, Rocky! Haven't seen you for a while," she said, without taking her eyes off a wagon filled with geraniums that she was watering. "Everything okay?"

Rocky said something to her in Cantonese. She looked up at me for the first time.

"Oh, hi." She waved with one gardening glove still on. "I didn't notice you there. I'm Rosie. Rocky's crazy cousin. Rocky says you're on some kind of spiritual journey?"

I went to shake her hand, but Rocky blocked my path.

"No, Desi! You must not interfere with her energy," he insisted.

"Rocky, it's all right."

She placed her non-gloved hand on her racketeering cousin's back.

"Why don't you guys go help yourselves to some tea in the apartment until I finish up here?"

Rocky grunted a nod of understanding and motioned for me to follow him back into the tenement building. The building looked as dreary and drab from the outside as it looked and felt bright and beautiful from the inside of Rosie's sprawling top-floor room. It was technically a studio apartment, with the kitchenette, bedroom, and living area all in the same space and a tiny bathroom tucked into the far corner, where it had obviously been added on years later. Shelves and shelves of books dwelled in the most creatively positioned corners, doubling the room as a kind of an avant-garde library. The subjects of the books all flowed together in a sort of spiritual Dewey Decimal System—from philosophy to religion, Chinese astrology to Greek mythology, San Francisco in pictures to the Holy Scriptures, beatnik novels to baseball history. Rosie walked in just as I was opening up a small book on the illustrated art of Kama Sutra. I disconcertedly put it back in its place.

"So," she said, washing her hands in the kitchenette sink. "How long have you and Rocky been together?"

Rocky Li laughed as Rosie handed me a cup of tea.

"Oh, I'm sorry," she blushed. "My gay-dar is so bad lately."

"Rosie has the gift," said Rocky. "It runs in our family for many generations. All the way back to the Han Dynasty. My grandmother had it too. She said she knew Rosie had it from the moment she held baby Rosie in her hands. She said she was surprised because she worried the gift might have to skip a generation. That it was gone from the family."

"That's because my mom wanted it to be gone."

"What kind of gift do you have?"

"Well, I knew Rocky was gay back when he was only two years old. That didn't go over too well with my uncle."

"Rosie does it all. Tea leaves. Tarot cards. Séances. Ouija boards. *I Ching*. Everything. And what's that other thing called? Xenography? You know, Rosie, from when we were little? When alls the sudden you be speaking in Russian and shit?"

"Xenoglossy," said Rosie. "That only happened once. A long time ago. And I barely remember anything I said."

"Is that all ancient Chinese stuff?"

"Not exactly. I always liked to experiment. It's funny. My grandmother always told me to pursue unlimited knowledge. And then she threw an absolute fit when she found out I was messing around with Western 'occult' stuff."

"That must be her," I said, pointing to a picture on the wall.

"Yeah. She was born here in Chinatown, but never spoke a word of English. Our family has San Francisco roots all the way back to the Gold Rush days. My great-great-grandmother supposedly tried to warn everyone about the bubonic plague before it broke out in the city. Everyone called her a quack. But then when it finally showed up a few years later, all of the sudden she was like a celebrity."

Rocky Li pointed to another portrait, this one a penciled sketch of a dreaming Chinese man with a butterfly floating above his head.

"Hey-hey-hey, Rosie! Tell Desi about this guy!"

"Oh, that's Zhuangzi. Chinese philosopher. My grandmother always told us that we're related to him. He'd be like our great-grandfather to the tenth power or something crazy like that. He believed in anarchy. Evolution. Reincarnation. He dreamed he was a butterfly but then woke up wondering if he was a butterfly dreaming he was man. Some people say he didn't even exist. But my grandmother insists he was 'one of us.'"

"Hey," I said, squinting at a baseball card–sized picture on an altar next to Master Zhuangzi. "Is that...*Tim Lincecum*?"

"Oh my God." Rosie pressed her hand against her heart and looked warmly over at the San Francisco Giants pitcher who'd been having a pretty bad year. "I love him *so* much. He's a beautiful man. His numerology and solar calendar, it's...it's just a really bad mix right now. Watch. He's *totally* going to pull it together. I know it."

Rocky Li and I both nodded our heads in agreement.

With casual introductions out of the way, Rosie asked Rocky to leave so that she could do a proper reading on me. Rocky left looking like his feelings were hurt—something I had never witnessed before. Rosie asked me to make two wishes and speak one of them aloud. I silently wished that Claire would call, and then vocally wished to be a Jedi Knight.

"You mean, like in *Star Wars*?"

"Exactly. I want to defeat my Emperor and my Darth Vader. You know. Blow up the Death Star."

Rosie handed over a deck of what I presumed were ancient Chinese Tarot cards.

"These must be your grandmother's."

"No, got 'em on eBay," she said, instructing me to shuffle them. "But don't worry. They'll do the job."

Rosie placed several cards face up in four rows on the table and began reading the images out loud in a kind of teleprompter tone.

"You are a good person who will not hurt anyone. You are a leader who likes to help others."

Rosie paused to think in the message from the next card.

"But you are struggling from the inside, searching and trying to fix something that many around you say cannot be fixed. Your anger. It stops you from finding out."

The next card was of a skeleton dressed in knight's armor riding on a white horse.

"The Death card."

I sighed.

"Don't worry. It doesn't mean you're going to die anytime soon. It can symbolize a spiritual death. Did you lose your job recently?"

"No," I laughed. "Not yet."

"Well, you might be better off if you do."

Next was the Magician card.

"You take action. In creative ways. But sometimes in manipulative ways. Your determination is strong. Your self-confidence blinds you."

The last card was the Star.

"Oh. This is good. You will soon find tranquility. Peace of mind. A spiritual resurrection or rebirth. Maybe a new career? You must first learn to trust the harmony and spirit already within you."

Rosie clapped her hands and stood up to signal the end of the session.

"Well, I hoped that helped."

Rosie refilled our tea.

"What about, you know, spirits?"

"Spirits? What about them?"

"Did you see any, you know…around me?"

"Desi, I was looking at the cards, remember?"

"Didn't you say you do some kind of séances?"

"Rocky said that. I haven't done any séances since all the cousins had sleepovers. But I've been studying past life regression lately."

"Yeah, yeah, yeah. Can we try that?"

"Desi, I'm a little tired right now. But I tell you what. Come back tonight. We'll do a session. After the Giants game. Rocky said you've been having some dreams about your mother, right? Can you bring a piece of jewelry or a photograph? If the Giants win, maybe I'll be inspired to do a séance. You never know."

•••

MY FATHER WAS NAPPING in his room, which was just as well. I didn't have the gall to grab any of my mother's belongings from my parents' room or disrespectfully remove her portraits off the dining room walls. I was ashamed to see no palpable representation of her in my old bedroom. Sadly, it was an accurate reflection of the fleeting intertwinement of our lives. The one possession of hers that was in my room was perhaps the most sweetly symbolic of our time together—the Peter, Paul & Mary "If I Had a Hammer" forty-five-rpm record. While pulling the record off the shelf above my old desk, out fell a heavy manila envelope folder. It was the one Howard left for me that contained the Bowie knife and silver cuff links that Charles Sansome had with him on the day he died.

"Life is all about synchronicity, Desi," said Jack Burnside's sexy voice in the back of my head, as I placed each of Charles Sansome's stolen belongings respectively into my backpack. "The universe is always sending us signs. And it's up to us to follow those signs."

•••

ROCKY AND I ARRIVED at Rosie's place with two outs in the eighth and the Giants protecting a comfortable lead. Tim Lincecum's strong seven-inning performance had placed Rosie in very good spirits. We ordered food—Chinese of course—free, from another cousin across the street. As Giants broadcaster John Miller described the final out, we raised our glasses of plum wine in the air and did so again and again during the postgame wrap on the radio with Kruk & Kulp and Fleming, in order to ease our nerves and soak up the pork buns. Rosie was delighted that I'd brought my mother's Peter, Paul & Mary record. She loved that song. It was the most apropos artifact, she said, as we listened to it over and over again and well past the bottom of a second bottle of plum wine. The metaphysical activities began with the opening of our fortune cookies. I read mine aloud:

"Keep the faith—you will be rewarded handsomely for your optimism, integrity, and perseverance."

"But not in bed," Rocky Li added.

Using my March 2, 1975 birthday, Rosie told me a little more about my predestiny. Element: Yin Wood. Animal: Rabbit. This meant my most positive attributes included patience and altruism while my negative feelings were dominated by anger.

No kidding.

We took a stab at an *I Ching* reading, but it proved too complicated as the third bottle of plum wine mixed with a touch of tequila had gotten the best of our concentration. Next, we began a past life regression session. This involved lying on our backs, conducting concentrated breathing exercises as we made our way through a series of spiritual tunnels.

Rocky Li stole the show. His past life visions were as a champion Greek wrestler and a pregnant teenage girl in nineteen-fifties…Cincinnati?

Unfortunately, I temporarily dozed off.

After sharing a pot of extremely caffeinated herbal tea, we convinced Rosie to conduct a séance. She placed a decorative heirloom tablecloth over the table, dimmed the lights, closed the blinds, burned some incense, and lit a circular line of candles. We held hands around a Parker Brothers Ouija board placed in the center of the table. We didn't use it. Rosie brought it out as a just-in-case, Hail Mary attempt to swing with the spirituals.

The first freaky thing occurred seconds before we began. The last verse of the Peter, Paul & Mary record began playing by itself. There was a logical explanation. A moderate earthquake. A 4.6 on the Richter scale with an epicenter about forty-five miles across the Bay near Hayward, as Doug the radio reporter immediately informed us from his living room. We had apparently left the record player needle circling indefinitely around the non-music grooves of the forty-five, and the small shake had cued it back to a constant repeat of Peter Yarrow's final fading guitar strums.

"Who do you wish to reach?" Rosie asked, closing her eyes.

"The rightful owner of these items."

I placed the Bowie knife, cuff links, and coins atop the Ouija Board. "I believe they belong to—"

"Don't tell me. I don't want to know. Let's see which spirits wish to visit us tonight."

With her eyes closed tight, Rosie began chanting calmly in Cantonese. This went on for about a minute while the quiet crackling at the edge of the Peter, Paul & Mary record continued. By the glow of candlelight I could see trancelike rapid eye movement below Rosie's brow. Rocky Li's hand shook in mine.

"I see two people," she said in a slow, slurred, and raspy voice. "It's a man. And a woman. The woman is. Me? The man. Is you? Desi. Yes, it's you. We are around this table."

"This table?"

"Yes. This same tablecloth. That's what I said. Tablecloth. I am telling the man. Wait. No. It's not me. It's my grandmother. No. It's my great-great-grandmother. She is very young. I have never seen her so young before. I recognize her face. It's definitely her. And it's definitely you."

"Me? How do you know it's me?"

"I see your face. Only you have a…"

Rosie looked as if she was about to faint.

"What?" I said shaking her back into the trance. "What do I have?"

"Uh…uh…a moustache."

"A moustache? That's impossible. Rosie, that can't be me. I'm not even capable of growing a moustache. I've been trying since I was twelve years old."

"It's definitely you, Desi. The moustache. It looks a little funny on you. Like from the Civil War or something. Not a full beard. You know. The kind that connects through the sideburns."

"What am I doing talking to your grandmother?"

"Great-great-grandmother!" said Rocky, his hands still shaking.

"You are asking her for help. She is trying to warn you."

Rosie gripped on to my hand as if for dear life.

"He's angry. Wants to leave. His coat. Pocket. He's looking for something."

"He? You mean me?"

"He wants to pay her. She won't take the coins."

Rosie said something in Cantonese and then gasped back to real life.

"Oh my God," she said, catching her breath. "That was *amazing.* I've never felt so...so...*possessed* before. That was incredible. Look at me. I'm shaking."

"What did you see? How do you know you saw me?"

"Desi, please. Give me a minute to let it sink in so I can interpret it."

"Interpret? What? Wait. Are you guys fucking with me? Is this a joke? Rocky, did you set me up?"

"Desi! Sit your dumb ass down! Rosie just dove into the motherfucking other side for you!"

"Can you both just tone down the testosterone? Please?"

"How am I supposed to calm down when you just said you saw my ghost?"

"I never said I saw a ghost," said Rosie, growing angry. "I saw a vision. It could be anything. All I know is that it came from the energy in the room. It could be coming from the objects you brought. My grandmother's tablecloth. It could've been my imagination. Look, I really don't know."

"Imagination?!"

Rocky Li pushed me back down to the floor as I arose in anger from the crouched position. I instinctively took a swing at his jaw, which he immediately karate-chopped away while jujitsuing me into a tae kwon do kill hold.

Letting out a deep sigh, I slowly extricated myself from Rocky Li's half-nelson and stood up to retrieve the Peter, Paul &

Mary single. Feeling dizzy, I walked toward Rosie's record player and thought of what Uncle Lalo always told me and Hector after every Sunday Mass.

"Remember, *chicos*," he'd say, lighting his first cigarette of the day. He only ever went to church as a courtesy for being a guest in my father's home. "Fear is just the soul's way of telling you that it's time for your life to change. You mustn't be afraid of being your own resurrection."

I lifted the needle and turned the record player off once and for all.

"Look, I'm sorry, guys. I didn't mean to yell. I just got a little freaked out. I think I understand what all this really means. Thank you for—"

Rosie had already stood up to leave for her rooftop garden. Rocky followed after her.

While unzipping my backpack, a scrunched up picture of Charles Sansome fell on to the Ikea rug on the hardwood floors. Stuffing the "If I Had a Hammer" record in the bottom of the backpack, I leaned down to pick up my picture and placed them atop the forty-five-rpm record along with the rest of my belongings.

Chapter 28

Waking up to the belief that you're the reincarnation of an obscure historical figure does not change your life in the immediate manner some might suspect. You still wake up with bad breath and bedhead hair. You still get phone calls from debt collectors for not paying your credit card bills. And you still feel guilty for forgetting your father's birthday. The only difference is that you do all of these things with the understanding that the countdown is on to the day when the whole world will finally know that you are batshit crazy. With that out of the way, an insane-laced lease on life can actually be quite refreshing. I embraced the new me(s) by reading everything I could about my past life as Charles Sansome.

When I was Charles, I was born on January 8, 1845, in the French-American community of Natchitoches, Louisiana. I, Charles, was the oldest son of eight children. Some say our mother, Alma, had

French aristocratic blood. Others suggested she was a prostitute. In 1854 our family boarded a steamer for San Francisco, where our drunk, ever-gregarious, and accident-prone father slipped through a railing, fell overboard, and drowned.

At age nine, I, Charles, supported our seamstress mother as a newsboy, selling and folding newspapers delivered to saloons, gambling rooms, and whorehouses of the Barbary Coast era. At age twelve, I, Charles, founded *The Educational Call*, which vociferously criticized what I, Charles, saw as the lackadaisical leadership of the city's school district. The superintendent implemented a successful moratorium on it after one issue. But I, Charles, didn't give up. Six years later, at the age of eighteen, we and our brother Michael, borrowed a twenty-dollar gold piece from a retired sea captain neighbor. With that loan, the first edition of *The San Francisco Call* was published and I, Charles, never looked back. *The Call*'s first big scoop was the news of President Lincoln's assassination, thanks to our "CLOSED: MEASLES OUTBREAK" sign. As self-righteous brothers, we used *The Call* as a crusading cannon aimed against what we decided were the right and wrong causes and the corresponding good and bad guys.

The New York Times wrote: "Charles Sansome grew into manhood with peculiar notions of morality, and looking upon human life as of comparatively no value whatever when weighed in the balance against an insult to Californian 'honor.' Charles had a profound sense of right and justice and an ever-increasing abhorrence of wickedness and corruption in high places. He never spared these evils and when once he had made up his mind to attack evil or evil-doers, no threats or persuasions from foes or friends could swerve him from his purpose. ... He measured men and matters at a glance and seldom did his judgment deceive him."

There were other common characteristics that did not require stretches of interpretation.

✓ Charles stood at five-foot-seven and weighed approximately 160 pounds.

✓ Charles had a dark complexion and carried a medium figure.

✓ Charles' eyes were black (✓) and were thoughtful rather than piercing. ✓ (According to one of Rocky Li's boyfriends.)

✓ Charles was raised by a single parent.

✓ Charles was liberal in his estimate of the value of news and was not considered to be the best of newspapermen. (Thank you, Janus.)

✓ Charles had pronounced opinions and was most emphatic in their expression and thought in the *Call*'s columns.

✓ Charles was always neatly dressed, usually in black (✓) and if he had a weakness at all, it was vanity in regard to his personal appearance. ✓ (Thank you, Rocky Li.)

✓ Charles was never married and had no children. (For now.)

✓ Charles' habits in money matters were the most businesslike. His business genius was Napoleonic and unerring. (?)

Apparently, some characteristics skip a reincarnated generation. I certainly hoped that the rest of Charles' fate would be different than mine. "It was often predicted of him that Charles would die with his boots on," continued *The New York Times*.

An elderly man had attacked Charles with his cane at the corner of Clay and Montgomery Streets. The assailant, a judge, was angry after discovering the news of his wife's evening whereabouts while reading the society pages of *The Call*. Rival papers teased Charles with detailed coverage of how he ran off in confused shame.

There were many other mêlées and maimings involving the Sansome brothers, the most significant of which sprung from an incident where the Sansomes received an overdosed taste of their own medicine. Benjamin Natoma was a sixteen-year-old street orphan who survived by reselling stolen newspapers along the waterfront. After serving jail time for getting caught, a raggedy young Ben showed up at *The Call* looking for a job. Impressed with the troubled teen's chutzpah, Charles hired him as an office assistant. Thanks in part to his background, Ben soon became a talented crime-beat reporter. After three years, the rival *Bulletin* offered Ben a higher-paying gig. When Ben accepted, Charles took it personally.

Ben's reporter stock plummeted dramatically when Charles spread rumors of Ben's tendency to befriend prostitutes. Ben insisted it was all part of gathering sources on his beat, but the damage was done, and for a while, no editor would look twice at his byline. Eventually, Ben was hired by a conman named Stefano Sol , who published a blackmail sheet called *The San Francisco Sun*. *The Sun*'s editorial content centered around unflattering stories of businesses that refused to pay for ads which Sol had presumptuously placed in *The Sun* on their behalf. Intent on getting back at Charles, Ben ran an in-depth feature in *The Sun* that shined a light on the Sansome mother's life…as a prostitute. The Sansome brothers flipped their lids.

Charles stormed *The Sun*'s Washington Street newsroom, accompanied by an armada of police, who wrangled several *Sun* employees into a paddy wagon. A day later, the suspects were released on bail and back to printing more copies of the story that newsboys were by then selling for upwards of five dollars.

Ben was arrested at his home and sent to jail, where he was charged with libel. At the jail, reporters gathered around asking for comment. As Ben began to speak, Michael Sansome approached from behind during the press conference. In Jack Ruby style, Michael raised his pistol from out of the crowd and aimed directly at Ben. An officer blocked the way just in time to save Ben's life. Charles was up next. Letting out a battle cry, Charles charged down the hallway, landing on top of Ben, who, in turn, broke loose and searched for cover in the safest place he could find—an empty jail cell. A police captain took hold of Charles, confiscating a revolver inside of Charles' jacket. While the Sansome brothers spent the rest of the day in jail, the local rival papers got to work.

The Evening Post described the scene as "Bedlam broken loose. Men were crouching in corners. Behind the safe, women were screaming, the prisoners in their cells were tugging at their bars, and every face was blanched with excitement."

The Daily Oakland News wrote: "The Sansome brothers have made asses of themselves by their bluster and bad shooting."

Screw *The Daily Oakland News*. These were definitely my people.

While all were out on bail, Ben republished the article yet again. An infuriated Charles stalked Benjamin for two weeks. However, Charles' distinct style of dark clothes and tall white hat served as a dead giveaway in the crowd, and Ben managed to evade him. Charles was eventually tipped off that Ben made a routine stop at a post office on Washington Street every morning. A hatless Charles set up a stakeout in the hallway of the building, using a copy of *The Call* to conceal his moustache. The moment he spotted Ben, Charles dropped the paper and fired his pistol from just a few feet away. As fate or skill would have it, he missed. The two former friends continued to exchange gunfire outside in the vicinity of Washington and Battery Streets, but kept missing one another. One of Charles' shots finally did connect—through the leg of a thirteen-year-old Western Union messenger boy. Out of bullets, the gunfire fracas finally ended when police took control of the area and arrested both shooters.

The matter was eventually settled rather peacefully in a courtroom. Benjamin convinced the judge to drop all charges against Charles, saying he understood and even admired Sansome's honorable motive. The judge dismissed charges against both men. Charles sent money and a note of apology to the wounded messenger boy's family. Eventually, Benjamin and the Sansome brothers buried the hatchet and renewed their friendship, with Ben even being invited to *The Call*'s newsroom Christmas party each year to reminisce over the ridiculousness of it all.

That should have been the end of the story. Unfortunately for I, Charles, it was only the beginning of our end.

The "Sansome mother is a whore" story resurfaced about five years later when the Reverend Isaac Judah used it to bite back at *The Call*'s unflattering coverage of his mayoral campaign. Just like Lester Braun always recounted in those *Call* newsroom tours, and no matter how many times I reread the 1880 newspaper accounts, that bastard Reverend Judah keeps calling our mother a whore. He still becomes mayor of San Francisco and always manages to kill me in the end. I mean Charles. I wish I knew how to edit it differently, but we still can't figure out how.

On April 23, 1880, at 7:30 p.m., the Reverend Isaac Judah walked into *The Call* offices at Third and Market Streets, where he methodically shot and killed Charles Sansome.

Nobody bothered to stop Judah as he casually walked by a *Call* clerk and approached Charles, who was leaning against the counter reading over edits for the next day's paper. When Judah lifted his revolver and pointed at the face of Charles, no one thought quickly enough to stop him from pulling the trigger. Judah said nothing as he fired a shot that just missed Charles' head. No one thought quickly enough to stop Judah as he fired another shot that again narrowly missed Charles. And as the predestined-to-be-doomed-to-a-death-with-his-boots-on publisher struggled to get his pistol out of his fashion-over-function overcoat, still "none of his friends had the presence of mind enough to seize the murderer," wrote *The New York Times*.

Once more, the silent Judah pointed his pistol into the face of Charles and fired. That last shot tore through Charles' mouth, knocking him to the ground. Still, no one did anything as Charles somehow rose to his feet to face his killer and then fell backward into the arms of his brother, Michael. Charles was dead in less than ten minutes. By the time someone thought to shout, "*After him!*" Judah was long gone from the *Call* office. At 10:15 p.m., when the coroner carried Charles' body out to transport to the morgue, Judah's supporters cheered, hooted, and whistled at the sight.

The coroner found the fatal bullet somewhere in the middle of Charles' moustache.

I read these details aloud while visiting my past life's grave at the Cypress Lawn cemetery just south of the city, where an 8'6"-high statue still stands in I, Charles', California honor. It captures a handsome Charles holding a cloth, editing pen, and newspaper in hand while in the motion of moving forward. In an 1880 editorial, *The New York Times* took offense at the tremendous tombstone that I was now leaning my back against.

"*The surviving Sansomes mean to vindicate the sacred cause of indecency by erecting a statue in honor of its martyr, for the worship of coming generations of hoodlums.*"

"You know something, Charles," I said, crumpling up the story and continuing in what was, fortunately, a one-way conversation with the bronze-eyed Sansome.

"Fuck *The New York Times*."

Chapter 29

No one in the newsroom would be spared the shots of venom coming from my newfound pontification platform. I, Charles, read every word of every story every day and sent corresponding reporters, editors, and photographers my unsolicited feedback. Most were shocked that someone was still reading the paper. Being editorially vocal was in direct contrast to the ominous climate where folks weathered the job stability storm by keeping heads down and mouths quiet. This reverse psychology initially impressed some of my most criticized targets, including Lilah "Quick Mix" Dee. She invited me to be a special guest at a top editors' quality control meeting in the publisher's special conference room.

Everyone who was anyone anymore was there. Janus. Leech. Judy Dorland. Maryanne Miller.

"Desmond here," said Lilah, twirling her cold black hair with a plastic pen, "is a passionate young man, who is, shall we say, *very opinionated*? I've invited Desmond to share some of his ideas with the rest of us."

Janus, Leech, Judy, and Maryanne rolled their eyes like synchronized swimmers. Most everyone else seemed to hold their hands against their mouths in a self-shushing manner, apparently to keep from commenting on my work-in-progress sideburn-connecting moustache.

The meeting was dedicated to discussing whether or not *The Call* should charge readers a fee for accessing content on the newspaper's website.

"The other day," said Lilah, starting off the debate, "I'm in the car and I hear this amazing song on the, um...*radio*? And I'm with my...*nephew*? And I'm like, 'Oh, my god, where can I buy this CD?' And my nephew, he just grabs my iPhone, and he's all like, 'Dude. You don't have to buy anything. Here, just listen to it whenever you want on YouTube.'"

Lilah paused, oblivious to the collective frozen stare aimed back at her.

"And then, I'm like, but wait," she continued. "I totally want to, you know, *support this band*? But then Jayden, you know, *my nephew*? He's all like, 'Dude this band's got like ten million views on YouTube. They're totally getting paid for that. They're doing fine. If you really want to support them, just click "Like" and comment on their Facebook page.' So it got me thinking, if this newspaper business is going to survive, we have to starting thinking like Jayden and his, you know, *generation*? I mean. But then again, I would totally buy that CD right now, because I got to hear their song for free, and it lured me in. I just can't remember the band's name. So, it's like, I don't know, like, maybe we should totally charge for our articles, you know, *eventually*? Or maybe just charge for some of them. I mean, if I'm being honest here, I could totally see myself going either way. Thoughts?"

I could feel my beard growing in anger.

Maryanne broke the silent ice.

"Well, I could totally see myself going either way, *too*?" said Maryanne, adopting Lilah's style of ending every thought with a question. "And by the way, I absolutely love the new Quick Mix… *feel*? It's perfect for when I'm on the go. It's an easy and breezy way to find the most important information I need to know at whatever moment I happen to be clicking *online*?"

To some degree or another, most everyone nodded in agreement as Maryanne reached the end of her infomercial.

"Carrie?" asked Lilah in the direction of the only online editor invited to the meeting. "What about you? I'd love to hear what you…*think*?"

"Well," said Carrie, clearing her throat and adjusting her posture in an attempt to recalibrate her awareness. "I, um, I suppose, maybe a good start could be if we at least charge for content that is actually coming from *The Call*? And maybe, you know, cutting back a little on the other…*stuff*?"

A growing majority of stories on our website were not of *Call* content as they were regularly filled in à la Yahoo! News style, with AP world disaster stories on top of that day's OMFG pop culture column of most-clicked gossip stories from newspapers across the country. There were also "Bay Area Celebrity" blogs written by freelance journalists who were being paid with "*Call* exposure" instead of actual money. This caused the biggest headache for Carrie, who was responsible for answering the stream of complaints that the local celebrity journalist blogs were generating. These blogs were littered with errors, uncorroborated innuendo, and personal agenda attacks. In some cases, these guest *Call* bloggers were on the payrolls of the private companies that they were "reporting" on. Readers presumed them to be the same reported facts as regular newspaper stories, since after all, they had

The San Francisco Call website logo at the top. Carrie repeatedly explained to those claiming to be victims of false information that these blogs weren't official *Call* stories and so therefore didn't require official corrections or clarifications.

"Well," said Maryanne. "I don't see anything wrong with it. I mean the whole point of the Internet is for it to be an aggregator of information, right? We're your one-stop shop for whatever information you need. You know. It's like, 'You want it? Come and get it. Because we got it.'"

"Oh my God! Yes! I like it!" said Lilah, rhythmically moving her shoulders from side to side, as if preparing to jump into an all-white editorial jam session. "You mean, like, an aggregator that like totally, you know..." Lilah snapped her fingers, fishing for another editor to rap along and finish her sentence.

"You mean...like a Costco? Like wholesale information?"

"Oh my God, Desmond! Yes! Exactly. Like a Costco! Wholesale information. That's actually *really-really* good, Desmond."

Lilah jotted down "Costco" and "wholesale information" in her legal-sized note pad.

"But the problem is," I said, pausing to allow Janus and Leech to take deep breaths, "that there are some things you just don't want to buy at Costco."

"What, are you kidding?" said Maryanne. "Costco's got everything. We just bought my grandmother's casket there the other day. Saved a fortune."

"Sure, but you can't save your soul at Costco, can you?"

"Oh Lord, there he goes again," said Maryanne.

Lilah attempted to play her own devil's advocate.

"Desmond. Could you like, name me one thing, that you would like, *really-really* never buy at a Costco even if it could like, actually *totally* save you a ton of time and, you know, *money*?"

"How about a journalism degree?"

"I find that interesting to hear," said Leech, leaning forward, "coming from someone who flunked out of City College."

The room's rumblings began to resemble a rowdy British House of Commons session. Lilah clacked her plastic pen against the conference table, calling things back to order.

"I think we all know that the real problem with newspapers is *the Internet*?" said or asked Lilah. "It seems like nobody's figured out the right journalism model *for it yet*? But if we really want to fix it, I think it's *really-really* important that we all follow three basic steps. Ask. Believe. Receive. If we want to make a profit online, than we all have to believe that the Internet—"

"The Internet," interrupted I, Charles, "is currently in junior high school. And *The Call* is wasting its time and good name pandering to it."

Leech threw back his head and groaned. Janus stood up and put his hand on my shoulder.

"Desi, that's enough. We've all got a lot of work to get back to. Nobody here has the time or interest for another Desi sermon."

"No, that's okay," said Lilah, the orgasm in her voice finally climaxed and gone. "We've invited Desmond to speak his mind. Let's hear him. Please. Desmond. Continue."

"You see. The Internet, when it first came out, it was like this newborn baby. Everybody wanted to visit it in the hospital and see what it looked like. Find out its name and all. Right? And then. Then it went through this nice little learn-how-to-walk-and-talk-with-one-another preschool stage. Innocent fun. Making friends with anyone and everyone who crosses the online path of your whole wide world. But now, now we're in the middle of junior fucking high school. The worst years of everyone's life. What we don't realize is that *it's supposed* to be the worst years of everyone's life."

I looked up momentarily and was surprised to see that I, Charles, had begun prowling around our conference room table like a lion.

"And just like in junior high school, the Internet's all about shaming this girl and embarrassing that guy, while everyone else runs for cover by reinventing themselves each week trying to figure out how best not to be made fun of. Some go on thinking like this all the way through high school while a few other kids... finally figure it out and say, 'Hey, you know what? Fuck you. I'm gonna dress however I want. Listen to whatever fucking music I want. And be true to my fucking self.' Those are the only ones who really, truly survive. Because the millions of others who think they're really living have already died."

"Oh-*kay*! Well, I think we've had *just* about enough of digging through Desi's buried childhood resentment."

"I'm not done, Leech," said I, Charles, turning toward Lilah Dee. "And you. You're the kid in junior high who throws the big party at her parents' house when they're out of town and invites as many people as possible, thinking the more who show up the more popular she is and therefore the more problems get solved."

Lilah slowly stood up to gather her things and leave.

"The next day, she's left washing down all the puddles of piss left on the porch. The vomit spewed between the dining room sofa cushions. There's that sticky mess from all the eighth grade guys who jerked off in your sisters' room. Dad's liquor cabinet is cleaned out. And all the expensive jewelry is stolen from Mom's closet."

Lilah had one foot out the door, but turned to allow me, Charles, the courtesy to finish.

"And then! Then, what does she do? She throws an even bigger party by inviting all the asshole high school kids to come, too. Because, you see, that way, at least she'll have a lot more clicks and comments to count the next time she has to clean up the despicable fucking mess destroying the name OF THIS ONCE RESPECTABLE NEWSPAPER!"

Lilah closed the door behind her. Everyone followed after, except for Leech, who, like a reporter on deadline, wrote down everything I had just said.

"You've really outdone yourself this time, Desi," he said, closing his notebook.

After Leech left, I, Charles, stayed behind in the conference room and stared at the intricacies of the expressions on the carved lion eyes hiding in the mahogany corners of the crown molding. This was the same room with the empty display case that Howard had broken into and stolen the personal belongings of Charles Sansome, including the cuff links that I, Charles, was now wearing. We had little time to enjoy this premonition as Armando walked in during the middle of it.

"Hey, where'd everybody go?" he asked, fiddling with his iPhone to tweet the announcement of his arrival. "I thought the meeting started at four."

We said nothing.

"What's the matter with you? Something wrong?"

"Oh, I was just having a little talk with Charles Sansome. He is very upset."

"I'm sorry, who?"

In the name of California honor, I could have killed him. With the knife in my pocket and just like Miguel from Nicaragua did with Dr. Millhausen, or if it came down to it maybe even with the tip of Lilah's plastic ballpoint pen left behind on the table. We could have killed him right then and there in our very own conference room. The thought crossed my overpopulated mind. But ultimately, I, Charles, decided that would be too easy.

Armando noticed my moustache and, pointing to his upper lip, laughed out loud.

And for the time being, we laughed along with him.

Chapter 30

I was never invited back to another meeting. Leech and Janus reassignedallofmyreportingshiftstounpaidinternsandredirected my stories to former *Call* reporters-turned-freelance-writers. There must have been at least fifty of these "retired" reporters who, after being laid off or bought out, continued to cover the same beats for *The Call*, collecting 100 dollar freelance payments for each story in place of their former salaries and health benefits. The biggest difference was that they were now writing ten times as many stories as they did when they were on staff. So I guess it all evened out for them in the end. Used to be that we distinguished these writers by placing "Special to *The Call*" in freelanced bylines. But Lilah argued that these words were taking up unnecessary and valuable print space. Now, these same writers—who used to demand they be identified as "Staff Writers"—apparently agreed that their edited attributions looked much better in print.

I meditated on finding a solution for my *Call*'s problems by routinely visiting the downtown vicinity of where Charles Sansome had either shot or was shot at by someone.

•••

I HADN'T RECOGNIZED HIM, as the brim of his Jamba Juice baseball cap was tipped downward to cover most of the top half of his face. My guess was that this positioning had been planned out earlier in front of a mirror in the employee break room. I immediately noticed the misspelled "Stanleey" nametag, but even then didn't make the connection. But there was no mistaking the sound of Stan Edelstein at work.

"Great. Great. Hey, Josh? Can we eighty-six the wheatgrass for now? Looks like we're all out. Umm kay? And hey. Joshua? I need you to grab me some more blueberries while you're back there. We're running low. I mean *really* low. Pom-pick-me-up ready for pickup!

"Stan?"

"Desi?!"

Stan took off his hat and put it down on the counter next to my drink, then delivered a big bear hug from across the cash register.

"Hey! I didn't recognize you with the…uh…the…"

Stan pointed to his own upper lip to help him find the words. "What is that anyways? A moustache? Sideburns? I don't get it. I mean. It looks. Well. It kinda looks like shit, Desi. But you. *You* look great!

"Thanks, man."

"Hey, I heard you told off all the editors in the publisher's conference room. Good for you, man! I mean, what the fuck are they doing with our newspaper? Do they really think the Bay

Area's gonna buy a quick mix *USA Today* bullshit paper, man? I mean. Jesus fucking Christ! They're running it into the goddamn ground. And everybody's just sitting around watching. What the fuck is wrong with everyone?"

"Stan," said a stern voice from behind the blenders. "Language, Stan, language. And please. Put you hat back on."

"Sorry, Ben, but I'm on my break."

Stan grabbed his mesh hat and ran around the Jamba Juice counter in the excited manner he used to around newsroom desks and photocopiers. I conveniently forgot to pay for my drink as we continued our conversation on the other side of the Washington Street storefront window.

"Goddamnit, Desi. It's so good to see you. I was getting worried. I haven't seen your byline in a while. Anyways, I can barely bring myself to read the fucking thing. But hey. Looks like you're surviving, right?"

"Surviving? Well, Stan. I hadn't thought of it that way. But now that you mention it, I think it's understood that I'm pretty much a marked man now."

"Hey! Don't you ever let those cocksuckers intimidate you, Desi."

Stan wiped a smoothie drop from the woolen lapels of my knee-length trench coat. The coat was custom designed by one of Rocky Li's friends. It was patterned from a photo I sent them of Charles. Stan lowered his head in shame.

"I mean. Lotta good it did me speaking up. Check out my new press pass."

He pointed to the typoed nametag pinned to his Jamba Juice logoed polo shirt.

"How long have you been working here, Stan?"

"Few months. But this is just part time. I've got a second job, too. Copy editing for some website that sells medical supplies that nobody ever fucking buys. Twelve bucks an hour. But I need that medical coverage for the kids. Jesus Christ. Just be happy you don't have any fucking kids right now, Desi. I swear to God. My kids are going to grow up thinking their father is such a loser. So long as I can at least take them to the dentist, maybe they'll still love me."

"Fuck that, Stan. You don't need the fucking *Call* to be a good father. And wait. How the hell can *you* not be writing about politics? That's just crazy, man. I mean, can't you start your own website or something?"

"What, are you kidding? Please don't tell this to anyone, Desi, but I'm about to file for bankruptcy. That's about the only way I can get my name in a newspaper anymore. My name—it isn't worth shit anymore."

"Come on, Stan! You've got what? Twenty-five years' worth of encyclopedic politics under that goddamn mesh hat, man."

"Yeah, well. Google 'Stan Edelstein' and you'll see what I mean."

Stan's manager poked his Jamba Juice hat out the door and gave us a dirty look.

"Five minutes, Stan, five minutes. And I thought I asked you not to take breaks in front of the store, Stanley."

Stan indignantly waved his manager back inside. He then pulled out a Blackberry to Google his name.

"Take a look at this shit."

He handed me the phone.

The top Google hit for Stan Edelstein brought up a blog posting.

> Not so heart braking-news: Stan
> Edelstein was the latest to get the
> Call axe. Word from our newsroom
> sources was that 'Mr. Anoyingstein,'
> as his colleagues effectionately
> refered to him, 'tried' to write about

> *politics until management finally figured out that noone's read a single one of his stories since, like, 1982? The Call newsroom just got a little less irritating; as we hear that Stan Annoyingstein was known to be, ahem, just a tad difficult to deal with.*

"Ah, Come on, Stan," I said handing the phone back to him. "Nobody reads this shit."

"What, are you kidding? My eighty-two-year-old mother read it! She's the one who told me about it. '*Stanley. I always told you that you were a difficult boy. But you. You never listened. Now this,*'" said Stan, adopting his mother's frustrated Yiddish accent. "My fucking mortgage broker read it! Said we can't refinance our house now because the bank's underwriter knows I'm 'too difficult' to hold down a job."

"Stan. Don't pay any attention to this shit, man. This blogger, or whatever the fuck he is. He's just living in a junior high school talent show right now man, that's all. Let him enjoy it while he can."

"Huh?"

"It's a junior high school talent show, man. You know. Those things were always rigged. The winners. They never had any real talent. They just lip synched and never actually played a real instrument, you know? This guy. He's not writing. He's not reporting. He's just lip-synching, man. He's just hosting a junior fucking high school talent show. It doesn't mean a goddamn thing. Stan, don't worry. I'm telling you, man. People will wake up to all this once the Internet finally graduates from junior high school."

"Junior high school? Look, Desi. I don't know what the fuck you're talking about. All I know is that this fucking *blog* cost me three job interviews already! I guess nobody's read any of my fucking stories since the Reagan administration. But lemme tell you something, Desi. *Everybody* reads this shit. *Everybody*."

Stan's manager came marching up toward us.

"Hey Mr. *Annoyingstein*. Your break was over five minutes ago."

"Hey, man," I said, talking back to the manager on Stan's behalf. "You don't need to be disrespecting my friend like that."

"Let it go, Desi," whispered Stan, placing his Jamba Juice cap back into the incognito position.

"Hey, *Annoyingstein*. Why don't you ask your friend with the moustache here to leave? Otherwise I'm going to have to ask you both to go. Got it...*Mr. Annoyingstein*?"

Stan said nothing so, naturally, I felt obliged to say something.

"Hey, fuck you, Jamba Junior."

"That's enough, Desi," said Stan, walking back toward his second job.

"Pardon me, sir. What is your name?"

"Charles. My name is Charles Sansome."

Stan stopped just short of the Jamba Juice door to do a double-take back in my direction.

"Well, Mr. Charles Sansome. My name is Benjamin. I'm the manager and I just happen to be Stan's supervisor. And, Mr. Sansome, I meant to ask. Did you in fact pay for that Pomegranate Pick-Me-Up™?"

It was then, standing beneath a Washington Street sign, when it occurred to me that Benjamin the manager was standing very near where Benjamin Natoma would have been during the great Washington Street shootout of 1874. Not wanting to let my defenses down for another second I, Charles, instinctively slung the smoothie at Benjamin the manager and watched the blood-red pomegranate juice splatter all across his face.

"Jesus Christ! What the hell? What are you? Some kind of psycho or something?"

The piercing, but still thoughtful, look in my black eyes must have suggested that I probably was.

"Stan, you're fired! And you and your friend, Charles Sansome here, better get the fuck away from my store before I call the cops."

Stan Edelstein didn't know whether to laugh, cry, or run. He settled on throwing his Jamba Juice hat and misspelled press pass at the white hospital-worker sneakers of Benjamin the manager. Without anyone saying another word, two newspapermen with nowhere to go walked back into the epicenter of the San Francisco skyline.

Chapter 31

Stan's dramatic throwing of the hat and nametag lost much of its buzz when, three blocks later, he realized that he forgot his backpack containing important résumé papers in the employee break room. Stan reluctantly retreated back to Jamba Juice, and I headed back toward *The Call's* basement to sleep on the blue vinyl couch. These angry "I, Charles" possessions erupting inside of me were exhilarating. But once passed, they would leave me depleted, with spiritualized hangovers.

My employee access card was denied entrance to the unmanned loading door that I normally used as a more direct route to the basement. I was too exhausted to think about why. Slowly schlepping my way through the back alley toward *The Call's* main entrance, I stubbed my steel toe on a rusting sheath of metal protruding from the sidewalk. Pedro, the security guard, had taken me through here a few times before. This metal section of sidewalk opened into a subterranean loading station that *Call* delivery trucks used back when the newspapers were still printed on site. Kneeling down, I used both hands and all of my force to pull the metal doors open, managing to lift them a few inches higher off the ground. This entrance was designed to only be opened from the inside. In shaking the heavy metal door, I could hear a chained hinge preventing it from opening further. Using my steel-toed boot to maintain the progress already made, I pulled out Charles' knife, reached into the abyss below, and sliced away at the chains blocking my way.

Inside my old *Call*'s den I slept through the night. On Sunday morning, I emerged from hibernation and headed to the nearby vending machines in the empty basement cafeteria. Using a plastic grocery bag filled with change taken from a broken newspaper stand abandoned in the basement, I stocked up on candy bars, stale sandwiches, Cherry Coke, and instant cups of soup from the vending machines.

"Well if it isn't little Mr. Shit-Disturber himself," she said, tending to her Pampered Chef container in the microwave. "Congratulations on your career suicide. I must say. That was a very creative way to go."

I didn't bother to hide my exhaustion.

"Desi, who do you think you are?"

"Charles Sansome," I said, pointing to my "moustache."

Maryanne shook this answer off as the esoteric joke that it was.

"Desi, do you have any idea what people are saying about you?"

I shrugged my shoulders.

"Don't you realize everyone in the newsroom is laughing at you right now? What, do think you're some kind of moral savior with you and your righteous vigilance? Don't you realize the whole world finally sees you for what you are?"

"Oh yeah? What's that?"

"A clown with his pants around his ankles."

"Oh, is that right?"

"Yes it is, Desi. I hate to be the one to finally break the news to you. But that's the sad truth you've been looking for this whole time."

"Well, all right, Maryanne. I'll remember that," said I, Charles.

"What?" she scoffed. "*You'll remember that?* What is that supposed to mean?

"I'll remember what you said—when my FUCKING KINGDOM COMES!!"

I collected the high-sodium snacks into my arms and retreated back to the basement apartment. I didn't know what kingdom I was referring to, either.

But I, Charles, would find out soon enough.

• • •

I WONDERED WHAT MY life would be like without newspapers. Once *The Call* finally found a way to fire me, it might not be so easy to get hired by another newspaper. Not that I, Charles, could ever join an enemy paper. To cheer up, I looked over a file I had been keeping of my favorite Yahoo! News headlines about perennially important things like where the oldest living man and woman now live, the current whereabouts of eighties sitcom stars, and the joy that infuses people's lives when they are reunited with wallets and postcards lost from fifty years ago and beyond.

Some of my favorite headlines:

CEOS WITHOUT DEGREES. WHY BOTHER? FIND COOL ONLINE COLLEGES.

ARE SKINNY JEANS HAZARDOUS? SYMPTOMS TO LOOK FOR.

OBESITY SURGERY THROUGH THE MOUTH LOOKS PROMISING.

IS IT LARD'S TURN TO SHINE?

WEAR SUNSCREEN INDOORS? MAYBE.

CAREERS WITH BAD REPUTATIONS. LOOK FOR THE WORST JOBS IN AMERICA.

TIPS TO HELP YOU LIKE SOMEONE YOU HATE

OBAMA BRINGS CUPCAKES TO WHITE HOUSE REPORTER

TRENDING NOW: MOUNTAIN DEW. MARINES HE- LICOPTER CRASH. HITLER. KINDERGARTEN BRAWL.

I longed to live a life not needing or caring to know anything more.

Closing the laptop, I decided it was finally time to shave the farce off of my face.

11:35 A.M. SUNDAY MORNING

Back in the abandoned pressmen's bathroom, I finished shaving the left half of my face and was one razor stroke into the right side when I was startled by the image of a uniformed security guard looking back at me in the mirror.

It was Pedro, my father's old soccer buddy.

"*Mijo*," he said, his hands shaking with adrenaline, "You no supposed to be here."

"Ahh. Come on, *Tio*." I returned to trim the right side of my face. "I was never supposed to be down here. *Mira*. I'm just going to finish shaving. Then I'll grab my things and go."

"No, Desi. You come with me now. They've been looking for you. They print your picture for us at the front desk. They say they catch you on video *con un cuchillo*."

Pedro put his hand on the top of his holster and without looking unsnapped the leather top, making obvious eye contact with Charles' Bowie knife that was hanging from my belt.

"What? This?"

I pulled out the knife.

"Look, *Tio*. This thing, it's like a hundred and fifty years old. Even my razor is sharper."

I was now holding both the sharper razor and the more menacing antique knife. Pedro pulled out his gun and, standing about six feet away, aimed it at my knees. He was shaking much more pronouncedly now.

"Put the knives down NOW! *CARAJO!* NOW! *AHORA MISMO!*"

I slowly placed both the knife and the razor down on the bathroom counter. I searched my scattered mind for the best way to reason with Pedro but had difficulty in finding the right words.

Before either one of us could say anything, else, Ernest Holloway walked in. A tall stack of plastic jewel-cased compact discs fell from Ernest's hands, loudly colliding with the concrete floor.

"Jesus Christ, Pedro! What are you doing?"

A startled Pedro quickly changed his aim to the vicinity of Ernest's denim crotch.

"Jesus Christ! Don't point that thing at me, man!"

Pedro pivoted his pistol stance back and forth between Ernest and me, like a basketball guard deciding whether or not he should look for a teammate to pass to, or just go for it and take a shot.

He took a shot.

The deafening blast, aimed toward the bathroom ceiling, ricocheted off a section of the basement's metallic boiler room walls. The bullet sliced right by the side of my forehead before crash landing into the bathroom door's frosty glass window. I looked in the mirror and saw blood dripping down the hairier side of my face.

I don't know why. But it felt awesome. As I continued to admire my more masculine half in the mirror, Ernest tried to take hold of Pedro by tackling him. With Ernest's proportionately unfair size advantage, this was easy for him to do. Pedro squeezed off another round. This bullet grazed Ernest's left arm and sounded as if it found a new home in the wooden section of the bathroom's wall. With his arm now bloodied, Ernest began slap-wrestling with Pedro as each attempted to pin the other down to the ground. Still in awe of my new two-faced look, I finally snapped out of it after seeing Pedro gather his footing and begin aiming his gun at Ernest, who was still on the ground. I instinctively kicked the gun out of Pedro's hand. The gun slammed against the tile sink counter and discharged another bullet. This one connected with Pedro's shin. Yelping in agony, Pedro began hopping on his unharmed leg while cradling his wounded leg with both arms. Three hops to the left landed Pedro directly into Ernest's pile of *Call* archived compact discs, sending the back of Pedro's head crashing down on the concrete floor.

"Dear Lord!" Ernest shouted, catching his breath. "What the hell just happened? Why was he pointing a gun at you? What's with your face? What the FUCK IS GOING ON?!?"

I grabbed a towel and wrapped it around Ernest's arm.

"Dear Lord! I've been shot? I didn't even know. Oh my god!"

Ernest began hyperventilating. His face was swollen and scratched from Pedro's pummeling.

"I know, man! Look. I just got shot in the head. But I'm totally fine. Can you believe that shit?"

I patted the wound on my head as if to demonstrate the audible depth of density within.

"See? Everything's going to be cool, man. This is it. It's just the universe sending us signs. Don't you see? All of this happening for a reason because all of this has already happened before! Trust me. Everything is all right forever!"

Ernest stopped hyperventilating and started laughing hysterically. Amidst the slow-motion confusion I convinced Ernest that the best thing to do would be to carry the unconscious Pedro out to the street, where we could call an ambulance. Momentarily forgetting about his own injuries, Ernest and I dragged Pedro out through the gates of the metal sidewalk.

"Wait, wait," I said, before closing the entrance. "Grab his keys."

Ernest did so without asking why. We placed the injured and groggy Pedro up against the wall and waved to a curious MUNI bus driver on his break and parked nearby. As the bus driver ran across the street to help, the both of us scurried back into the basement maze, slamming shut the metal doors behind us.

"What about me? Desi? I think I'm gonna need an ambulance too, man."

"Ahh," I said, waving my hands in an annoyed fly-swatting manner. "It's just a flesh wound. You'll be fine. Follow me."

I ran as Ernest lurched over to the windowless storage room that Pedro had given me a tour of years before. As if it wasn't the first time, I instinctively identified all of the keys and unlocked the loculus storage shed. Once inside, and without allowing time for Ernest to ask another question, I pressed all of the red and green "Total Lockdown" buttons.

And then the walls came down.

• • •

LIKE THE NATURAL EDITOR that he was, Ernest asked lots of good questions. I answered each of them with my actions.

"What did you just do?"

We walked over to the see that the concrete walls dividing the basement and presumably the rest of the upstairs were in complete Sansome lockdown mode.

"How are we going to get out of here?"

Squeezing at his arm, Ernest followed me back into the old pressmen's bathroom.

"Desi, what in the hell are you doing?"

I picked up Pedro's gun and placed the Bowie knife back in its position on my belt.

"And why is your face only half-shaven?"

I affixed Charles' cufflinks back onto my shirt, made sure the two Morgan silver dollars were still in my pants pocket, and put on the eighteen-eighties-era knee-length coat that Rocky Li's famous designer friend tailored for me.

"Goddamnit, Desi! What have you been doing down here all these years?"

I went back into my *Call* studio apartment, which was now separated from Ernest's archive room by a concrete wall. I stuffed a laptop, cell phone, and two thick folders with lots of notes into my backpack. Lastly and before Ernest could ask another question, I pulled this recorder out of my coat pocket. I turned it on and, as best as I could remember, started repeating the questions Ernest had most recently asked me from "Goddamnit Desi! What have you been doing in the basement all these years?" to "Jesus Christ! What are you doing, Pedro?"

Climbing up the secret stairs to the cordoned-off newsroom, Ernest was far too enthralled with this newly discovered maze that he had walked on the other side of maybe a million times to ask any follow-up questions. The maze ended through the wall of the Emperor Publisher's room that Armando had allowed Lilah Dee to expropriate as her office. With the exception of Darth Vader's conjoining office, all of the other doors entering into it were blocked by concrete walls. I re-familiarized myself with the two offices as Ernest searched for a first aid kit. We could hear the muffled commotion of exasperated Sunday-shift copy editors pounding on the other sides, looking for a way out. They sounded more sarcastic than panicked, just as they always did whenever rudely interrupted by a routine fire drill.

Lilah Dee had recently redecorated the publisher's room by, among other quantumly vile things, plastering pastel wallpaper over all of the original redwood-paneled walls. I, Charles, began tearing down sections of the wallpaper to unveil a vast library of built-in bookshelves, each decorated with dozens of dusty Sansome artifacts perched alongside framed historical front pages of *The Call*.

Using the Bowie knife to cut down the last section of Lilah Dee's hair-raising decorations, I uncovered a portrait of Charles

Sansome. It was mounted at my exact eye-level. I felt it smile back at me, like the Mona Fucking Lisa.

Pilfering through Lilah Dee's desk, I found a printout of an email beneath a yellow and black copy of *Journalism for Dummies*. The subject line read:

> *Acceptable Comments for Armando*

The body of this email read:

> *Armando, in case of media emergency or if sudden need arises to discuss The Call business in elevator or hallways, please stick to these comments:*
>
> "This is truly unchartered territory."
>
> "We are still playing to win."
>
> "We always <u>ask</u> our readers what they care about most and we <u>believe</u> they <u>receive</u> an abundance of all of this and more."
>
> "Our Google analytics are looking great!"

On the publisher's shelf was a thickly stapled packet that, according to the many pen markings, bent pages, and tattered corners, had been referenced quite a bit. It was an alphabetical list of every *Call* employee. This list, prepared by R. J., R. L., and L. D., included categories for race, sex, age, and date of hire. Next to each name were comments on such things as "H.R. grade," "expendability: pros. vs. cons," "non-age-related medical/health concerns," "temperament," "physical appearance," and "social media credit." The names of those previously laid off were highlighted with fluorescent pink ink.

Grabbing these sheets, I went out to meet and greet the marooned newsroom. It was the usual Sunday skeleton staff with the only added muscle coming from those unbalanced enough to show up to work on their day off. None seemed surprised to see me when I walked out of Darth Vader's office.

Among the staff were:

Harte, Zeke: 35. Reporter. H.R. grade: 4 (out of 5) stars. Talented. Tireless. Mostly keeps to himself. Has turned down multiple job offers from outside agencies. Con: Known to criticize editorial and news judgment in emails to colleagues. —Janus.

Codiroli, Taylor: 49. Editor/Writer. Guild loyalist and steward. Set to collect $102,936.00 in Guild rep salary. Buyout negotiation in process. —Janus.

Diaz, Anna: 52. Photographer. HR grade: 2 stars. Spends too much time working outside of newsroom. Has ignored multiple warnings to speed up photo sessions. Expendable. —Leech.

Kearny, Esther: 27. Reporter. 4 stars. Pros: African American. Attractive. Youthful (personality). Good candidate for *Call* TV appearances. Cons: African American (see Apperson medical study). Possibly pregnant. Known to be combative when counseled. —Janus.

Mueller, Ken: 49. Copy editor. Graphic designer. HR grade: 2 stars. Heavy smoker. Military injury. See recent medical activity. See outsourced copy desk study. —Leech.

Richards, Charles: 43. Copy editor. No additional information available.

Sherman, Cyrus: 45. See forthcoming layoff list. (?) Popular in newsroom. Need to consider emotional reaction. —Leech.

Zambini, Roberta: 63. Copy editor/Designer. See Apperson outsourcing copy editor study. Unpopular in newsroom. Lump detected in left breast last year (benign). —Janus.

• • •

I WAVED HELLO TO the group, clenching these HR notes in the fist of one hand, forgetting that I still had Pedro's gun in the other.

"Jesus H. Christ!" said Ken Mueller. He put out his cigarette against the concrete. "Put that gun away! Have you gone insane?"

"Look. I can explain," I said to Ken and everyone else who was now backing away from me. My smile reflected, sadistically, in their eyes.

"For Chrissake, Desi! What the fuck's gotten into you?" Taylor said. He stood at a defensive distance. "Please tell me this is a joke."

"We heard gunshots," said Ken, circling a defensive perimeter around me. "Was that you?"

"It was an accident. But it's ok. This is all meant to be."

Before Ken could decide whether or not to ambush me, a self-bandaged Ernest hobbled out of Armando's office, his puffy face making it difficult for him to navigate past the newly placed walls.

"Jesus Christ, Desi, what did you do to him?" said Ken as he ran over to help Ernest into a swivel chair.

"Ken, I'm fine," said Ernest, collapsing into the chair. "It really was an accident. Look, Desi, I think he got shot in the head, too. But he's fine. I don't even know how to explain what just happened."

"Oh, uh-uh, I don't think so," said Esther Kearny, shaking her finger. She pounded on every wall to try and find a way out. "They are not paying me enough to put up with any of this bullshit. Gunshots? I don't think so."

Security guards shouted out to us from the other side.

"We're in here. Desi's got a gun," Roberta yelled back to them, her sarcasm penetrating right through the concrete walls. "But don't worry. He's even shot himself in the head. Everything's going to be *fine*."

Esther continued to pound on the walls.

"Esther," said a calm Zeke Harte, wearing sweats and holding a basketball in his hands. He always played an early game before showing up to his Sunday shift. "I don't think there's any way out. Why don't we just all stay calm and wait until the fire department shows up?"

"The fire department isn't going to be able to do anything," said a woman's voice approaching from the far end of the newsroom. Her timing was like that of a member of the *Scooby Doo* gang ready to finally solve the mystery. Unfortunately, it wasn't Daphne or Velma. It was Judy Dorland. "The only way we're going to get these walls back up is to find out who brought them down. And I think we all know who that was."

"Listen. I know you guys think I'm crazy. And I admit that I probably am a little, you know, *possessed* at the moment," I said, illustrating my words with the gun-wielding hand. "But you know something? I really believe we're all in this newsroom together for a reason."

"Yeah, Desi, D.," said Cy. "That's 'cause you gotta gun. Now why don't you do the right thing and put that thing away. Come on now. Let's make your pop proud."

"Oh hell no. I don't give a damn about your daddy issues," said Esther, continuing to try and pry a way out.

"Hey, Esther. Aren't you pregnant?"

"Excuse me?" She put both her hands on her hips. "I don't care if you have a gun. Didn't your mother teach you *never* to ask a woman if she's pregnant?"

"Well, if you wanna keep your job, you better not be," I said. "And your skin color. I dunno. Could be a good thing. Could be a bad thing."

Roberta gasped.

"How dare you talk to her like that?"

"What? You don't believe me? See for yourself: '*Roberta Zambini. Unpopular in the newsroom and lump recently detected in left breast.*'"

I waved the packet in front of them like a Bible-thumping preacher warning of the coming apocalypse.

"Ken. That smoking habit may or may not take your life. But says here it might cost you your job! And Cy. Congratulations. You're getting laid off next month. And Taylor… Holy shit! Wow. Is this right? Says here you're all set to make over a hundred grand working for the union? *And* you're taking a buyout package? Well, hot damn. Taking the money and not running. Good for you. I guess you'll be fine… Judy! I see you hiding there in the corner. How about we skip to the Ds. Aha! '*Dorland, Judy. Parked in Armando's spot TWICE! TERMINATE in the Fall,*' signed by Lilah Dee."

"Charlie. Let's see. *Richards, Charles*... Actually...for some reason. They don't have anything on you."

"I knew it!" said Charlie, pounding his fist into his palm. "They know about my buyout strategy. I swear to God, you can't hide anything from them!"

I threw the HR profile packet onto the desk in front where everyone gathered around to read it.

"Let me see that thing," said an uncharacteristically vulnerable-looking Judy. "*What?!?* But he's hardly ever here. And Fraze said I could use Armando's spot during off hours. Lilah! That bitch!"

"*African American? Combative?* What is this? Some kind of sick joke?"

"Esther, you bet your Nubian soul it is, sister! And this whole time, the joke's been on us. On all of us! Now let's show these bastards who this newspaper really belongs to! This is our newspaper! This is *San Fran-goddamn-cisco*'s newspaper!"

And the crowd sort of went wild.

Chapter 32

Without those HR files, I think it's safe to say that Ken and Taylor would have proceeded with stage one of my Shanghai-ing—a plan that they had obviously begun formulating via telepathic eye contact the moment they saw Pedro's gun in my hand. It doesn't really matter, though.

Because I am going to die tonight. I know this for certain, because I've never felt more alive.

I still don't know if I will die a good person or as a bad person. And try as I might, I am pretty sure Janus and Leech were right all along about my never becoming a very good newspaper reporter.

Ah, well.

I still believe in *The Call*. Chronicling this story is the only way I know how to truly test my beliefs. It's my hammer. It's my bell. It's my song to sing. And it's all that I've got left.

I just replaced the double-A batteries in Uncle Lalo's tape recorder and I am in the publisher's bathroom right now. I've been locked in here for the past hour and a half, since handing off those HR files to Judy and the rest of *The Call* crew. I made my way into the bathroom while Zeke, Roberta, Ernest, Esther, and the others began sifting through Armando's and Lilah's computers and files.

I've always loved this bathroom, if you can call it that. Tuscan marble floors. Greek Gods acting out their tragedies on the mural walls. Mesopotamian mosaic tiles across the skylight ceiling. There's a beautiful Oriental rosewood writing desk with etchings of old Chinatown carved down the sides.

Alma Sansome designed this as a "place to pace."

"Son," she used to say with her loud little laugh, "you can only find yourself when you're truly alone. And what better place to be alone than when in the commode?"

So here I am. Alone again, or…at least, together alone, with I, Charles.

I've used the bathroom desk today to transcribe and update our notes and recorded memories into this chronicle that we began so many years ago. I suppose this is the last installment—or, "the diary of a resurrectionist," as I, Charles, like to call it.

There's an old brass mail chute next to the bathroom window that drops directly down onto Ernest's desk in the archives room. I will leave these digitally inscribed memories for Ernest, and trust that he will archive it in the right place for the next me to find. Or you. Or us. Or whoever we turn out to be. ▶

Epilogue
Death Is Not the End ▶

ℭhe San Francisco Call

SF CALL REPORTER TURNED GUNMAN FATALLY SHOT IN NEWSROOM

QUESTIONS LINGER FOLLOWING DEATH OF NEWSPA-PERMAN

By Ernest Holloway
Call Archivist

SAN FRANCISCO, APRIL 24— No one cried the night Desmond de Leon died. Neither were any of us all that surprised when we finally pried open the door to find Desi dead on the floor in a pool of blood, his eyes still open wide and emitting a sustained sense of contented pride.

Desi was shot and killed by a team of state and federal officers who, for two hours beforehand, had surrounded the Call Building in an attempt to penetrate the antiquated concrete fortress that Desi had triggered earlier that evening.

The sniper's fatal bullet reached Desi from a rooftop across the street through a small window in the bathroom of the publisher's office on the top floor of the Call Building where Desi had holed himself up. The bullet appeared to have sliced through the shaven side of his inexplicably half-bearded face.

We had always been told that the windows of the Call Building were bulletproofed. It was among a number of misconceptions that Desi helped uncover about *The Call* that evening, as the nearly dozen entrapped *Call* employees sifted through confidential files found in the publisher's and executive editor's offices.

Among these was a file called "Armando's Associates," found on the computer desktop of Executive Editor Armando Attis, which included a list of nearly fifty names. A description at the top of this list instructed that news stories containing these names be forwarded and reviewed by top editors before reaching print. Included in the names of "Armando's Associates" were several key players in the Countrywide mortgage and Enron energy scandals.

Call staff also located Apperson Corporation earnings statements listing the salaries of those on *The Call*'s executive masthead. At the top of this list was "Executive Associate Publisher and Editorial Consultant at Large" Lilah Dee, whose earnings showed upwards of five million dollars in annual salary, bonuses, and consulting fees. An accompanying human resources file referred to Dee as "The Alchemist," for her "unprecedented ability to destabilize unions."

Call employees knocked on the bathroom door after blood began seeping onto the publisher's room floor, prompting myself and two other *Call* employees to break open the door.

Lying lifelessly on his back, Desi had his cell phone in one hand and a gun in the other. There were no shoes on his feet. A rusty knife was attached to the side of his black Levi's. Two silver coins appeared to have fallen from his knee-length coat pocket. A pair of tall nineteenth-century-era black leather boots was by his side, with keys dangling from the buckle.

A bright spotlight shone through the bathroom window. A voice blaring through a megaphone atop the building across the street warned us to step away from Desi's body. As the light momentarily flashed off, I grabbed Desi's cell phone and keys. Then we left the bathroom.

The ensuing chaos of hovering helicopters and blaring police sirens grew exponentially outside as the authorities struggled to find a way to break through *The Call's* concrete walls. The top floor windows of the bathroom and newsroom were initially deemed too dangerous for law enforcement to climb through. As the authorities attempted to break through the concrete walls, the rest of the marooned newsroom continued to occupy themselves by sifting through and photocopying confidential Apperson files.

In the basement, we found meticulously organized sets of audio recordings, handwritten notes, and typewriter-printed documents chronicling what appeared to be Desi's life and times at *The Call*. After reviewing excerpts, we made the decision to print excerpts in this special edition of *The Call*, along with this report and several of the key findings from the staff upstairs. *Call* Newsroom Assistant Cyrus Sherman tinkered with the antiquated printing press in the basement for us to print and prepare the special edition.

I called the number from the last conversation Desi had on his cell phone.

The phone number belonged to a woman in New York. The woman said she was an old friend of Desi's and was not aware of the violent circumstances he was engaged in when she called. Desi made no mention of the day's events during their approximately seven-minute-long conversation, she said. The woman agreed to speak to *The Call* but asked that her name not be printed.

"We hadn't spoken to one another in a very long time. We were catching up and making plans to meet up soon because I was traveling to San Francisco with a theater group," she said of what is believed to be the last conversation anyone had with Desi. "He said he was busy at work and about to finish up for the evening. I was telling him about how my mother had recently died, and so he began consoling me. He said, 'Just remember. Death is not the end...' And right then the call ended."

Acknowledgments

This book exists thanks to the love and support of my wife and best friend, Tiffany Vigil.

Thank you also to Montgomery and Paloma for helping me keep those serious-writer-dad-moods to a minimum.

Mil gracias to: Delfin Z. and Kathleen Vigil, Bob and Bonnie Schroth, Esther Hassard and Rosie Lucchesi... And Manny.

Thank you...Agente Especial y Editor Mark Burstein...to Tyson Cornell, Julia Callahan, Alice Marsh-Elmer and all at Rare Bird Books.

Thank You Jedi Journalists: Charles Darren Richardson, Simar Khanna, Joe Brown, Steve Gibbs, Raul Ramirez (R.I.P.), Don Menn, Debra Hollinger, and Dave Weinstein.

Supernatural Thanks to Herb C. and Charles d. for all those basement séance sessions. Thank you also to Simon Read for the definitive biography, "War of Words," (Union Square Press, 2009) which was an invaluable resource in researching the real life of Charles de Young.

Thank you to editors Hillel Black, Joe Loya, and Alan Rinzler. Thank you...Daniel Lee Crowell, Tony DuShane, K. C. Staubach, Mikel Delgado, I. A. Nimmo. Vince Johnson. Daniel Alarcon and all at Radio Ambulante. Chris and Nina Gruener at Cameron + Company. And thanks to all at 10,000 Degrees LAM and RadioValencia.fm.